The Science of Understanding

T0376227

THE SCIENCE OF UNDERSTANDING

A Novel

Polly Kronenberger

FLARE BOOKS

Published by Flare Books.

© 2025 Polly Kronenberger

All rights reserved.
No part of this book may be used or reproduced in any manner whatsoever without written consent from the publisher, except for brief quotations for reviews.

For further information, write to info@catalystpress.org.

You can find out more at catalystpress.org.

In North America, this book is distributed by
Consortium Book Sales & Distribution, a division of Ingram.
Phone: 612/746-2600
cbsdinfo@ingramcontent.com
www.cbsd.com

First edition, first printing
9 8 7 6 5 4 3 2 1

ISBN 978-1-963511-13-0
Library of Congress Control Number 2024951886

"We are our breath. Without it, there would not be life.
Nature reminds us of this every time we breathe.
And we all breathe."
—Charlie Greene, Siler, IN, 1987

"Lots of people talk to animals ... Not very many listen though ...
That's the problem."
—A.A. Milne

"Speak to me: I will spend my lifetime trying to understand you."
—Kamand Kojouri

Chapter One

I knew I had to be completely silent. The darkness of the walk-in cooler made me feel safe somehow. Well, I suppose as safe as I could feel as I watched my friend die. I sat there on the blood-soaked floor, holding him in my arms. I saw the life move out of him. A gunshot. Most likely the one to his neck. The metallic smell of his blood rose up around both of us. I kept my eyes locked with his, and I never left his gaze. Andy looked so scared at that moment, gasping for air, struggling to stay alive. And then, in the very next second, it all changed. He was gone.

Someone was still in our lab. I could hear him moving outside. I let go of Andy, got up quickly, and hid behind a stack of food boxes. Three boxes high, dates, plums, and other fruits. I hunched down so tightly under the back shelf and slid the boxes in front of me. And waited.

Perhaps only minutes had passed, but it felt like hours. The entire ordeal came crashing in on me when the door swung open with a thud. The person there, breathing hard, called out loudly, "Clear!" That is when I spoke, softly at first, then louder, telling them not to shoot. I realized then it was the police who had finally made their way to our floor. They cuffed me immediately and led me out into the main area. I explained I wasn't the shooter and nodded down to my identification badge hanging around my neck. It didn't matter. It would be hours until everything got sorted out.

The trouble started a couple of months earlier. Our work at Corrington and Ames Research, funded, this time, by a United States governmental grant, had been focused on communications with animals. CAR's purpose, our mission, was to figure out how animals and humans might communicate most efficiently on a peer-to-peer level.

My name is Victoria Greene. Rory is what most people call me. I'm a human, first and foremost, a citizen of the planet. And secondly, I am a scientist. When I first became interested in science, in finding out how and why the world works the way it does, I never expected that I would be caught inside some tangle of murder and kidnapping. Ape-napping, more to the point.

It all started so harmlessly. I think it does for all people. In life, we begin so new, so fresh to the world. We are innocent, blameless, and so pure. Our lives are so new to this place, and as we draw each breath in, we learn. We find out about the world around us. I was born in 1984 in Siler, Indiana. It was the only place I ever knew or lived until the year I turned 18. I didn't move too far away. Just slightly east, from Siler to Bloomington, where I attended the University of Indiana and lived on campus. I stayed in the dormitories for a couple of years. I couldn't stand the Greek life there, and my family really couldn't afford for me to get my own apartment in the early going of things. Regardless, I went to school and earned a double Bachelor—one in Communications and another in Biology. I worked like crazy in school and couldn't decide which route I wanted to take. My communications degree had been inspired by Oliver, our family pet while growing up. And in the way of biology, I had followed in my father's footsteps. Charles Greene. And then there was Magdalena Porter.

I suppose Siler was a perfectly nice little town, but all anyone talked about was getting out of there. I don't know why. It was clean and quaint. There was always plenty of work, as the Patel Microcircuits factory was located in our county. We had very little crime, if any, and the sheriff never had much to do but walk around town and look smug.

My sister and I dutifully attended St. Ignatius Catholic Grade School and, later, Holy Rosary Catholic High School. Ruth. My sister. Ruthy, as everyone knows her. She is two and a half years older than me, and while we get along okay these days, she was always a little bossy and controlling when we were kids. I suppose the same is true in our adult lives.

I can't tell you much about growing up Catholic other than that is what I did. It was the only thing I knew. We wore uniforms to school and went to church four days a week, on Mondays, Wednesdays, and Fridays at school, and on Sundays with Mom and Dad. Afterward, on Sundays, we always went back home and fixed a big breakfast of fried eggs and bacon, toast, and fried mush. I loved those breakfasts.

My parents are Charles Edward Greene and Corine Anne Ladner. Everyone referred to my dad as Charlie. I take after him, of sorts. He worked in the lab at Siler Community Hospital, running blood samples, or body fluids, or whatever came his way. I'm not sure if it was truly what he wanted to be doing, but his options for working as a scientist were limited in Siler.

It was Mom who wanted to live in that small town, after all. Not Dad. That's where she was born, and Grandma and Grandpa Ladner gave us our house, or else sold it to Mom and Dad for a little bit of nothing. It stood two stories tall, made of dark brick from the bottom up. The front porch wrapped all the way around, and we had two extra bedrooms. The place had enough space for a family of ten, let alone just us, a family of four. I liked it that way. In the wintertime, especially, I could always sneak off to some corner of the house and be by myself, even to places like the creepy attic or the semi-creepy basement. But I loved being in those rooms by myself, reading or thinking or just plain old sitting.

We never had a cat or a dog or even a rabbit or hamster. Ruthy had no interest in animals, and while I always thought it would be fun to have a dog, I was completely happy with the one pet we did own. A bird. A beautiful African Gray Parrot named Oliver. My dad brought him home from work one day. Someone's aunt or something had died where my dad worked, and no one in her family wanted her bird, so Dad took him. They said Oliver was 41 years old. Anyway, I loved that bird. I'd pull up a kitchen chair and stand at the front of his cage, talking to him for hours. I'm guessing he knew about 50 words. Maybe more than that.

Oliver, most likely, changed my life. He came to our house just after my eighth birthday, and for the first time, I started thinking about communicating. I started to wonder if this bird really understood what it was saying, or was it just good at mimicking? Then, I began to think about people talking to one another. What made people want to say things to each other? Sometimes out of need. Other times, out of personal wants or wishes. Learning about communication became a diversion for me. I tried to teach Oliver new words, holding up objects like pencils, a baseball, an apple. Then I'd say the word over and over, hoping he would catch on. One day, I didn't say a word. I just held a fork up to his cage. He'd seen that fork a hundred times before and had heard its name. He popped off a couple of his regulars, like "hello" and "hold it right there." And then it happened. Oliver rocked back and forth on his perch, as quiet as could be. He then made his way over to the front of the cage, took one peck at the utensil, and said out loud, "Fork." I felt completely convinced that he understood the meaning of the word. I ran through the house screaming with delight until Ruthy slugged me and told me to quit being an idiot.

Ruthy. My older sister Ruthy. It's not that we dislike each other. It is more along the lines that she never wanted to be bothered with having me around. For almost three years, she was the only child in the family, the center of attention. And then I showed up. Of course, I had spoiled the fun, and she let me know about it. Now she's married and lives in Carmel, a suburb of Indianapolis. Her husband is a dentist, and they have two sons, Trent and Scottie. We send our yearly birthday and Christmas cards and see one another most holidays when we visit Mom.

Anyway, back to my job and the trouble at my lab. My bonobo had been stolen, and I wanted him back. Lazzy. Most people aren't familiar with bonobos. But they are somewhat similar to chimpanzees. The main point to note is that bonobos are smaller in size and much less aggressive than chimps, which makes them ideal for studying in the lab. Especially where human communications and personal interactions are concerned. Both of those things are mandatory for our current investigations.

Nonetheless, Lazzy wasn't actually "my" animal but a part of our primary studies there. Eons ago, when I was in college, my professor told me never to get attached to the subjects. But guess what? I did back then, and I have ever since. I can't help myself. Sure, I'm a scientist, and I should be able to separate my emotions from the content of the research. But, as circumstances would have it, I'm human, and since the time I could sit up and look around me, I've loved animals.

I know they say parents shouldn't have their favorites. I can't help myself there, either. I love my Lazzy. He isn't like the other bonobos, I don't think. Della and Gloria are smart, don't get me wrong. But they find it easy enough to get back to their ape brains rather quickly. They are easily excited over things like bananas or anything else they deem as treats, be it food or otherwise. Also, Della and Gloria get distracted. One minute, we'll be carrying on a conversation about the weather, and the next minute, they will be trying to put their fingers up my nose, or pull at the buttons of my shirts. Gloria has a thing for sparkly objects, like earrings or necklaces. Della loves the color blue.

But then there is Lazzy. Anyone with half a brain can see how completely intense he is when they look into his eyes. Lazzy is thoughtful. When I say thoughtful, I mean considerate. He will offer you half of his food, or he'll let you go first through a door. I also mean he is heavy in his thoughts. He's pensive, almost. Absorbed. Engrossed. Rapt. Somewhere in there, Lazzy is always considering something. Oftentimes, I'll ask him through signing. "What are you thinking, Lazzy?" And he'll respond with something like, "I is wondering why rain comes out." Or "How come cars make big smells?" Always something far removed. Things you'd never expect a primate would be thinking.

The day he went missing, he'd been gone an hour. There'd been no word from anyone. All the staff had been accounted for in our department except for Martin. No one signed out Lazzy on the board, and Martin hadn't signed himself out of the area either. Before I raised a global, corporate-wide alarm, I had all the lab techs search the building. We employed several techs per shift who were responsible for the general care of things in the lab, including the feeding, bathing, and housekeeping of the bonobos. There were just three of us who were considered researchers. Myself, Martin Boyle, and Andy Turner. I report directly to Dr. William Barber. Dr. Barber was out on vacation that week, so everyone else in the department was aware of Lazzy's absence, and all of them went out searching, except for Martin Boyle, who was still nowhere to be found.

One little quirk about Lazzy. He loves corners. He would rather sit with his back to a corner than anywhere else. I'd scoured every corner I could find on our floor, under counters, behind desks, everywhere. But no luck. Fear overcame me. The more time passed, the more my chest began hurting. I could barely catch my breath even though I was standing perfectly still. None of us found even a trace of him, so after 71 minutes, I made the call to the head of our division, Dr. Aubrey Keegan.

"Keegan," she answered.

"This is Rory, Dr. Keegan, in the Animal Communications Department. I'm calling to report that one of our bonobos is missing. We've been searching for more than an hour," I said.

"What do you mean it is missing?"

"Just what I said. He's not in his cage, which is where he's supposed to be. No authorized personnel have signed him out. We do not know his location."

"Do you have any idea how serious this is?"

Her question ran through me like a knife. What did she think I was, some kind of idiot? Of course, I knew how serious this was. More than she'll ever know. Keegan had never even met Lazzy. But this went much deeper than Lazzy's disappearance.

There had been an unspoken rift between Dr. Keegan and me. The tensions between us date back to a time before I was even born, back to a grievance between Keegan and an old friend of mine. I tried to set all of that aside and behave in a professional manner. Even still, most days, I felt she was a callous, uncaring administrator. And a bit of a narcissist to boot. I always behave cordially toward her, but beneath it all there lies a pool of animosity.

Now she was asking if I had any idea how serious this situation was. I swallowed hard.

"Yes, Dr. Keegan. I do."

"Well, then. Find the damn thing. Do whatever it takes, but keep it quiet. We don't want this getting out, especially to the press," she huffed. I could almost see her rolling her eyes or inspecting her nail polish as she spoke.

"But, Dr. Keegan, how do you suggest we keep this quiet? I'm ready to sound a corporate-wide alert and lock down the exits."

"You'll do no such thing, Dr. Greene. You can call the head of security. Tell him your situation, but make sure he knows this is strictly need-to-know. Put an extra guard at the main exit."

I hung up the phone and called Morris Mott, head of security, and repeated Keegan's instructions to ensure that I was following the rules from the high-and-mighty offices above. I had known Morris since I began working at CAR. When we met, he hadn't advanced to the head of security yet, but he was on his way up. On my first day, he loomed large behind the counter to issue all my security clearance information. He took my photograph, my fingerprints, issued my badge and my key fob. Morris stands at about 6'4" and looks a bit like a young Danny Glover, especially with his mile-wide smile. But he's built like a rock. Even in long sleeves, you can tell his biceps are bigger than logs. Yet, despite his daunting physique, Morris is probably one of the nicest people I've ever met. Not that I'm around him all day long, but I've never heard him say a disparaging word about anyone. He's always smiling and waving at people, and he looks like he is genuinely glad to see them.

Given the current situation, I was glad it was Morris who picked up the phone and not one of his underlings. I explained the circumstances, and, as always, he offered a sense of calm and reassurance, telling me they would be on the watch for anything suspicious. He felt fairly certain that no one had walked through the exit with Lazzy that day, which hopefully meant that Lazzy was still somewhere in the building.

Chapter Two

Stories connect us. Stories are how humans have communicated since the beginning of time. Even before we were humans, we told each other the things we needed to express. Stories have been around long before words were ever written down. We tell stories, first and foremost, with our minds, our voices, and our hearts. Stories have been moving through time. From one moment to the next. For thousands and thousands of years. We know because someone told us so.

I realized this early on with the help of many people. But it wasn't until Magdalena Porter came along that I knew just how important stories were.

I first met Magdalena Porter in the fall of 1994. The world seemed good to me at that time in my life. Looking back, it was simple. My pursuits centered around one of three things. I either went to school, completed my chores, or played. That was about it.

My fourth-grade year had just started, and the school gave us a week off because they discovered the entire heating system had quit working since the last time they had turned it on during the school year before. It had to be replaced, and the school decided to do major repairs on the ductwork at the same time. As a result of our time off, Mom and Dad took me and Ruthy down to Red River Gorge. They rented a cabin for the week, and we were all set to do a lot of exploring.

We visited a couple of natural bridges in the area for the first few days. On about the fourth day of our little adventure, my parents decided we'd just hang around the cabin for the most part. Do little hikes. Or we could read. I was allowed to take a short walk on my own. As I ventured out, I went a little further than I intended and got a bit turned around. I couldn't get over how, all of a sudden, everything looked the same. The afternoon got long, and so did the shadows. I was worried, but not quite to the point of being panicked. The bottom line, though, is that I couldn't find our cabin or my family.

By the time I started to swing into full panic, I smelled smoke. Campfire smoke. A few steps more and a clearing appeared. And that's when I met Magdalena Porter. Standing straight and strong, her back to me, she was tending a fire in a stove off to the side of a hefty-sized cabin. A couple of small outbuildings lingered in the rear. The smoke smelled especially sweet.

"Excuse me, ma'am," I said.

"C'mon over here. Closer," she said without turning one inch.

I slowly walked in her direction, moving to where she could see me.

"I'm sorry to disturb you and all, but I'm a little bit lost."

"Little bit? Or a lot?"

"A lot." My eyes dropped toward the ground. I felt embarrassed and still a little terrified.

"Well, young lady. My name is Magdalena Porter. My friends call me Maggie. And seeing as how you seem okay to me, you can call me Maggie."

"Thank you, ma'am."

"Are you hungry?" she asked, finally turning her head. She had striking green eyes, crystal clear, and strong features. She smiled lightly, a good smile.

"I don't want to bother you any. I was just hoping maybe you knew where there might be another cabin around here."

"I know of a couple," she said. "Come over here and sit down for a minute. Here."

I sat down on a large boulder near the stove. She handed me a grilled sandwich with some kind of beef between the two slices of bread.

"Tell me what you think," she said.

I was quite hungry, and I bit in immediately. The beef tasted slightly salty, but in a good way, and was dense yet soft. I took another bite and then another. I realized I was really going at the sandwich hard and stopped mid-bite. She smiled again.

"What do you think?" she laughed.

"I think this is the best sandwich I've ever eaten."

She got up and walked to a nearby well pump, cranking it a couple of times and holding a cup underneath. She handed it over to me.

"Good cold spring water. Drink it all," she told me.

The sky continued to darken as the day was giving way. I knew my parents had to be worried sick by that point. I decided I should tell her, but Miss Porter spoke first.

"Finish up. We need to get moving."

She handed me a large flashlight, already flipped on. It didn't seem necessary at that moment, as there was still plenty of daylight left. She had a flashlight too, and she waved it at me, prompting me to follow along. She walked through the forest swiftly and sure-footedly, as if she knew every rock and branch on the ground. Occasionally, she looked back over her shoulder at me. I did my best to keep up her pace. She never hesitated once or stopped to get her bearings. Once, she lifted the whistle she wore around her neck and blew it a few times in quick succession. Then she said, "Bears."

One moment, we were in the denseness of the trees, and the next, we stepped into a clearing. The campsite where my family's cabin was. My dad was just climbing in the car when we stepped through.

"Charlie, wait! She's here," my mom yelled out as she came running to me. "Rory!" She threw her arms around me, squeezing me tightly. A moment later, my dad joined in, both of them hugging me. My sister stood a few feet away, shaking her head. She mouthed, "You're a dipshit," and gave me the finger.

"Where have you been?" Mom held me at arm's length. "We were worried out of our minds."

"I was just walking, and all of a sudden, I didn't know where I was," I said, shrugging.

"Well. Don't ever leave this campsite again. Not without Mom or me. Do you hear me?" Dad said, his voice cracking.

All at once, we looked over to Miss Porter, standing a good distance from us.

"Mom, Dad, this is Miss Porter," I said.

"Maggie, please," she laughed, stepping forward, her hand extended. "But you know that." She shook her head, still chuckling. "What are the chances? I can't believe it. I have a little cabin not too far from here. Victoria stumbled across my little glade."

"Maggie Porter! I can't believe my eyes. How have you been? And more than that, how can we ever thank you for finding Rory?" Mom asked.

"No need to thank me. Coincidence. Luck. Serendipity. Whatever it might be, I was happy to help. I'll let you all get back to the reunion. And I'll be getting back to my cabin."

"So you guys know each other?" I asked. Clearly, they did.

"We go way back, sweetie. We met Maggie back during the IU days," Dad said.

"It has been quite some time, that's for sure," Miss Porter added. "But I really should be getting back before it gets much darker." She pointed at me. "No souvenirs, though. I'll need my flashlight back," she said.

I walked over and handed it to her. I gave her a hug, which she did not wholly return. She simply patted me on the shoulder.

"You folks take care," she said and turned, walking back in the direction we came from.

"No. Please, wait," Mom yelled. "Tomorrow night. Why don't you come by for dinner? We only have a couple more nights here. We'd love to have you."

Miss Porter looked down at the ground, not answering at first. Then, she finally spoke.

"That's very kind of you. What time would you like me to be here?"

There was something about Magdalena Porter that struck me from the start. She had a calm about her, a peace. It showed in the way she moved. It seemed as if she glided from thing to thing, even simple things, like making that sandwich for me or cranking the handle of the water pump. I wanted to be like her. I'd only felt that way one other time, and that was when I read the book about Babe Didrikson, this woman who was an excellent athlete in every sport she played. I wanted to be somebody like that—good at whatever I did.

The next evening, Miss Porter showed up exactly at 5 o'clock. She was dressed mostly the same as she had been the day before, blue jeans and a dark green pullover sweater. She carried a bouquet of not-quite flowers. It looked more like a gathering of pretty plants, and something in them smelled awful good. Miss Porter handed them to my mother.

"There's something useful about every one of these," she said. "That's the beauty of being right out here in the woods like we are." She smiled and nodded her head.

"Do I put them in water?" Mom asked.

"If you like. Or you can hang them upside down to dry. Either way."

We sat around the campfire, a little awkward at first. At least, it seemed that way to me. I liked Magdalena Porter so much I could feel it in the bottom of my ten-year-old heart that I wanted everyone to get right back to being the best of friends. We talked about the weather and how the nights were starting to get so much cooler. Mostly the grownups were the ones doing the talking, but every so often, Miss Porter would look at Ruthy and me and ask a question. She asked where Ruth and I went to school. For some reason, I didn't want to tell her that we went to a Catholic grade school. I didn't want to give her any cause not to like me or think that I was different from her. But Mom blurted it out right away.

"Do you like going to St. Ignatius?" she asked us.

"It's alright. It's school," Ruthy answered right away.

I poked my stir stick into the campfire and watched the sparks float away into the nearing dark.

"How about you?" Miss Porter bobbed her head at me.

"Yeah. To be honest, I kinda like school. And I've always gone to St. Ignatius, so I suppose it's of a pretty good caliber, as schools go."

For some reason, Miss Porter laughed.

"Good to know," she said.

That was the last I would see of Magdalena Porter for a while.

Yes. A while.

A hard turn of events happened in the winter of 1995. The January part of winter. My father died. I'll never forget the day, as I had been totally excited in the morning. A winter storm, just off to the west, came pushing through earlier than expected. During math class, Sister Marianne's voice came over the loudspeaker to tell us we were being let out of school early because of the storm and that everyone should report to their homerooms. Mom was there, waiting to pick us up. I can't imagine the logistics of calling all those parents.

There were no words big enough to describe my joy of getting out early and having the chance to go home and watch daytime

TV. Mom agreed to my plan halfway. Studies and chores were to start at 3 p.m.

As always, she fixed dinner. We were going to have spaghetti that night, one of my favorites. I set the table and then began reading a book, waiting for Dad to come home. But he never did. He got into his car, as always, which was parked in space number 124 in the hospital lot, as always. He even shut the door behind him. But he didn't turn the key in the ignition. Instead, his heart exploded. Some guy named Roy Halbertson found him slumped over his steering wheel about three hours later. Roy worked as one of the late cleaning crews at Siler General, and he went out to his car to get a pack of cigarettes. That's when he saw Dad.

Waiting for Dad to come home while the storm was raging, Mom and I were frantic. I suppose Ruthy was too, but she wasn't showing it like we were. She just sat in front of the TV, watching some comedy show. I could hear the laughter coming from the living room, and it made me angry.

Mom eventually called his lab. The person who answered the phone that hung on the wall right by their office door said no one was there. Mom thought perhaps he had a town council meeting, but it was the wrong night of the week. We didn't eat. We just watched the platter of spaghetti sitting at the center of the table, listening to the wall clock in the kitchen make its ticking noise.

And then, around 8:15, the phone rang. And that was it. Our lives changed in that minute. I would never be the same. Mom would never be the same. Ruthy didn't say a word. She just kept watching TV. I don't remember another single thing about that night. Not one thing.

Before that minute, I never thought about bad things happening. My 11-year-old life was just that—some kid skipping through the everyday of things. The only moments I ever worried about were getting my homework done quickly so I could get outside to play. My life felt happy and normal. Then the air got sucked right out of everything. Life became a vacuum. A space devoid of all matter. An airless container with me trapped inside.

Mom changed. I changed. Ruthy seemed upset, but somehow, I always thought it was on the surface. Like maybe it didn't matter to her one way or the other. And then I'd feel guilty for thinking such a thing. But deep down inside, I knew I never wanted to be like her. Not in any way.

Dad filled our days with goodness. He moved through every minute with energy, always smiling or singing or whistling. He asked questions. But underneath, it seemed like he knew the answers to most everything. He knew how to fix things. He'd tinker. He'd look with curiosity. He sought. He discovered. Dad walked through life like everything around him was in a precious space. Even when certain situations must have unsettled him, he approached them calmly, with understanding and compassion. He knew how to be at peace. But the thing that he did the best was to make the simple things seem like the grandest experiences in all of life. The way he'd draw our attention to a snail in the grass. We'd all get down on our hands and knees, bowing our heads over, looking closely at how it moved, seeing its little face. Or the way he made a peanut butter and jelly sandwich, with such precision and care, spreading the jam all the way out to the crust perfectly, then the peanut butter, not missing one millimeter of that white bread. He'd place the two slices together, shifting them so they lined up precisely. And he always cut his sandwiches on the diagonal. His sandwiches always tasted better.

There were a million other things about him, all gone.

Eventually, we emerged from our stupor of losing him. We never could go back to the way we were before his death. We had to learn, by some means, how to be ourselves in a different manner from that point on. I'm still learning how, and he's been gone for 27 years. That's how grief goes. It never leaves. It just goes somewhere and lays down for a while, and, just when you don't expect to see it again, it creeps out from the shadows and knocks the wind out of you.

For the next seven years, I made my best effort to be Dad's replacement. I thought I owed it to everyone. I worked hard around the house, always trying to do more than what Mom asked. I started doing the jobs that Dad usually did, like taking out the trash, or sweeping out the garage, or locking the doors at night. I kept a cheery disposition, always the people-pleaser, attempting never to step out of turn, despite my sister's rotten tendencies. I swear. Ruth. She can truly be a nice person, but most of the time she seems dedicated to pressing everyone's buttons. I'm not sure why, but she was steadfast in her mean-spiritedness. With everyone. Even with Mom. Mom and I always gave it our best in shrugging her off. We still do.

We continued residing in our house, which, looking back, I think was a big mistake. I'm sure, financially, it was the easiest thing for Mom to do, but everywhere we'd turn, there'd be a memory of Dad, a patched wall, our height marks on the doorjamb, or the attic hideaway he made for us, like a little clubhouse, tucked away up there.

Mom never remarried, and she still lives there, all by herself. She's only 65 years old, but it feels like it might be getting harder for her with each passing year in the way of taking care of things. And Ruthy still has a way of getting under my skin. "When are you going to get married?" she'll often say, or "Have you ever thought of getting your teeth whitened?" She obviously whitens her teeth, or should I say, has her husband whiten her teeth.

But, despite my dad dying, I had a good childhood. Mom loved me. I lived in a good home and always had plenty to eat, clean clothes, and a warm bed. I attended quality schools. We always had plenty, and I never wanted for anything. Except to have my dad back. I always wanted that. The truth is, I still talk to him. Sometimes, I will look up and ask him to help me with something or to lead me to an answer. I kind of believe he is listening. The problem is, though, I'm not sure I am.

Chapter Three

The next few days that followed Lazzy's disappearance were exasperating. The police were eventually notified once Aubrey Keegan approved the call. They came and questioned all of us, everyone in our division, not just our section of the lab. I pointed out that one of the three main lab techs, Martin Boyle, was still missing too.

It seemed obvious to me that Martin was the one who took Lazzy. When the police officer questioned me, I told him so. The coincidence was too great to indicate otherwise. Then the officer pointed out that this might be a case of missing persons. Perhaps whoever took Lazzy also made off with Martin Boyle. The thought had never occurred to me. That particular officer. I wish I could remember his name. As with any of these things, at the outset, it seemed that everyone under the sun was involved in the case. The police had at least four different officers or detectives there, questioning all of us. But I knew that in a couple of days, if things lasted that long, there'd just be one who got the assignment. And this whole thing would just be another manilla folder on his or her desk in a pile of other manilla folders. I'd seen it happen years before when I was in college, working a summer job as a teller at a bank. Someone came in and held up the place and gave a note to the teller at the next window down from mine. At first, the police swarmed the bank. Then, a few days later, our "hold up" had been replaced by more recent crimes, and we simply faded from their scope.

From the time my father died, I've been doing things for myself. This situation with Lazzy was no different. I felt pretty certain if I wanted to find him, I'd have to take an active part in the searching. But I also knew I couldn't do it alone. I would need some of my colleagues to help as well.

In our lab, there were three of us working on the main path of our grant studies: Martin Boyle, Andy Turner, and myself. We got along for the most part, but in truth, Andy and I were much closer to one another, and we trusted each other in our work. I felt confident in him and his dedication to the program. And then there was Martin, who could rub me up the wrong way a little bit. I had the feeling that he considered the work as nothing more than a job. It was a thing for him to do from eight in the morning until five in the afternoon.

Conversely, with me? This was a life goal, a mission, a purpose. It reached far beyond the scope of having a job. As corny as it sounds, this was my calling.

Martin once asked me what I wanted. I looked at him, questioning his question. And he said it again. "What do you want? You know. Out of life."

What does any of us want, really? I think, at the core of most people, we want to be "somebody" in our own lives. We want to "find" our own meaning and move that purpose forward. Maybe it lies in fame or finding fortune. Perhaps the thing is having children or finding the perfect husband. Some people want to climb the highest mountain. Others might wish to dig in the dirt and look for old bones. Maybe they want to dig in the dirt and plant carrots. But whatever the thing may be, I believe people, at their very core, simply yearn to find their purpose in this life. Some say our purpose in life is to be happy. I'm not sure if I believe that is true.

It always amazes me when I hear a person say, "I knew I wanted to be a doctor ever since I was five years old." Or whatever the path may be for that particular person who has found their meaning at an early age, be it a doctor, or a mechanic, or a professional bowler. I look back on the revelations I had with Oliver and the possibility that he had a higher understanding of words. And with that, while I wanted to figure out his words and mine, I wasn't thinking of lifelong goals.

If I had anything close to that kind of epiphany as a kid, it didn't come to me in the form of knowing a future profession. Rather, I used to say things a lot, like, "I just want to be a good person." Maybe it was the Catholic thing, the fear of not wanting to go to hell. You know, conflict avoidance in the biggest way.

All my life, I've been a pleaser. I've always tried hard to be liked, always working to say or do the right thing in any given situation. I never wanted to rock the boat. Call it what you will. Spineless? Weak? Soft? It isn't necessarily what I want. But that is how I evolved, how I came along, for whatever reason.

I'm 38 years old now, and I'm still not sure I've found my purpose in life, but I feel like I'm coming pretty close. I'm not sure what you would call me. A research biologist, I suppose, but my main work is in communications. I'm a bit of an anomaly. During my sophomore year at Indiana University, one Dr. Miles Whitmore received a government grant to conduct research on the communications of animals. They needed seven students to help with the program, which would be voluntary. I thought I would just waltz in and ask him when I should start, but much to my surprise, Whitmore's reputation had preceded him. There were more than 50 applicants. Thankfully, my double major and my good grades nudged me through the door. For the next three years, I worked in those labs every day. It captured my heart.

We mostly worked with birds and chimpanzees, though a few other universities had been awarded the same grants. At the

University of Hawaii, they got to work with dolphins and belugas. At Florida State, they were doing work with sea lions, and at Harvard, their entire study was on dogs and cats. Truthfully, I would have been happy at any of those places, but I felt lucky to be at IU, in the program with primates and birds.

Throughout those three years, we used a variation of American Sign Language with the chimps. With the parrots, we relied predominantly on visual association and verbal recognition. We had three chimps and seven parrots, all of whom needed care and attention. I loved what I did, but it was no cakewalk. We put a lot of hours into that program, all the while having to maintain our course schedules and at least a B average. Of the seven who signed on, four quit during the first year. By the second year, there were just two of us who had stuck it out, me and Maxine Mason from Halston, Georgia. She was a sophomore also, and the two of us persevered as we watched the replacements filter by. For that reason, Dr. Whitmore gave us the "higher" jobs on the ladder, even allowing us to do our studies in the living quarters with the chimps. That was my favorite part.

Lula, Camilla, and Cletus were the chimps. I knew the lab rules about not showing favoritism with the animals, but Cletus was my boy. I loved that silly primate, and I'm fairly certain he loved me too. He'd light up when I walked into the room and vice versa. First, he'd jump to his feet and start tugging on his left ear. Then he'd begin signing my name once he learned how, and held his arms open wide. My heart sprung a happy leak every time.

From the first day we met, Cletus and I had a connection. I liked all the chimps and all the parrots, but Cletus and I clicked. I walked over to the holding cage on the chimpanzees' first day, and all three of them stood near the middle, looking us over. I stood close to the bars and spread my hand out flat against them, smiling all the while. Cletus walked over, pulling on his ear, and the next thing I knew, he was pressing his hand against mine. We stood and stared at one another, and that bond never changed from that day forward.

Dr. Whitmore had walked up behind me. "I think you have a friend there, Ms. Greene."

I turned slightly, still holding Cletus's hand. "I hope this is okay," I said.

"Well, people. Gather around." He motioned for us seven lab techs before continuing. "I'll give you your first lesson here in caring for the animals. Do not get attached. I'll say it again if you need me to. Here is your reality. Eventually, either you will be leaving, or they will be leaving. In the meantime, you'll be spending an extraordinary amount of time with them, doing things probably neither one of you will like. So. Do not get attached," he said, looking over his glasses at me.

I leaned my head forward, placing it on the bars. Cletus leaned his head in so that our foreheads were touching. It was the first time in my life that I felt like I wasn't pleasing someone. In this case, Dr. Whitmore. In fact, I felt almost defiant. Cletus and I stood for a moment like that until I stepped back from the bars, looking over at Whitmore, smiling.

"This isn't going to be a problem for you, is it, Ms. Greene?"

"No, sir. It won't be a problem for me at all."

From that moment onward, I felt, for the first time in my life, that I had some direction toward a purpose. A reason. I wanted to figure out how to communicate with that animal, with Cletus. Not to leave out the other two. Or any of the parrots. I hoped to be able to liaise with them as well. But there was something completely extraordinary about him, and it seemed we both knew it. I vowed to myself, standing there, that I'd work my tail off to figure out new ways to speak with these animals, to communicate in ways that brought about a more significant understanding. A connection had been formed instantly with Cletus, and I can't explain it other than it took hold of me with great weight.

~

Back to the problem at hand: Lazzy's disappearance. The entire day had felt off to me. It had been one of those days when things started out abnormally peculiar from the moment I opened my eyes. I get up before 5 a.m. every day. I don't even need an alarm clock, but I set one anyway, just to be safe. I like to be at the lab early, before seven, and have that first hour with mostly no one else around. Yet here was the thing. On the day of the kidnapping, I woke up just before seven. No alarm sounded, and my internal clock must have been unplugged too. So there I was, in a major scramble, getting ready for work, showering, dressing, and scooting out the door as fast as possible.

Normally, I like to fix my eggs, bacon, and bagel, sit at my kitchen table, and read through my emails. Not so on that day. I drove fast through town and stopped at McDonald's for an Egg McMuffin, coffee, and juice. By the time I got to work, I was wearing half of my meal on the front of my shirt.

That's another bit of big quirkiness about me. I'm a neat freak. I have to have a tidy house, a tidy lab, and tidy clothes. The Tidy Bowl Man has nothing on me. The fact that I had coffee and orange juice stains sent me to the restroom to make an attempt at removing them. By the time I got to the lab, it was well after eight.

And that's when I noticed Della was gone. Her cage looked normal except for the fact that she wasn't in it. The safety latch on the front was engaged, so I checked my schedule to see if someone had signed her out for some activity or test that morning, but nothing was on my board. I tried not to panic, but I've always been extremely protective about my work friends, and Della was one of them. Initially, I reached for my phone, and then I thought better of it. I walked back over to the cages and looked at Gloria and Lazzy. Gloria crouched down in one of the back corners, flipping through a book, and Lazzy had his arms crossed over his face, lying on his bed.

"Hey, you two, can you come here for a moment, please?" I asked.

Lazzy came right over, but Gloria stayed hunched down, flipping pages.

"Gloria?"

She turned and looked at me before getting up and ambling over.

"Where's Della?"

Lazzy shrugged, flopping his hands on top of his head.

Gloria took a couple of steps backward and wrapped her arms around herself.

The panic hit me like a bolt of lightning.

"Gloria? Tell me what happened?"

She pointed toward the door and shook her head. Then, she made the sign for "man, or male."

"A man took Della away?" I asked.

At that point, I tried not to show how upset I was to either of them, but I could barely contain myself. It had been one of my longtime fears, losing one of our "subjects" to someone outside of the research. Even when I worked in the college labs, I worried about this without cause. But at Corrington and Ames Research, we had plenty of reasons to be concerned. The threats were real. Someone had been working to intimidate us. Or menace us.

I had worked at CAR for more than five years after a series of other stepping stones at science institutions. In fact, I had made my way to up the ladder here too. I'd recently been named the supervisor of our division, and with that, I took my responsibilities seriously.

A year prior to Lazzy's disappearance, we landed a government contract, and while the motives of the United States Military were theirs to keep secret, we were given specific terms of our contract, and we were handed precise tasks to perform. We had to film almost everything we did, and those files went directly to whatever branch of the government hired us. About two months ago, we started receiving threats. At first, they came in the way of bomb scares, but those subsided after a couple of weeks. Most recently, there had been warnings about the safety of our animals. We knew we were in danger. We just didn't know why.

To me, it didn't make sense: why would someone call to say they were coming for the animals? In my mind, these calls were nothing more than ways to disrupt our workflow. And disrupt they did. Every time something like that occurred, we had to follow a series of strict protocols, which included massive amounts of paperwork. One little episode could wreck an entire day of work.

But there I stood, staring at two of my bonobos in my own lab, wondering desperately where the third one might be. I ran to the assignment board to see who was on shift. Just then, the door opened, and Martin Boyle walked in, smiling as always and guiding Della along.

"Jesus! Della!" I shouted, feeling suddenly relieved, nearly to the point of tears.

"What's wrong, Rory? You okay?"

"Where have you been? Why'd you take Della?"

"I was just getting her weight and vitals. Remember? Last week, I mentioned I planned on increasing our measurements to every three days?"

"You didn't sign her out," I said, turning and walking toward my desk.

"Good lord, Captain Quicksand. Don't get so bent out of shape. She's right here," Martin put his forehead to Della's, rubbing their heads together.

"It isn't funny, Martin. From now on, sign the bonobos out. Period."

"It was just for a weigh-in. We were gone maybe five minutes."

"Sign them out. Always." I sat down at the counter, pushing a couple of papers to the side, though I had no idea what they were. I could barely contain my panic, the thought of losing Della, or any of them.

Martin flipped open the latch on the cage and put Della inside with the other two. He turned around, shaking his head, and walked over to one of the counters, mumbling under his breath. I almost spoke another warning but decided to leave it. Martin and I didn't always see eye to eye, and while I appreciated the pay increase for being a supervisor, I found it hard at times to fulfill the role. I wasn't built to be a manager, even though I had more knowledge and experience than anyone else in our lab.

Chapter Four

The disappearance of Lazzy completely shook me. In the days following the incident, I felt disoriented, unable to think clearly. It's possible that my emotions were clouding my judgment. In hindsight, visiting the warehouse that night may not have been the wisest decision.

I think it was the second morning that Lazzy had been gone when the note came under my office door at work. I rarely stepped into my office during regular working hours. It was more important for me to be in the lab with everyone else, especially with the bonobos. They needed to see me as much as possible. They needed to trust me and know I was working right along with them.

Regardless, Lazzy had been missing for at least 24 hours by then, and I needed a moment of private time to think. So I sat at my desk, head in my hands, in quiet contemplation. Then I heard it—the note—sliding under the door. By the time I got up from my chair to have a look, there was no one in the hallway.

The typed note was plain and simple: white paper, white envelope. "Wilkerson Metals Warehouse. By yourself. No police. 10 p.m."

After placing the note on the desk, I realized that my fingerprints were all over it. I regretted not using gloves. To preserve the evidence, I carefully sealed it in a baggie and pondered my next move. I had more than 14 hours to decide if I would go to the meeting alone, go to the police, or go to Drs. Keegan and Barber.

I made my decision just before ten o'clock that night, and that was to venture out to the warehouse district alone. Wilkerson's had long since gone out of business, and the building was dilapidated. As I walked through the open area of the main floor, the broken windowpanes let the streetlights filter in. Plants and vines had taken over the interior, creeping up the walls and ceiling and even covering parts of the floor. For certain, I did not feel alone, standing in the middle of that warehouse. Someone was in there with me, even though I could not hear or see them.

I walked a few more steps forward and called out. "Hello? Is anyone here?"

Silence.

Then, a figure appeared. The person stood at the far end of the building in a long dark coat and hat. They wore a mask that looked a little bit like Richard Nixon, but I couldn't quite tell from my distance.

And they held a gun.

"Don't come any closer." The voice was clearly disguised and low.

"Where's Lazzy?" I asked.

"Alive for now."

"Take me to him."

"Look, lady, I'm calling the shots here. And I'm doing you a favor, so shut up. I didn't sign on for this to be killing anyone, but that's what's going to happen. I'm just warning you. They aren't going to keep your monkey alive for very much longer, so you just better do what they ask."

"He's a bonobo, not a monkey."

"Don't interrupt me again, or that monkey won't be anything at all."

I couldn't stand the thought of Lazzy being held by strangers in some strange place, let alone the thought of them hurting him. I took a deep breath before I spoke again, trying to sound steady. "What do you want? Nobody has told us what you want."

"You'll be hearing from them soon."

"Then why are we even here? What do you want from me?"

"Like I said, I'm doing you a favor. I don't want to see anyone dead, so just do what they tell you to do. Like you did tonight." He turned slightly as if walking away, then stopped and faced me again. "They might be having a slight problem."

"What's wrong? What happened to Lazzy?"

He looked around for a moment and then finally spoke again. "He's not eating." The Richard Nixon face cocked his head to the side. And then, "What does he like to eat?"

"Bananas. And figs. Those are his two favorite things. He also likes milk. Like from a baby bottle. Not cold milk. Let it get a little warm. And he likes Wheat Thins, but not too many, okay?"

"Enough already," he held up his hand, shaking his head. He turned again and began to walk out.

"Don't try to follow me," he said over his shoulder.

I stood there helplessly and started to cry. "You better not hurt him," I yelled into the empty darkness. My voice echoed. I was all alone.

I went back to the lab that night and pulled out an air mattress along with one slim blanket that I kept stored in my office closet. I wanted to sleep in front of the cages. As I was settling in, both Della and Gloria kept a watch over me. When I finally laid down, Gloria walked over to Lazzy's cage, reached through, and pulled out one of his books. She came over to me and pressed the book against the cage.

"That's his favorite. You want me to read it? Or do you want to?" I asked.

Gloria sat down, cross-legged with the book in her lap, and started to turn the pages.

I watched her and smiled whenever she looked up at me. "You're reading great, Gloria," I said and put my hand against the cage. She reached up and pressed her hand against mine. I held back my tears, as I didn't want anyone to see me cry, especially not Gloria and Della. Gloria reached her hand through the bar and ran her finger alongside my nose, the path where a tear would fall.

As I looked at Gloria and Della, sitting there quietly on the floor near the front of their cages, I looked back on all my involvement with these animals. All the years of my work. I knew exactly when it all started. When I was just a little girl. With Oliver and the fork.

There were probably 40 other words or so that he prattled on with endlessly.

"Hello."

"Hey, good looking."

"Buddy, can you spare a dime?"

"Howdy, partner."

"Beep, beep."

"Rock-a-bye, baby."

And on and on it went. When we first got him, it was obvious someone had worked to make him memorize these things. But Oliver had no idea what he was saying. It was just chatter. He didn't know a baby from a dime. Or a rock from a buddy. And he certainly didn't get the joke.

Our next-door neighbor was this old baggy-pants guy, Mr. Patterson, and he lived all by himself in his big house, along with his dog Howard. Howard was a scruffy mutt, but by God, he was smart. He and Mr. Patterson would amble around their backyard, Patterson smoking his pipe, inspecting tufts of grass with the toe of his shoe. But if Mr. Patterson told Howard to "get your bone," the dog would leave for a few moments and then come trotting back with it. If the command was "Get monkey man," Howard would lope off and retrieve his sock-monkey toy. It went on. Howard knew how to sit, shake, lay down, roll over, and more. At a young age, I realized this dog knew what things meant, and I wondered if our bird could understand the meaning of words too.

This became a fascination of mine. When Mom or a teacher would use a word I didn't know, they always said the same thing. "Look it up." The dictionary became my fast friend, and I started looking up things I never knew existed. We, humans, need to name our "stuff" so that everyone knows what everyone else is talking about. It has become so elemental and second nature to our existence and everything around us. We forget that, somewhere along the line, someone had to name everything. When life started out, nothing had names. Language did not exist.

Then things really started clicking in my young brain. I started to wonder if animals had names for things between themselves. Does one dog say to the other dog, "I'm going over there to piss on that tree"? Can cats understand dog language? Do rabbits have a dialogue with deer? What about birds? Do mourning doves speak to robins? Or do they only know how to communicate with other mourning doves?

This leads me to my current situation. Throughout much of my adult life, I have endeavored to understand these matters, not just with humans but also with animals. I often find animals to be more intelligent in many ways. Long before my time, individuals have researched this subject with different degrees of success. My deepest desire and hope is not merely to "study" this topic but to truly understand it.

I see it like this. There have been two approaches. The first is trying to teach animals the human language, giving them our words. Koko the Gorilla and so many more have learned hundreds of human words. Even Oliver, my kitchen parrot. But animals aren't human.

The second way is observing how animals communicate between themselves. Like Jane Goodall spending all that time sitting in the jungles of Tanzania, observing chimpanzees in the wild. Or Dian Fossey in Rwanda with the gorillas.

Somewhere between the two, I believe there is an unknown primal understanding where we can communicate freely with the animal kingdom. Perhaps we humans had it at some point in time during our 300,000 years here on Earth.

My father used to have an incredible interest in Oliver, and that is undoubtedly what started my fascination with that bird. I loved my dad, and he died too young. He died when I was too young, and it has impacted my life ever since in many ways. But I wanted to know what he saw in Oliver, because he would stand in that kitchen, in front of his cage, and not say a word. And wouldn't you know? That bird, who usually blathered on endlessly, would be completely silent too.

The two of them, Oliver and my dad, would bob their heads and shift their weight. Always silent. This would go on for long periods of time. Whenever I asked my dad what he was doing, he'd always tell me he was talking with Oliver.

I knew then I wanted to learn to talk to the animals. And at my young age, one would think that I had the image in mind of Doctor Doolittle with his top hat walking around chatting with his macaw or the pushmi-pullyu. Instead, I saw my dad standing at that cage in the kitchen, making silent movements right alongside Oliver.

About six months after Dad died, my efforts to "hold" the family together started to dwindle. My grades dropped. Once, I even skipped school because I wanted to be alone. I took off and sat down by Three-mile Creek all day long. My absence caused quite a stir. Mom even called the police. Along with that, I quit eating as much as I usually did. I started moping around most of the time.

Then, one day, when I got home from school, Miss Magdalena Porter was standing on our front porch. "How goes it?" she asked as I walked up to the porch.

"It's going okay. What are you doing here?"

Miss Porter laughed. "Is that any way to greet an old friend?"

"Sorry. It's just … Well, I didn't expect to see you standing on our porch."

"Your mom invited me over. She thought you and I might go and do something this afternoon. So, what do you think?"

I felt a little bit self-conscious, recognizing, even back then, that this was some sort of mini-intervention.

"I guess that sounds alright," I said.

"Good. Well, then. Let's go. Put your books inside and let your mom know we're leaving. We'll be back before dark."

We got in her car. I didn't know the make, but it was older, like out of the 1950s or something. A white sedan with turquoise and white paneling on the sides, the design outlined in high-polished chrome. The entire thing was immaculate, inside and out. I got in the passenger seat and ran my hand along the dashboard. It was white too, maybe even leather.

"Do you like her? she asked. "Her name's Lola."

"What? You named your car? Why Lola?"

"A couple of reasons, really. I like the name for one. Don't you think this car looks like a Lola?"

I shrugged. "I suppose so," I said.

"Well, I think she looks like a Lola. But the reason I named her Lola was after an actress named Lola Lane. She was born in Macy, Indiana. Right near the place I grew up. In fact, my mom and my grandparents knew the family. Her real name was Dorothy Mullican. Her dad was a dentist there. At any rate, she was in a bunch of old movies."

She looked over at me and smiled. "Don't mind me. I'm full of old, useless facts. Now, buckle up."

We drove for a while, not really talking about too much of anything. She'd see something interesting and would point it out. Or we'd drive by a restaurant, and she'd ask if I'd ever eaten there.

Those kinds of things. Finally, we pulled into Monfort State Park. I'd never been there before.

We drove down winding roads and through dense woods. All I could see were endless acres of trees. She drove by the lake and the lodge. Then we pulled up near horse stables, and she parked in the small gravel lot near the back. "You like horses?" she asked.

"I think so. I've never really been around too many."

"How do you feel about taking care of some today?"

"I guess that would be alright," I said, not quite sure about what she meant.

We walked around the gate and into the stable area. A man was working on a saddle that was slung over one of the stalls. "Hiya, Berle. What's happening?" she said to the man.

"Oh, slow day today. You here to take a ride?"

"Not today. I thought maybe we could pitch in and give you a hand for a while."

"Thanks, Maggie. I never turn down the help. Fuller and Jussie need their stalls cleaned. Everybody's due for clean water. And there are some apples over there if you want to give anybody a treat."

"Thank you, Berle. We'll take care of those stalls."

I followed Maggie around, taking it all in. She went to the rear of the stable and grabbed a wheelbarrow. A few pitchforks leaned up against the far wall. She handed one to me and took one for herself. We walked down to the third stall.

"This is Fuller. He's an old man, a good horse. Never complains. Berle puts all his beginners on Fuller. That's because Fuller knows how to take it easy on them. He keeps it nice and slow."

We both petted the horse for a moment before she handed me his lead. "We're going to put him in this stall over here while we clean his," she said, pointing.

I stood with the lead in my hand, shaking my head.

"Well, what are you waiting for? Take him on over. Be sure to latch the door once he's in."

"You want me to take him?" I asked. I looked at the size of that horse and considered the size of me. I wasn't sure who would be taking who.

She nodded. "That's a big yes," she smiled.

I led the horse to his new stable and closed the door just as she asked. And I felt like I'd just successfully walked on the moon. I tried not to show my elation, but I couldn't get the grin off my face.

"Alright," she said, "let's get to shoveling."

We worked on both stalls until they were fully cleaned out and freshly bedded with straw. Then we led both horses back into their homes, filled the water, and, at the end, gave apples for treats. That, of course, was my favorite part. It was getting late, and we thanked Berle for letting us spend time with the horses. I should say Miss Porter thanked him. Before we got in her car, she had me take my shoes off, and she put them in the trunk along with hers.

"You hungry?" she asked.

I was, in fact. It was the most I'd felt like eating in a long time. We left Monfort and found a mom-and-pop restaurant not too far from the park. I swear it was the best cheeseburger and fries I'd ever eaten. We both had apple pie with vanilla ice cream for dessert. On our way back home, I nodded off. Miss Porter woke me when we pulled into the driveway.

As I look back on that day, on my mom calling Miss Porter, I think of three things: One, that my mother loved me and could see that I was struggling. Two, that my mom thought Magdalena Porter was the person who could turn me back around. And three, that Miss Porter would take the time to drive over to Siler and help some kid she barely even knew. And she was clever in all of that. I'd come to find out just how clever Miss Porter could be in life, as over the years, she and I became good friends. She taught me things about this world that I would have never noticed otherwise.

And that was the reason I decided to pick up the phone and call her that night. Gloria and Della watched me dial the number. "Can I talk?" Della signed to me as it rang. She held her hand up to her ear. I had to smile.

Chapter Five

I talked with Magdalena Porter for nearly an hour on the phone. Anytime I had called Maggie for advice over the years, she had a way of gently guiding me, showing me the positive side of doing this or that. I always appreciated her advice. At the end of our conversation, we made plans to meet sometime during the week.

I hung up the phone, then dialed the number of the detective who handed me his business card before leaving the lab on the day Lazzy went missing. "Call me with anything," Glenn Vargas had said. At the time, I wasn't overly impressed with his enthusiasm, or rather lack thereof. Regardless, I left him a message, not realizing that it was past one in the morning.

The next day, first thing, he called me back.

"Detective Glenn Vargas here, Dr. Greene," he said.

"Please, just call me Rory."

"What can I do for you?"

"Well, yesterday someone slipped a note under my office door and wanted me to meet them in the warehouse district. I went and met them. They were very specific about not calling the police, but here I am, calling you."

"Trust me, Dr. Greene, you made the right decision. Do you still have the note?"

"Yes. I fingerprinted the heck out of the thing. I didn't know what it was until after I opened it."

"That's okay, we'll still need it for forensics. But you should have called us before going to the warehouse. Were you harmed in any way?" he asked.

"No. I'm fine. And the man, or, at least, I think it was a man, didn't really want anything from me. It was like he changed his mind about meeting me, and then, at the last minute, he changed his mind again."

"How so?"

"Well, he just told me to follow their directions. Then he started to walk out, but he turned around. And that's when he told me that Lazzy wasn't eating."

"Anything else?"

"No. Not really. I just told him what Lazzy liked to eat and how to give it to him," I said.

Detective Vargas and I talked for a few moments longer. He ended the call by saying he'd send someone over to pick up the letter within the hour. I wasn't too impressed when he didn't offer to come over himself, especially since our city isn't very large and its crime rate not that high. Crime in Columbus, Indiana, is well below the national average. I doubted they had ever encountered a kidnapping case like this before. If indeed they were treating it as a missing persons or kidnapping case and not a theft. Just as I hung up the phone, two lab techs walked in with Andy. It was the first time I'd seen Andy since Lazzy went missing.

"Andy, when you have a few minutes, we need to talk. In my office."

He instructed the lab techs on their tasks, and we walked to my office together. Once inside, I asked him to close the door. I took my seat behind the desk, and Andy sat in the chair closest to the wall across from me. I always wonder what someone's choice of seat means. If they choose to sit closer to the door, are they looking to leave as soon as possible? Are they settling in for a chat when they sit closer to the wall?

"Thanks for coming in, and I'll get right to it. Do you think Martin took Lazzy?"

Andy glanced down and chuckled a bit before answering. He leaned forward in his chair and looked me straight in the eye.

"No doubt about it. Martin took Lazzy."

A wave of fear rushed over me, hearing Andy's answer so quickly and without reservation. It caught me off guard.

"You sound pretty sure."

"Look, Rory. Can we talk openly here? Just you and me?"

"Sure," I said, nodding, trying to appear as trustworthy as possible.

"I can't stand Martin, and I guess it probably shows at times," he said. "From the first day I met the guy. He doesn't care about science. And he sure doesn't give a shit about those apes, or any of the animals for that matter. He doesn't even like us. Martin cares about one thing. And that's Martin. Bottom line."

"Well, I'm glad you're being frank."

"Do *you* like him?"

Again, Andy caught me by surprise. I was supposed to be both of their supervisors. Their boss. I hesitated in answering.

He leaned forward. "Be honest, Rory. Do you like the guy?"

I took a deep breath. "I don't care for Martin. Just between us," I said.

"See? I knew it," Andy pounded his fist lightly on the desk.

"He's just no good. And here's my theory on the whole thing. I don't know who's behind it, but they approached Martin. They needed an insider to take Lazzy. And Martin saw a way to make money for Martin. Case closed," Andy sat back in his chair, nodding slightly.

"Well, I hate to say it, but I think you may be right. Why else would he disappear?" I said.

"Right."

"Although, one of the detectives did speculate that maybe Martin was kidnapped too. Maybe these people took both of them?"

Andy cocked his head and furrowed his brow slightly. He looked like a little boy, even though he was at least six feet tall, and looked like he spent a lot of time at the gym when he wasn't at the lab.

He took a few moments before speaking again. "I hadn't thought of it that way. But," Andy stopped for a moment, rubbing his forehead, "but I doubt it. I'd be willing to bet next week's paycheck that he's in on the whole thing."

I leaned forward, nodding. "I tend to agree. Had someone taken Martin, I think there would have been signs of a scuffle, at the very least," I said.

"So what do we do?" Andy asked.

"I've been going over all of this. Over and over. I'm afraid the more time passes, the worse our chances of seeing Lazzy again. And it makes me sick. Literally sick. Besides that, I think the police aren't too concerned with our little case here. So I'm planning on doing some investigating of my own."

I told Andy about the note I received and my trip to the warehouse and that I was planning on going back in daylight hours to see if I could find any clues. Anything at all. I had some ideas on how Andy could contribute to the cause too.

"So, I'm hoping you'll be willing to help me," I said.

"Sure. I'd do anything to help find Laz. What do you want me to do?"

"Well, the big thing is that I'd like you to search Martin's work area. Check around his desk and his paperwork. See if there's anything on his computer. His schedule, any contacts that look suspicious, anything."

Andy nodded. He looked eager to help.

"I'm asking you because I think you'd be the least conspicuous of the two of us. I'm hoping nobody will notice anything."

I explained that if I were to go over there, snooping around, it would look like I was snooping around. Even if I'd try to do it early in the morning when I got to the lab when only a few people were there. But as it was, Andy and Martin's desks were side by side and pushed right up against one another.

Andy continued to nod as I talked. "Got it. Anything else?" he said.

"Well, I guess the big thing is what you pointed out. We don't know who's behind this. So I'm being suspicious of everyone around here."

"Including me?" Andy asked.

I laughed. "No. Not you. I trust you, Andy. Why else would we be in here talking right now?"

Andy headed back to the lab. I felt charged up after our discussion, so I decided to head out for a drive to the warehouse district to look around. But then I stopped myself. I'd been so absorbed with Lazzy's disappearance that I hadn't been getting much else done in the way of work. I put on my lab coat and headed to see Della and Gloria for our daily communication exercises. I needed to focus on the work that was still in front of me. And the communication exercises were some of my favorite things to do, after all. We had developed a specific signing language. It was similar to American Sign Language, but our spelling signals were slightly different.

I pulled them both out of their quarters, and we sat at our "chat table" at the far end of the lab. A few partitions had been put in place, making it like a little room where we had some privacy. Not only that, it blocked out distractions and made for better focus. On a normal day, all three bonobos would have been there.

Gloria started out by asking why Lazzy was gone.

Gloria: "Lazzy, bye."

"Yes, Gloria. Lazzy is not here. I don't know where he is," I answered using both my voice and hand signals.

Della: "Why not know?"

"Oh, Della. I wish I knew. I'm trying to figure out where Lazzy is. Someone took Lazzy."

Gloria: "Man."

"A man took Lazzy? Did you see him? Do you know who it was?"

Gloria nodded her head quickly. Della followed too and began nodding.

Gloria: "Black man."

I needed to be careful about interpreting what they were saying. "He was a black man? His skin was black? Like Curtis?" I asked.

Gloria looked at me and didn't answer. Then she ran her hand down her face, then her arms, sort of patting herself.

Gloria: "Everywhere black."

Della nodded again. I never intended for our session to be an interrogation about Lazzy's disappearance. But the information provided by the bonobos greatly surpassed any evidence we had gathered thus far.

"Black clothes? Like my lab coat is white. But this man had black?"

Della: "Black everything."

"Could you see the man's face? Face?" I pointed to my own.

Della: "No face. Black."

Their responses made me think that whoever it was must have been wearing a mask. I was writing notes as we went, but I didn't want to linger on this topic too long; as I could see, the subject matter upset them. The two of them missed Lazzy, and it was evident on their faces. But especially Gloria.

The three bonobos were all so different. Cognitively, Lazzy was sharper and more aware than the other two. He picked up on words and symbology much quicker. He had a better memory. Lazzy was the thinker of the group. He appeared deep in thought even when we weren't working on our exercises or activities. Sometimes, when

Lazzy was on his own, without anyone else around, he seemed to be pondering. Pondering what, I did not know.

Gloria, on the other hand, was a bit of a kidder. She joked around. She liked to hide things from everyone and make it all a game. She thought "peek-a-boo" was a riot and would laugh whenever she made the gesture. She was also the most sensitive of the three. She loved to hug. And it always appeared as if she was trying to be friends with the other two, always rubbing their backs or sidling up right beside them.

And then there was Della. Della had attitude with a capital A. Della liked Della and thought everyone else was subpar. Sometimes, she'd put her nose up in the air and look away when you were talking to her. She kept more to herself than Lazzy or Gloria. She's a little uppity if you ask me.

As I watched Della and Gloria start to get upset, I turned our conversation back to exploring new words in their vocabulary. The word of the week had been "favorite." It was a concept we'd been working on lately.

Abstract concepts. They are quite a thing in communication. I can show the apes a hammer, and they'll know it is a hammer. They can spell it out. I can demonstrate what its action is. But I cannot show them a "favorite." I can't pull a favorite out of my pocket. So, the concept is harder to teach. Same with so many words, like "worst" or "guess."

That afternoon, I worked on trying to learn what their favorite fruits were and go about teaching the concept that way. But I remained distracted by the information they'd given me, and I could barely wait to call Detective Vargas. At that point, I had more questions than answers.

Chapter Six

Glenn Vargas seemed to be around my age, maybe in his late thirties. He was probably a little shorter than the average man, and while he wasn't overweight by any means, he had a slight paunch about his waistline. It didn't seem to bother him, as he always left his suit coat unbuttoned. His suits. They never seemed to fit him quite right. I can't really put my finger on it, but they looked like they belonged to someone else. And they were always grayish. Dark, light, or in between, maybe with a tint of blue or green. But, basically, always gray. I hadn't been around him long enough to gauge his personality, but in my brief interactions, he acted mostly uninterested in what I had to say. Regardless, I wasn't going to let him off the hook.

"Vargas."

"Detective Vargas, this is Rory Greene at CAR."

"Yes, Dr. Greene. What can I do for you?"

"Well, I was just talking to the bonobos, Della and Gloria, and they said they saw the person who took Lazzy."

There was a pause. "You were talking to the monkeys?"

"Well. Technically, they are bonobos. But yes. That's right, Detective. That's what we do here."

I heard the phone muffle for a second. I could just imagine the gestures on the other end of the line. We were probably a big joke throughout their office.

"And what exactly did your monkeys have to say?"

"Again, they aren't really monkeys. They are a species called bonobos. They're closer to chimpanzees than monkeys, though. But that's beside the point. To get back to your question, they didn't have a whole lot to say. But what they gave me might be helpful. They told me it was just one person and they were wearing all black. They had a black mask on, too, of some sort."

"Okay. Got it. Perp was wearing black. Anything else?"

"As a matter of fact, there is. I was thinking about how we videotape our sessions to study their movements and facial expressions. Anyway, it reminded me of the cameras. Have you checked the security footage for the building?"

There was a long pause.

"Well, we're working on that," he said.

"Here's the thing, Detective. I asked Dr. Keegan if I could review it, and she told me that activity was better left to the police. I was hoping to find out what you'd learned."

"As you well know, Dr. Greene, there aren't many security cameras in your lab areas. There seem to be more in the hallways and entrances."

"And?"

"And I'm not sure that the footage will tell us much."

I couldn't believe what I was hearing from this guy. "You're kidding, right? Whoever took Lazzy had to leave by the only door to the lab. And that door leads to the hallway. And so on. You don't think seeing a video of a person walking a bonobo out of here will be helpful?" I could hear my voice shaking.

"If you'd calm down there a minute. We watched the tape for the hallway outside your lab. We saw a few people walking through that area during the hours that Lazzy may have been taken. But we didn't see anyone with a monkey. We did not get a visual on anything suspicious."

I wasn't sure how to respond, but my heart dropped. "You didn't see him?"

"No, ma'am. I'm sorry."

I felt like he might have been lying to me and that no one with the Columbus Police had taken the time to review the footage. I swallowed my anger, but not my doubts, as I cleared my throat. "Do you still have the tapes?"

"We still have all of them."

"Can I come down and have a look?"

There was no response, so I offered more. "I promise I won't get in your way. Please. It would really mean a great deal to me if I could just have a look at those tapes."

"Uh. Sure. I guess that would be alright. Jack, our video guy, is here during normal work hours. Let me switch you over to him, and you can set up a time."

The line cut to music playing. He'd put me on hold without asking if there was anything else, without saying goodbye. I didn't want a friend in the guy, but I did hope for a little bit of enthusiasm or interest in our case. Regardless, I talked to Jack, the video guy, and scheduled an appointment to see him the next day, first thing. I then made a point to file a request for two personal hours for the following morning. My immediate supervisor happened to be on vacation. I'm guessing by now he knew about Lazzy's kidnapping. In fact, he might have been trying to come back early from Costa Rica at that moment. But at the moment, he was still gone, and I could never be too sure about Dr. Aubrey Keegan signing off on the paperwork for my personal hours. So I wanted to make sure I had all the forms in perfect order for her.

Keegan. Ever since she came to the CAR organization, the two of us hadn't quite seen eye to eye. It was my opinion that she had a preexisting chip on her shoulder. Or maybe she thought she had something to prove. At any rate, she's one of those women who give women a bad name. There's that old phrase, "When a man gives his opinion, he's being assertive. But when a woman gives her opinion, she's being a bitch." I'm fairly certain whoever came up with the phrase had Aubrey Keegan in mind because, in her case, the bitch part seemed true.

She was short with people, gruff, abrupt. Whenever she'd give you instructions to do something, it felt like there was always an "or else" attached at the end. Even her body language was blunt. She was always crossing her arms and jutting her head sideways. But what I noticed most about Keegan is that she liked to be in charge. She seemed to thrive when she had power over someone else. It wasn't the greatest trait for a boss to have, especially when I was on the receiving end. And she acted this way from the very start.

Like the one day when she used the restroom on our floor and thought it smelled like cigarette smoke. Moments later, every female employee in the wing was crammed into the meeting room, where we received a fifteen-minute thrashing about smoking on CAR property. She threatened us with the firing squad—if you're caught, you'll be fired.

This was just one of many incidents. Most people tried to steer clear of Keegan. I, for one, would be glad when Dr. Barber got back from vacation. Now, there's a nice guy. William Barber. His accent was always a telltale sign that he was born in Germany, although I have never directly asked him about his birthplace. Dr. Barber was slightly older than most of us in the department, perhaps in his late fifties or beyond. Nevertheless, he possessed an affable demeanor that put everyone at ease. He was genuinely kind-hearted—easy to see from his rapport with the animals. Although he no longer worked with them directly since being promoted to Department Head, the bonobos all liked to cling to him whenever he visited our lab. In a way, I think he might be a little bit like my dad when it came to his "communications" with the animals. He seemed just to have a "thing."

His vacation to Costa Rica had finally been approved once Keegan filled the Head of Animal Research Division spot. Barber had long wanted to go someplace he'd never been. He wanted to see some of the Costa Rican wildlife interacting in their normal environs. Even still, he picked a bad time to go. I wish he had been at work to help.

The next morning, I arrived early at the Columbus Police Department for my meeting with Jack. He greeted me warmly in the waiting area, then ushered me back through their building, walking through a little maze of messy desks into a room near the rear. It wasn't large, but it was his, as evidenced by the nameplate on the wall: "Jack Everton, Digital Investigator." He kept the area especially clean. Everything was organized, shelved, labeled, and well-ordered. He went to a large cabinet and pulled out an envelope, a portable hard drive enclosed.

"This is a copy of their files from the night of your incident. A total of five cameras are in that immediate area of the building. As you probably know," Jack said.

"Actually, I've never paid much attention," I said.

"Let me get this set up, and then I'll let you move through the videos as you like. There's the time stamp right there in the upper corner, all the time, and you know the rest of the controls, stop, play, fast forward, and so on."

"Got it."

"I'll be right over here if you need anything, okay?" he said.

I started watching the videos, fast-forwarding through the tapes of blank hallways. Finally, I saw some activity: people I knew just walking through on their way to whatever work thing they were doing.

But no sign of Lazzy.

Then, there was one person pushing a small cart. I believe it was Kim Avery, a lab tech for the birds. When cleaning or working on the different animal cages, the techs need to bring supplies in by cart. They clear waste via these carts also. To cut down on contamination between labs, carts must be draped with a special material that does not allow the transfer of germs and such. I couldn't see what was under the opaque polypropylene draping, though it didn't look large enough for Lazzy. I dismissed Kim Avery's activity.

I was almost through all the files when I viewed someone wheeling a large cart down the hall. The cart in question was our biggest variety, typically used for transporting cages or large, bulky items. Again, this one was covered in polypropylene. But the person was unrecognizable. They wore a dark hoodie under their lab coat, which is typically frowned upon by corporate. Not only that, their face stayed turned away from the cameras, and sometimes off to the side of the cart, as he or she pushed. It had to be him. It had to be Lazzy.

"Jack!" I said too loudly. "Has anyone seen this?"

Jack came over to where I was sitting, a pleasant look on his face. He leaned over and took control of the mouse. After running it a couple of times, he finally spoke. "I think they have. I'm pretty sure Detective Vargas and Detective Patterson went through all the footage the other day. But you might want to check with them."

"Are they here?"

"I don't know. I could have them paged."

"Could you please?" I asked.

A few minutes later, the door opened. I felt embarrassed as I assumed Detective Patterson would be a man. But a woman walked in: tall, neat, professional, and young.

"Whatcha need, Jack?"

"Detective Patterson, this is Dr. Greene from the CAR Laboratories. She's here looking at the videos from the other night when one of their animals was stolen."

I stood up and shook her hand.

"Nice to meet you. You all can call me Rory if you'd like," I said. I continued right in with my question. "I was wondering if you or Detective Vargas had seen this clip of this person with the cart."

Jack ran through it again, first at regular speed, then in slow motion. Patterson leaned over, watching. As she stood, she nodded her head slowly, then looked at the floor.

"Yes, ma'am. We've seen this."

I could feel myself getting upset. I pointed back at the still on the screen. "This is him." I tried to calm my voice. "This is Lazzy. It has to be," I said.

She hesitated in her answer. "Well, we did review that portion of the tape. Yes. And, uh, Detective Vargas, he thought it was inconsequential."

"Inconsequential? How does he figure? Good lord! This has to be Lazzy. There's no other way he could have gotten out of there. And just look at this joker pushing the cart. He's all covered up. He's got a hoodie on, for crying out loud. He's keeping his face hidden."

"Yes, I can see the person's appearance is obscured."

"Darn right, it is. Look, you have to admit. This looks terribly suspicious." My reaction came out with far too much emotion attached. I could see Detective Patterson's apprehension about my assertions.

"I suppose it could be possible that the bonobo is under that tarp," Patterson looked away as she spoke.

"Jack, what do you think? Don't you agree?" I nodded my head toward him.

"I'm just the technical guy around here. I leave the crime-solving to the detectives," he smiled, shrugging.

"Well, I'm calling Vargas. This is ridiculous."

I got his voicemail and left a lengthy message.

It wasn't until late in the day that Vargas called me back. I'd been checking in on our parrots, as Kim Avery had just come on shift, and I wanted to ask her some questions about the night Lazzy was taken.

"What can I help you with, Dr. Greene?"

"The tapes. I watched every second of those tapes. And toward the end, there is the segment where someone is pushing a large cart down the hall. The hall that leads to the elevators. All three of the elevators, two public, and one service."

"Yes, we saw those tapes. But we didn't see any evidence of that monkey on the film. Is there anything else you need?" Vargas's voice trailed off as he spoke.

"Yes. I need you to figure out who that is, for crying out loud. It's right there in front of your eyes. Lazzy has to be on that cart!"

"Dr. Greene, there is nothing there that would indicate that the monkey was on that cart. There is no visual. The person doesn't seem hurried or panicked. There's just no hard evidence there."

"Are you kidding me, Detective Vargas? In science, we call this a hypothesis. A hypothesis means you are suggesting a viable explanation based on limited evidence. It is a starting point for further investigation. That's how we go about proving facts."

The phone was silent, so I started back in. "There isn't any other footage that shows Lazzy leaving. This is the only plausible explanation. This is the probability."

"Yes. But the tape doesn't show us anything. We've got no monkey. No ID for this person ..."

I interrupted him.

"You have a probable weight and height. A walk. A clothing description. Can you zoom in on the hands for tattoos or rings? At the very least, review the tapes for the elevators, the lobbies, the service entrance. Can you at least request those from Dr. Keegan?"

"That's a lot of footage, Dr. Greene. It would take a lot of man hours to review all those tapes, and frankly, we don't have the personnel to handle this."

"We're in freaking Columbus, Indiana. What are you so busy with? Jaywalking? Littering? Jesus!" I'd completely lost my cool.

"Look, we're doing our best right now. We'll let you know if we come up with any leads."

"Wait!" I yelled into the phone. "What if I did it? What if I went through the tapes?" I tried to calm myself.

There was another long silence on the phone. I waited, holding my breath.

"I'll have to check into this and get back to you," he finally answered.

I felt a glimmer of hope. Despite that, everything else about this investigation seemed off to me. It was clear that Vargas wasn't motivated. In fact, he seemed to be edging on the side of indifference. I had to wonder why.

Chapter Seven

I've had the pleasure of living in both small towns and big cities. They each have their advantages and disadvantages, but as I look at myself and my levels of life contentment, I'd say I'm better off in small towns.

Columbus isn't tiny. The population is around 50,000, which is a pretty great size if you ask me. We have things that tiny towns don't have, like good grocery stores and an assortment of restaurants. And we also have advantages of small-town life, like less traffic and a lower crime rate. All in all, Columbus, Indiana, fits me pretty well.

I moved here around five years ago when I landed the job at CAR. I bought a house first thing. As I shopped around, I fell in love with this place, a two-story brick with a nice front porch and a decent-sized lot. I especially liked that it had a fence in the backyard, because I had hopes of getting a dog. And besides, I liked the name of the street, Broadmoor Lane. Everything just seemed to fit.

The day after I moved in, I got up early to start unpacking boxes and working on some of the minor repairs that were needed in the house. Not long after, there was a knock on the front door. Standing there was Sarah, a woman I'd met the day before at the grocery. She and I were probably about the same age or pretty close. We had been in the produce section, standing at the apple bin, and we reached for the same Fuji apple. We did this whole back-and-forth thing of "no, you take it," and the next minute, we were in the middle of a 15-minute conversation. I told her I was new to this side of Columbus, having just moved. As it turned out, we only lived a few streets over from one another. Maybe a mile or so away.

And there, that morning, she stood on my porch, wearing blue jeans and a bulky white sweater. The day before, she looked so put together. She appeared the same way then, smiling so easily. Everything about her felt genuine.

"Would you like to come in?" She was holding a small bag and a thermos.

"I brought coffee and banana bread. Are you up for it right now?"

Sarah and I sat at the kitchen table, talking, eating the delicious banana bread, and drinking coffee for the better part of an hour. Our conversation flowed easily. Sarah bought her house a few years prior. She was full of interesting stories. Like when she told me about a few of the neighbors, including Mr. Thurman Finney, who made a point of yelling at her, almost daily, for stealing his flowers. In his mind, everyone had been guilty at one time or another of stealing his flowers, and Sarah said he could be quite insistent. His wife would often stand at the screen door and wave her hands back and forth as if to say, "Don't mind him." Sarah added that I'd probably have some version of my own Mr. Thurman on this street.

From the very start, I enjoyed every minute as we sat there chatting away. And since that day, Sarah and I have been best friends. We frequently eat dinner together, trading turns on cooking, although Sarah cooks about five times to my one. We watch movies or play board games together. A lot of evenings, most evenings, one of us is hanging out at the other one's house. I think the world of Sarah. On the one hand, we seem to have a lot in common. But on the other, we are also very different. She has a perspective that proves, most of the time, to be incredibly unique from mine. That is one thing that I especially liked about her. She always gives me a fresh point of view, a way of seeing the world with a fresh set of eyes.

The night after my phone confrontation with Vargas, Sarah and I had made plans to have dinner at my house. I didn't quite feel like cooking, so instead we headed out to one of our favorite restaurants, The Deep Dish. Sarah and I split a large pepperoni and tossed back a couple of beers along with dinner.

"So, how long is it going to take you to tell me what's wrong?" she asked.

I leaned back in my chair, exhaling deeply. I wanted to appear calm about the whole thing.

"It's that detective. Vargas. I get the feeling that he's intentionally dragging his feet on this entire case," I said, crumpling my napkin on the table.

"Could it be that you're just upset about Lazzy, and he's not moving quick enough for you? Or do you really think he's not doing a very good job?"

I thought for a moment. "Well, I'd say both things are probably true." We both chuckled, but I continued talking. "Honest to God, trying to get Vargas to follow a lead is like pulling teeth. I've been reviewing the security tapes from the lab. The only way in or out is through the hallway. There could only have been one person on that tape who did it. The guy pushed a large cart out of the lab. His face was completely blocked, and he was wearing a hoodie. I mean, come on."

Sarah nodded, listening.

"I wanted them to get the footage from the other areas of the building. The elevators. The main entrance. The service area. He said he'd look into it."

"Well, that's good, right? That he's going to look into it?"

"God, you're infuriating. Why can't you grab your battle axe and club this guy with me? You always have to give the other side the benefit of the doubt," I said.

Sarah cocked her head to the side, smiling. She didn't say anything. She just crossed her arms, smiling.

"Okay, Okay. We should always try to see things from all sides. I know, I know, dammit. But do you always have to be so open-minded about things?" I sat back down in my chair, not realizing I'd gotten to my feet in all of that.

"I'm on your side, Rory. I am. It's just that you are awful close to this whole thing. You let yourself get attached to all of those animals, and I know how much you love Lazzy. So it feels like people are putting hot matches on you every time they don't agree with you or aren't moving fast enough for you."

Sarah was right. "I know," I said. "But I'm so worried about him. He has to be so scared. He's used to living a certain way and seeing the same people every day. Seeing me every day. And Della. And Gloria." I drifted off in thought.

After a moment, Sarah sort of sprang up to her feet and pushed up her sleeves.

"Maybe we should look at this from another angle. You've been focusing on the person who took Lazzy out of the lab, right?"

"Yeah … but …"

"But think about it. That person probably isn't the one behind it all. I'm guessing whoever took Laz is just some minion way down the ladder. Someone else is behind this. They wanted Lazzy, but why? Let's look at what we know and don't know."

She flipped over the pizza cardboard and asked me for a pen.

"They took Lazzy. Did it have to be Lazzy, or was it random? Was he just closest to the door, or did they want him specifically?"

"I don't know," I said.

"Guess."

"Well, by far, Lazzy is the smartest. He is further along than the other two in all the areas. I mean, his command of gestures that follow human linguistic rules is remarkable. He's excelled in other areas I've been trying to push, like our ability to communicate concepts with one another. Or the way he conveys his emotions. Everything from joy to sadness. Or fear. Even empathy."

"Okay, so Lazzy is the golden boy."

"Yes, he's the golden boy," I smiled. But truthfully, I felt like crying.

Sarah pushed on. "Who knows this?"

"Everybody in the lab. Everyone in the program, from the cage cleaners, all the way up to Dr. Keegan. I'm not sure the higher higher-ups know. Like the big bosses we only see during their thank-you speeches at the Christmas party."

Sarah scribbled on the cardboard.

"And who are your enemies? Would they know about Lazzy?" she asked.

"Our enemies? You mean like The Penguin or The Joker?"

We both laughed.

"You know what I mean," she said. "Who's the opposition? Who wins if you fail?"

I leaned forward on the table, looking at the pizza cardboard filled with words and arrows and exclamation points. I had to think about it.

"Well, most people out in the real world don't even know what we do. Most people don't even care about us, except for the handful that protest the treatment of animals in research labs. So there is that possibility. But, if I were guessing, I'd say it was someone in the same field. And God knows, everyone in research is always vying for grants. And awards. It really is competitive, even though every company puts on the air of 'we're all in this together for the advancement of science.' That's hype. Most of those people want to be number one in the field. Without a doubt."

"So, who's in the game?"

"Well, overall, we are pretty big—CAR. But, bigger than us is Krembold Research. They do a wide variety of things, but they focus a huge amount of their research on animal behavior. Some of the lesser ones are Moser Labs and The Seaton Institute. Then there's Shining Shores. Those are the most significant ones, I'd say."

"Don't you think it makes sense that someone in the industry took him? To slow you down or to toss your program in the ditch? Or maybe, by taking Lazzy, they gain in theirs?"

"I guess that could be. You know, every so often, you hear someone talk about moles in the organization. Stealing secrets. Gathering data. That sort of thing. I never gave it much weight. I figured it was just people gossiping or starting rumors out of boredom. But I suppose there might be people working at CAR who are working for someone else, too. I guess there is always that possibility that it all could be tangled up together. And, of course, I told you that Martin Boyle is missing. He's probably been a mole all along."

"Now we're getting somewhere. You need to broaden your focus. Try to figure out who is pushing this. Have they asked for a ransom or anything?" Sarah asked.

"Not yet."

"Well, if they don't, it probably means we are heading down the right path."

"You may be right about all of this. You know what else? I am seeing Maggie Porter in a few days. She knows this industry better than anyone. I'm going to talk with her and get her take on things. I bet she'll have some great input about all this. At least, that's what I'm hoping."

It started drizzling on our way out and had gotten dark much earlier. As we got in Sarah's car, a man was pulling away from the restaurant's pick-up window. I could have sworn it was Martin Boyle in the passenger seat.

Chapter Eight

Maggie Porter had moved to Indianapolis sometime about ten or 12 years ago. She went from years of teaching full-time at Indiana University to working part-time at Butler University. I told her I would drive to Indianapolis for lunch, and we ate downtown at Harry and Izzy's, one of my favorite spots in the city.

As I sat across the table from Maggie, a huge wave of gratitude washed over me. It always did every time I saw her. To look at her, you would never guess she was in her early sixties. But the big thing is her eyes. Those eyes held the vibrancy of discovery. Everything looked new to those eyes all the time. She questioned. She thought. She cared. Maggie was one of those people in life who sort of glows everywhere they go. I watched her sip her Diet Coke, nodding as we talked, knowing she was taking in every word and processing it deeply. After all these years, my respect for her had only grown.

"So, what's the update on Lazzy?" she asked.

I told her Aubrey Keegan hadn't been open about sharing information, and I wasn't sure why.

"That's Keegan for you. I have never liked that woman," Maggie said.

"I know you two go way back. Unfortunately."

"And I know you know the story, but some things are hard to forget. And others are hard to forgive."

I did know the story. Maggie had told me the details many times before. Almost two decades ago, a joint study was being conducted at a research center in Indianapolis. Tryon Institute. At the time, it was one of the most respected institutions regarding animal communications in the world. They had asked experts from all over the country to contribute to this study, a huge project focusing on gorillas and signing. One of their gorillas, Kiko, had already made headlines with Francine Patterson in California. Tryon Institute wanted to get in on the research. So they set up accommodations at a sprawling ranch west of Indy. There were two gorillas—Mimuh and Bradda—and ten different researchers contributing. But Maggie and Aubrey Keegan were two of the four scientists doing the actual work with the gorillas. They made great strides, especially with Bradda. In fact, he was surpassing any language skills that had previously been recorded, largely due to a technique Maggie had developed using a combination of sight cues accompanied by sound, mostly low vibrations of the voice.

Everything was kept tightly under wraps despite the repeated requests from the press for interviews. The heads at Tryon wanted to do a grand release of their findings, along with a huge press junket at the pavilion. Each researcher was to prepare their own dissertation to be presented to the board by a certain date. Keegan asked to turn hers in two days prior to the due date, saying she had another mandatory engagement at her university. The paper Keegan turned in was based completely on Maggie's findings. Keegan had written about the research like she'd somehow gotten a hold of Maggie's personal notes.

Maggie had no idea her work had been stolen. And when she gave her report to the board, they questioned her validity. It became a case of she said, she said, despite the support of the other two researchers for Maggie's findings. The board cited that testimony as hearsay and also made reference to the fact that Maggie and the other two researchers were close friends. The long and short of it?

Aubrey Keegan received recognition for Maggie's groundbreaking research and, in the months that followed, amassed several awards from the scientific community for her work. She's managed to ride the coattails of those honors ever since, getting high-paid offers for her presence at several different companies over the years.

"If I were you, I probably would have shot Keegan on the spot. I'm not kidding you. Even after all these years, I can't believe she got away with it. And look at her now. Corner office at CAR, a spot on the board, and pulling in the money hand over fist," I said, pushing my plate forward. The entire situation still disgusted me.

"She'll get hers some day, I bet. I'm not sure if that karma thing works the way people say it works. But somebody like Keegan? She can't keep doing the things she's doing without someone getting wise to her. Sooner or later." Maggie looked out across the restaurant before continuing. "But let's not talk about all that again. How can I help with Lazzy?"

"I'm not sure how anyone can help at this point. We haven't heard a word from the people who took him. Keegan doesn't want me to be meddling in the investigation. Her words, not mine. And this detective, Vargas, just seems uninterested." I had to stop talking because I felt a huge lump forming in my throat. My eyes welled up. I hadn't seen that coming. It took a deep breath and started again.

At that moment, my phone buzzed in my pocket. I ignored it, as I always do when I'm with someone else, whether it is a meeting or a lunch date. Two seconds later, it buzzed again. And then again.

"Take it," she said, nodding.

I pulled out my phone and saw four text messages from a number I didn't recognize. I opened them, and there he was.

Lazzy.

A video segment of him in a cage, just sitting, blinking. Four times over. I texted back.

Who are you?

At first, there was no answer. I hit it again.

Is Lazzy okay?

Still no answer. Then it came.

Wait for our call.

I turned my phone toward Maggie and handed it across the table.

"It's hard to see if he's doing alright," she said. "Will you forward it to me?" She handed the phone back. "But right now, let's get moving. I'll follow you down to Columbus. Call that Detective Vargas on the way. Send him the video. Tell him we'll be there in less than an hour."

I motioned for the check. I was about out of my mind seeing Lazzy in that small cage, just staring, blinking. Like he wasn't thinking at all. Then I felt a sense of reassurance, of confidence, knowing that my friend, my mentor, Magdalena Porter, was coming with me. Good old Maggie. Miss Porter. She had my back. Ever since I was little, she always seemed to have my back.

We arrived at the Columbus police station some 45 minutes later. An officer escorted us back to see Vargas, who was sitting at his desk, probably playing solitaire on his screen. Without getting up or barely looking up, he acknowledged us.

"What can I do for you, Ms. Greene?"

"It's Dr. Greene," Maggie said, standing tall.

"And you are?" Vargas cocked his head.

"I'm Dr. Magdalena Porter."

"And how is it I can help you two?" he asked.

"Didn't you get the video?"

"I did."

"Well?"

"Well, what, Dr. Greene? I see it is a monkey. I'm guessing it could be Lazzy, but it could be any other monkey on TikTok, or Instagram, or anywhere else for that matter," he shrugged.

I pulled my phone out of my pocket.

"I gave you the number. Did you run a trace on it?"

"Look, it would be a waste of time. I'm sure they used some burner phone. They'd be stupid not to. There's nothing about this video that helps at all. For all we know, it could be a fake."

Maggie stepped in front of me and leaned her hands on Vargas's desk.

"Look, Detective. Dr. Greene here has to be polite to you. Because of her job. But it is apparent you are not doing yours. She knows her subjects. The bonobo in the video is Lazzy. He's not a monkey, but how could you possibly know that? If all of this is above your head, call in the FBI, or at the very least, call in someone in this department who might be smarter than you or willing to figure this thing out. We are never going to find Lazzy if you are not looking. Run that damn phone number. At the very least, see what it brings. If it is a burner, find out where it was purchased. Do your job, Detective." She stood back up and stepped away from his desk.

Vargas sat in his chair, not saying a word, staring Maggie down.

"Listen, lady. I don't appreciate you coming in here and telling me how to do my job. I looked at your little video, and I don't see anything that can help us. So, if you got a problem with me, our Chief of Police sits in that office right there." Vargas motioned over his shoulder to an empty office a few yards away. "Captain Eugene Huffman," he continued smugly. "I'm sure he'll be happy to talk with you about all of this. Now, if you'll excuse me, I have work to do. Good day."

I started to turn and walk out, but Maggie grabbed my arm. "I will have a little chat with your captain. And some other people too." She looked down at his nameplate on the desk. "Detective Glenn Vargas."

Maggie looked around the room for a moment before heading for the door. I followed her outside the police station, hoping we hadn't just made a huge mistake.

Once outside, I stopped in the middle of the sidewalk. I had looked to Maggie for guidance my entire life. After my father died, she stepped in and filled a big portion of his role in my life. She taught me the ins and outs of everything. From changing a flat tire to replacing an electrical wall outlet. From frogs being able to hold their breath for seven hours to the fact that there are more than two dozen states of matter. On and on it went. How to swing a bat. How to patch drywall. And I probably wouldn't be working in the field of animal communications if it weren't for Maggie.

But the way she spoke out in the police station wasn't like her. I couldn't help thinking that her response to Vargas might have hurt my cause more than it helped. I felt the need to tell her.

"Maggie?" I tapped her on the elbow. "About what happened in there."

"Oh, I know. That Vargas guy is an idiot. He totally pushed me over the edge. I don't know how you've put up with him," she started walking again.

"Maggie, wait. I, uh. I don't know how to say this, but that guy is all I have. He's my only hope of finding Lazzy. And, well, I hope we didn't just burn that bridge."

She turned and looked at me, furrowing her brows.

"I just don't want him to shut it down completely," I said, rather meekly.

Maggie looked down at the sidewalk and shook her head. Then she looked at the sky. It took her a long time to gather her words.

"At some point, Rory, you have to speak up for yourself. I've watched you all these years. And so many times, you are as quiet as a mouse when it comes to confronting someone. I've always believed in trying to follow a peaceful path. Honey attracts more flies than vinegar and all that crap." She stopped for another moment and chuckled before starting in again.

"The fact remains. You seem to stand down when someone brushes up against you. And I realize that I've been guilty of this too. Look at me and this whole thing with Keegan. If I had been more aggressive back then, I would have stopped her right in her tracks. But I stood there in front of that review board, calmly telling them it was my paper. And through that whole entire hearing, I kept trying to convince myself that goodness would prevail and the truth would come out. Well, guess what? It didn't. That was my whole credo, all my life. Good will prevail. Justice will prevail. The truth will prevail, and on and on. But as much as I hate to say it, the real world just doesn't work like that a lot of the time."

"I just want Laz to be okay," I whispered.

"Me too."

Chapter Nine

We had nearly got to the car when someone called out behind us. "Excuse me."

I turned to see Detective Linda Patterson. She looked over her shoulder while striding toward us.

"Listen, Dr. Greene, I'm sorry about what happened in there," she said.

"Thank you. Detective Patterson, this is Dr. Maggie Porter. She is a professor at Butler University and a longtime friend. She's been helping me try to figure out this thing with Lazzy."

"Nice to meet you. Uh, I'm sorry to interrupt you two, but I just wanted to apologize about Vargas. He can be a little short sometimes, but he's a dependable officer," Patterson smiled.

Maggie nudged my arm. I looked at her, not knowing what she wanted.

"How long have you been with the Columbus Police Department?" she asked.

"Oh, this is my third year here, but I'm a rookie detective. I just got promoted about a month ago."

"Congratulations. How's it going so far?"

Patterson hesitated, looking down for a moment. "About as well as can be expected," she said.

"Let me guess," Maggie looked around the parking lot. "There's probably a handful of detectives on the force, and you are the only woman."

"Yes, I, uh. As a matter of fact, that's true."

"And you probably aren't getting much in the way of cases of your own," Maggie replied.

"Like I said, this is my rookie year. I'm mostly supposed to watch and learn."

"Well, Detective. Let me give you a little advice. Don't watch and learn too much where Vargas is concerned. The world doesn't need any more indifferent people. Indifference kills the soul."

"He can be difficult sometimes," Patterson said, shifting her weight. Suddenly, she looked very uncomfortable.

I stepped in. "Thank you for coming out here. I know you want to help. And I hope you can. Anything you can do for our case will be greatly appreciated. Lazzy means a lot to me. I just want to bring him home, safe and sound," I said.

"Listen, here's my card. My cell phone and email. Why don't you send that video to me? The whole text message. I'll have a look."

I took her card and thanked her. "I'll send it right away," I said as I watched Detective Patterson head back toward the building, hoping, once again, that the good guy would win.

Maggie followed me back to the lab in her car. I showed her around our facility, giving her a full tour of the area while pointing out cameras and exits. We finally went back to my office, where we continued our talk. She convinced me we should go to the Chief of Police, Captain Huffman. I sat at my desk, replaying the video of Lazzy. That's when I saw the sign.

"Look. Oh my gosh, look," I said to Maggie. "There's a sign on that back wall, back behind his cage. But it is out of focus."

I handed Maggie my phone, and she watched the clip a few times in a row.

"You need a video specialist," she said.

"There's a guy at the police department. Nice guy. Helpful. His name is Jack, I think," I said.

"Let's go see Jack. Maybe Captain Huffman will be back too," Maggie said, pushing out of her chair. "You drive."

I wished I had seen this sign behind Lazzy before we left the station earlier, but there we were, back a second time. As we walked through the offices, Vargas, still at his desk, did not look happy to see us, though he was determined to find out our business.

"Now, what can I help you with?" he said, shaking his head.

"We're not here to see you," Maggie said and walked right past his desk and directly toward Captain Huffman's office. His door was open.

"Hang on. Do you have an appointment?" Vargas stood up, holding out his arm.

"No, we do not. If we need one, I'm sure Captain Huffman will let us know."

Maggie knocked lightly on the door frame of his office.

"Come in."

We went through the introductions and the explanation of the case. Huffman may have been Maggie's age, but possibly slightly older, in his late sixties, I'd say. His hair was snow white and thick, and his teeth were as white as his hair. He was a good-looking, average-sized man, and his clothes were pressed sharply. He looked more like California Sunshine than Indiana Hoosier. He nodded as we spoke.

"I understand your concerns," he said. "And I'm sorry to hear that things haven't been going as well as you had hoped. But I have to tell you, kidnapping cases can be very problematic. They're often delicate situations. But mostly they are uncertain, as we have to rely on what the perpetrator gives us. Now, I'm sure Detective Vargas is gathering as much information as possible in this case, and while it may not seem like he's working through this, I can assure you he is committed to solving this crime." Captain Huffman had continued nodding the entire time he spoke.

Maggie and I looked at each other. I hated being brushed off like this, but I didn't see the point in arguing with him. Rather quickly, I stood up. "Thanks for your time," I said and walked out the door. A moment or two later, Maggie followed.

"Where are you going? You should have let him have it, Rory. He totally blew us off," she said.

"I don't know what we expected. He's covering his own rear, taking care of his people, doing what he has to do to keep his police department shiny and clean. We're wasting our time with him."

"So, you're just giving up?" Maggie asked.

"No, I'm sidestepping a little. Let's try to find the video guy. If he won't help, I'm not sure what to do next."

Every desk in the detectives' area was empty, and I saw this as being our first big break of the day. I motioned Maggie to follow me, and we made our way back to the video room. Jack was sitting at a counter, his back to the door, headphones on. He was watching a scene of a convenience store on the monitor in front of him. I didn't want to scare him, so I called out his name loudly. He jumped slightly as he turned to take notice of us. He slipped off the headphones and stood. "I'm terrible with names," he said, holding out his hand.

I walked over and shook it.

"Rory. Rory Greene."

"Jack. Everton."

"This is my friend, Maggie Porter. I'm sorry to disturb you, but I have a video of Lazzy, my missing bonobo, and I was hoping you might be able to look at it and help us with any clues."

He looked down briefly before answering. "I'm sorry, Rory. My work orders have to come from someone with a badge. That's just the protocol around here. Otherwise, I could get into big trouble."

"Are you sure there's nothing you can do?" Maggie asked.

"I'm sorry." He truly did look sorry.

We thanked him for his time and apologized again for intruding. We were about out the door when the next thought hit me. I stopped and turned around.

"What about helping me on the side? I could pay you. You know, after hours. Like, if you had any of your own equipment, not police equipment?" I asked.

Jack looked toward the door, which was now standing open. He returned his eyes to us for a moment before going back to the counter. He leaned over and wrote something on a slip of paper, handing it to me quickly.

"Call me," he said. "Not tonight. I have another engagement. But give me a try tomorrow. I should be home. We'll talk then."

I squeezed the paper tight in my fist. I wanted to hug the guy but thought better of it. We thanked him and made our way to my car.

Maggie headed back to Indianapolis late that afternoon. My feelings about the day were split down the middle. I felt skeptical about getting much help from the police department, but at the same time, felt promise in the connection with Jack.

I worked late into the evening, making up for the time I'd been away during the day. When most of my tasks were completed, I asked Gloria and Della if they'd like to come out and sit with me for a while. They both said yes, so we went to their play lounge, a room filled with some of their favorite toys and a mini fridge for treats. We sat at their table, eating bananas. I asked them how they were feeling, giving them options—happy, sad, bored, tired?

Della chimed in. "Banana. Happy."

Gloria kept eating but shrugged her shoulders.

"You don't know?" I asked her.

She shrugged again, then set the remainder of the banana on the table.

"Not word," she signed.

"Not word? You are not happy, sad, bored, or tired? None of those? Is that what you mean?"

"Yes. Not word." She picked up the banana and turned it around in her hands before putting it in her mouth.

"Do you miss Lazzy?" I picked up one of the stuffed animals and hugged it.

She shrugged again.

Sometimes, I didn't know how much they really understood. "Miss" was a new concept for us, and I had worked on it the other day. But I couldn't be sure either one of them knew its true meaning. I got up and found a stuffed monkey animal. I pointed at it.

"This is Lazzy."

Then I put it behind my back.

"Lazzy gone."

I pointed back at Gloria.

"You miss Lazzy?"

Gloria sat looking at me for a long time, but surprisingly, Della got up and walked behind me, retrieving the animal. She handed it to Gloria and sat back down. Sometimes, I felt like our communications flowed incredibly well, and other times it felt like I was climbing Everest. At that moment I wished I had more clarity about all of this. I wished my father were sitting there to explain to me what he did with our parrot. With Oliver. I sensed that I was going about this all wrong, like a hundred others before me. We all thought we were making great strides in this field, but in reality, we were missing the link. The connection. The bigger picture.

Gloria stood up and sat back down. I could tell she was getting agitated, so I decided to stop talking about Lazzy. I reached for the box of blocks when Gloria signed to me again.

"Gloria stay here," she said, pointing to her chest. "Gloria home," she signed it once, paused, and signed it again.

I went over, put my arms around her, and hugged her tight.

"Gloria's staying right here. I'm not going to let anyone take you. Della either. You both are home. Gloria, home. Della, home," I said.

Chapter Ten

Sometimes, we speculate. We might be going to a party, and we imagine how things might go. Or, we have a job to do at work, and we think about any possibilities that might arise. That's how humans are. We try to see into our futures. That was the case with me when I thought about meeting Jack to view the video of Lazzy. He asked me to be at his house by 6 p.m. I tried to imagine what his place might look like. Maybe some old dusty computer sitting in the corner of his living room, with the two of us on folding chairs, squinting to see the screen. Or perhaps a laptop on his kitchen counter amid a pile of dirty dishes. A few more scenarios ran through my mind.

I got to Jack's house a few minutes early and rang the bell. He lived only about five minutes from me on foot, surprisingly, in a neighborhood much like my own.

"Hey, Rory, come on in," he smiled, opening the door wide. A cat stood in the entryway, staring up at me.

"This is Bootles," he said. "Bootles is a bit of a stalker. I hope you're okay with cats?"

"I love cats. Nice to meet you, Bootles," I leaned over and let him sniff my hand.

"Can I get you anything? Something to drink? Coffee, water, a beer?" he asked as we walked through the living room and dining room toward the back of the house.

"No thanks. This is a nice place you have here," I said.

"Thank you. My dad gave it to me." He didn't offer any more. "Right through here," he continued.

He opened a door that led to a large room. "Oh, my God." I didn't mean to say it, but it just fell out of my mouth.

The room looked like it had been pulled from the interior of Microsoft or Apple, modern and sleek. Large screens lined the back wall, transformable into six different screens or combined to form one huge image. A large console sat in the middle of the room, with three computers there, each with a screen of its own. In front of that sat four oversized leather chairs with cupholders and footrests, all facing the screen. Large speakers were built in at each corner of the room, barely noticeable, blending in perfectly with the walls. Two office chairs sat behind the console.

"I built this onto the house about a year ago. Do you like it?"

"I feel like I'm standing in some secret room of the Pentagon."

"Well, it's probably not far off," he laughed. "I'm a bit of a geek. I've been playing video games since I could stand up and grab the controller off the coffee table. The old Nintendo NES. Thank goodness my mom was a gamer."

"Your mom?"

"God, yes. She loved video games. We used to sit for hours and play Zelda or Super Mario. Metroid. Any of them, really. My dad used to get so mad because most nights, I hadn't done my homework by the time he got home. He'd walk in front of the TV and flip it off mid-game. Mom and I would go berserk. It was our little happy family ritual."

"Where are they now?" I asked. I imagined them growing gray together somewhere, holding hands, laughing at old memories.

"Hmm. Well, my dad lives down in Florida now. He's at a retirement community there, and it seems to fit him. And my mom has passed. She was a Columbus police officer. The only woman officer ever killed on the job. You might remember it. The bank robbery downtown. She was walking by as the robbers were coming out of the building. They shot her on sight. She had her lunch in her hand. She'd just bought it two doors down at Irene's Kitchen. A grilled cheese sandwich." He paused for a moment. "Anyway, that was that. My dad couldn't stand to be in the house after that. He said I could have it if I wanted it. And I did. And here I am."

"I'm sorry, Jack. I didn't mean to pry."

"Oh, it's fine. Don't worry about it. I miss her. I miss them both, but it's a pretty healthy grief at this point," he said, smiling. "Alright, enough about me. Let's see that phone of yours."

I reached into my pocket and handed it over. He motioned to the two chairs at the console.

"This is the captain's chair," he laughed, sitting down. "Please, have a seat here."

"The reason I want the text from your phone is because I want to have the cleanest path of data on this message. Once I start to hack into things …" he stopped and looked over at me like someone had just jabbed him with a hot poker.

"You do understand how I have to go about these things. That I sometimes have to go where I don't quite belong. To get the information we need?" he asked.

"I don't understand how it works, but I figured we might have to cross some lines this evening," I said.

"Okay. I just wanted to make sure we were upfront with this. I'm a hacker. White hat hacker, but a hacker, nonetheless. You will be an accessory to the crime," he motioned toward the computer screens, smiling.

"Understood," I said, crossing my chest.

"Good. So, yeah, okay. Once I start hacking into things, it is much easier if I have the original path from your phone. Say, if you sent it to me or to Vargas, and I went from there, I would have an entirely new set of parameters to deal with." His fingertips worked the keyboard in front of him wildly as he talked. As if the two things were seamlessly intermingled in his brain.

I stayed silent so as not to be a distraction, but every so often he would say something out loud, like, "Okay, there," or "Now I got you. I see you, you little bastard."

He gave me a sheepish look. "Sorry. I like to talk to the code."

He continued to tap away. "I've triangulated the signal on this, the time stamp and such. The ID markers from the towers. It looks like it was sent from somewhere just north of town." He quickly pulled an Indiana map up on his screen and circled just above Columbus, showing me the area.

"That's a start," he said. "Now, let's take a look at that video."

It suddenly flashed up in front of us, one solid movie image divided on the six screens. A huge scene of Lazzy opening and closing his eyes. Lazzy looked distressed, blinking as if his eyes were bothering him.

"Let's try to zero in on that sign you wanted to see," Jack nodded, pointing. "What is that? Is that a face on the sign? Is it looking at flashlights?"

I recognized the sign immediately as Jack brought it into focus.

"It's an eye-washing station sign like in labs or factories. Anywhere there are chemicals in use. It's an OSHA thing. You have to assign clearly marked face-wash areas if you use certain chemicals. Anything that might be classified as eye irritants," I said.

"It would be nice if we could find something else," Jack continued, looking at the screen.

"Actually, this might be just the start we need. Right after Lazzy was taken, I got a message to meet someone at the old Wilkerson Metals Warehouse. It happens to be north of town in the warehouse district. Maybe that's coincidence, maybe not. The place is run down now. Empty. But there are other working factories up there. A lot," I said.

"So now what?" Jack looked at me, cocking his head sideways.

"So now I need to know something else. From you. I know we don't know each other that well, but I'm going to ask you to be completely honest with me."

"Okay, shoot."

"Do you trust Vargas?"

Jack looked down and scratched the back of his head. He looked at me over his arm, squinting one eye.

"That's a tough one, Rory."

"I'm sorry. Never mind I asked," I said, shaking my head.

He took a deep breath, looking forward. "No," he said.

"No, like I shouldn't have asked you? Or no, like you don't trust him?"

"No. Like I don't trust him. Not as far as I can throw him."

I sat back in my chair.

"I hate to say it out loud, but I've had this gut feeling like he might be in on this thing. Or, at the very least, he's covering for someone," I said.

Jack looked at me, tightening his lips.

"Are you sure you don't want a beer?"

"I'd love one," I said.

A small refrigerator stood along the back wall, along with a small counter that looked like a place for easy food preparation. Jack opened the cupboard above and pulled out some pretzels and chips, pouring them into a bowl. Then he retrieved two beers from the refrigerator below.

"Sustenance!" he said, holding them up as he walked.

We popped open the beers and sat quietly for a moment, looking at the screens on the large wall.

"I decided to work in law enforcement because of my mom, I suppose. Maybe it's my Freudian way of honoring her. I don't know. But I'm a layman there. No badge. There are a few of us like that in the department that aren't actually officers. But still, there's an unspoken code of honor among cops. You look out for your brother. Or sister. Even those of us who are on the outside of things still adhere to this standard. You know?"

"I sort of figured as much."

"At any rate, some of those officers are good to the core. They are golden. Honest. Brave. They freaking ooze integrity," he said. "And with them, it is easy to maintain that code." He laughed a bit before continuing. "Probably because they never do anything wrong. But guys like Vargas? You can just tell. Maybe they entered the force with good intentions, but somewhere along the line … They took a wrong turn. I'm not sure what his deal is, but he just doesn't seem to be above board. His partner quit about six months ago. I'm not sure why. It wasn't like they were on some big case or anything. There wasn't any kind of scandal that I know of, and that office is pretty small. But one day, he came in, walked into Huffman's office, and handed him his resignation. Two weeks later, he was gone. The guy packed up his family and moved out of Columbus."

"No explanation?"

"Oh, around the office, he'd say things like, 'Time for a change,' and such. But he never said he had a new job somewhere or anything like that. Since Ray left, that was his name, Ray. Since he left, Vargas has been working alone mostly. Except for lately. Huffman put Linda Patterson with him now that she's been promoted. She loves that," Jack said.

"Seriously?"

"No. Heck no. She's never said it out loud, but she can't stand the guy. You can tell by the way she looks at him. I'm pretty sure she has her own ideas about Vargas."

I took a long drink of beer.

"Well, maybe I need to do some research. I need to check what kinds of warehouses are located in that district and which ones are still active, also see what other labs might be around here. I need to figure out where they're keeping Lazzy, whoever they might be."

Jack spun around in his chair, facing the keyboard again. He began typing wildly again, and the screen went all white with a list of addresses. "There you go. There are the warehouses, at least the active ones. I'll send this to you." He went back to typing. "The lab list is going to be a lot bigger. So we're going to get medical labs, scientific labs, mechanical labs, robotic labs, on and on. I mean, I can't really narrow the search unless you're sure of what type of lab he might be in. I'm giving it a 50-mile radius, unless you want me to widen the circle," he said.

"No. Fifty is good. A good place to start."

"What else," Jack said, smiling again.

"You don't know how much I appreciate your help, Jack. Thank you. How much do I owe you for all of this?"

"You don't owe me anything, Rory. This is just what I do."

I felt overwhelmed by Jack's kindness. I never expected him to go to such lengths. But even still, I couldn't help but wonder why he would risk helping. "Well. Doing what you do is awfully nice, Jack. But I have to admit I'm a little curious as to why. Why would you stick your neck out for me like this?"

He didn't answer initially. He looked down at the table and began working the edge of the label from his beer bottle. After a long pause, he spoke. "My mom was a good cop. A darn good cop. She was as by the book as they come. Not only on the job but in all parts of her life. She taught me so much about integrity and honesty. And, well, I suppose I try to carry that forward when I can. I feel like Vargas isn't giving your case the attention it deserves. For whatever reason. So, I'm just trying to do my part to make sure it does get the help it needs."

"Well, it means a lot to me. I'm very grateful," I said.

Jack smiled and nodded. "Think nothing of it," he said as he got up. "Are you sure you won't have another beer?"

"No. Thank you. I've got an early morning tomorrow. But thanks. I mean it. Thanks for all your help."

As we walked toward the front door, he spoke again. "I'm going to do a little more poking around. It seems like when you have a whole bunch of dots on a page, there might be a connection somewhere. Isn't that how the game works?" he asked.

"I think so. I hope there's a bigger picture in there somewhere."

I walked out the front door, and, as the light from the porch caught my attention, something else clicked. "Jack? Can I ask you one more thing?"

"Name it."

"Do you think you could find me the address of Martin Boyle?"

He looked at me, rolling his eyes as if I could ever doubt his abilities for something so simple.

"It'll be on your phone in a couple of minutes."

Chapter Eleven

We were under a time-sensitive contract with the government for our advances in animal communications, and all of us were well aware. Every two weeks, we had to submit an extensive report, mostly a form they had provided, telling them of our progress, or lack thereof. CAR scheduled regular meetings to discuss progress and strategies. The pressure from above about the pace of our work came at a steady flow.

With all that bearing down on me, I got to work by 5 a.m. the next morning, to make up for some of the time I'd been investigating Lazzy's disappearance. The first two-plus hours went by quickly.

Around 7:30, people began filtering in slowly. Della, awake in her cage, worked on stacking her favorite colored blocks, but Gloria stayed fast asleep. She definitely did not classify as a morning animal. The smell of coffee started filtering through the lab, as well as food. People often carried in some sort of breakfast for themselves, eating at their desks as they worked. I hadn't eaten yet and went to the cafeteria to pick something up.

I took the elevator back up to the lab since I was carrying a container filled with my egg, cheese, and bacon bagel. As the doors opened, I noticed the light in the hallway. Somehow dimmer, I thought. Just two steps into the hallway and I became abruptly aware.

Smoke.

I ran toward our lab, and the air seemed to clear out some. I retraced my steps and headed back to the area down the hall. The smoke was thicker there. I pulled the nearest alarm on the wall, and the piercing screech of the siren filled the building, echoing onto itself.

I sprinted back to our area and found most people standing around, not knowing whether to leave or not. Most people are funny in these situations. It's like they don't want to be disrupted from their routine, to go outside if there might not be a catastrophe at hand. They seem to be willing to take that gamble with precious time in the event that the emergency might be real. That wasn't true with our lab staff. Everyone was well trained and knew of the importance of getting the animals to safety.

"Grab what's important to you and get out!" I yelled. "Go, go!" I ran toward Della and Gloria, flipping the lock on the cage area and motioning them out. "Thomas, help me with these two. I'll take Gloria, you take Della," I said, putting her hand in his. "Go, go." Many labs have an underground safe room area for animals. Ours did not. So in the event of fires, we had to evacuate to a designated outdoor area away from everyone else.

We all made our way to the stairwell and down to the main floor, where we exited out to the street. Within a few moments, police and fire were there, making their way into the building. I instructed Thomas to follow me with Della, and we hurried directly to our safe location, a large grassy area located a comfortable distance away from everyone else.

As the first responders worked, I assessed our side of the building. I could see smoke filling one of the windows. I tried to place the location, and it looked like it could be one of the men's restrooms. As far as I could tell, that was the only smoke-filled room. Thomas, the girls, and I sat on the grass and watched as the commotion played out before us: firefighters hauling hoses, police officers directing vehicles and a sea of white lab coats flapping in the breeze as everyone looked on.

Gloria bumped me. "Why outside?"

"There's trouble inside," I answered.

She pointed to herself and to me. "Okay?"

"Yes, Gloria. We are okay. We are safe." I gave her a hug.

Della was still clutching two of her blocks. She saw me looking and held them up, grinning.

"Way to be thinking, Della. You brought your blocks."

Gloria bumped me again and showed me her hands. These little beings made me so happy just about every time they spoke.

"It's okay, Gloria. It's okay not to have any blocks. How about if you help me keep track of my pen." I handed her one of my pens to hold.

Within another 20 minutes, the building had been cleared of danger, with minimal damage occurring on our floor in the men's bathroom, as I had guessed. As I walked near the front door of the building to reenter, I stopped to talk with one of the firemen, who seemed idle at the time. "How'd it start? There's not much flammable in the men's restroom," I said.

"One of the guys said an accelerant was probably used. It started in the trash can, but it spread across the floor and toward that wooden door rather quickly. The state fire marshal will probably get in on this one," he continued to nod. Just then, someone called for his attention.

"Sorry, gotta run," he called over his shoulder as he walked away.

I walked with Gloria, holding her hand. "Well, Gloria, it looks like somebody's really trying to upend things around here. I bet you a hundred bucks Vargas doesn't even come down here to see what happened. But if you ask me, and I think you did, this fire and Lazzy disappearing are related. All I know is somebody better be checking the security footage again." I leaned over and said in her ear, "And guess who's going to ask about it?"

Gloria pulled back slightly and patted me on the cheek.

"Don't worry, Gloria. I'll be careful."

We approached the crowd waiting at the elevator, several bodies deep. Per protocol, we had to wait at a distance until everyone had cleared the area.

"How do you feel about the steps, Gloria? Want to do some climbing?"

The rest of the day felt pretty useless around all the CAR labs. Everyone seemed more interested in talking about the fire and less interested in work. Since Martin Boyle went missing, the staff in our immediate lab rotation consisted of me, Andy Turner, and two research assistants, Brad Reynolds and Hannah Schultz. A couple of times when I walked through, the three of them were huddled at one of the counters chatting. Whenever I showed up, the trio spread apart quickly. On the third occasion, I walked over to see what the ongoing dialogue was all about. They appeared to be a little embarrassed, having been called out by their supervisor, but that wasn't my intention.

"What's the good word?" I asked.

The three were quiet at first, trading glances. A moment later, Andy spoke up. "Oh, we've just been talking about the fire and about this place. Things are a little edgy lately," he said, "what with Lazzy getting kidnapped and Martin going AWOL. And now this, today."

"Yeah, I'd say edgy is an understatement," I added.

"So what do you think, Rory? Why's all this crap happening right now?"

"I wish I knew," I said, pausing. "I've been trying to figure things out on my own, especially with Lazzy. But I'd really be interested in hearing what you all think." I paused briefly, looking at the three of them. "So. Come on. Spill it. What do you think?"

Again, they fell silent for a few seconds. Then Hannah spoke up. "I was on the phone with my dad last night and told him all about this. He's a cop in Houston. Anyway, he thinks someone's trying to derail our research. Espionage. Moles. All that. He watches too much TV," Hannah said. She let out one of her giddy laughs.

"He might be right, though. Since this is a government project, who knows how far the implications might go," Andy said, leaning in on the counter.

Brad made a funny scoffing noise, shaking his head.

"What, Brad? You think they're wrong?"

Brad and Hannah were at least ten years younger than Andy and I. They were both out of college by a few years, both with degrees in Biology. Brad planned on returning to work on his Master's, and Hannah seemed to be content with her current path. One thing was certain, though. Both always had strong opinions, with Brad leaning to the liberal side of the aisle, while Hannah was more conservative.

"So, I'm not sure our current administration would be setting fires in little laboratories in Bumfrick, Indiana. Personally? I think somebody is seeing a chance to make some money right now," Brad said, rubbing his fingers together.

Andy piped in again. "Isn't it always about the money? Money and power?"

Brad broke in, eager to speak. "Well. If it were me and I was running the show? I'd start with the obvious. Martin. He's been missing since Lazzy was taken. And not only that." Brad stopped and looked over his shoulder and around the lab. "The guy is just plain creepy. Seriously." The three of them agreed about their dislike of Martin. I could see it on their faces.

Just then, the fire alarm went off again.

"You've got to be kidding," Hannah said. "Really?"

"Let's go. You know the rules," I said, corralling them toward the door.

"Andy, get Della. I'll grab Gloria."

All of them complained as we walked toward the stairwell, with the exception of the bonobos. As we joined others shuffling down the steps, comments ran rampant about the absurdity of this. Again.

A moment later, everything changed. The building shook, and debris came raining down on us. Several people lost their footing from the immensity of the movement. The saunter down the steps suddenly became a rush. Gray dust fell on us from above, people started yelling. Screams could be heard from the floors above us.

Once I got outside, I ran clear of the building with Gloria loping along. I turned and looked back. A gaping hole had appeared at the side of the building. Chunks of concrete and twisted metal hung out this side, suspended by paper-thin threads.

A bomb.

Someone had planted a bomb.

Chapter Twelve

I sat in my kitchen, phone in hand, looking at Martin Boyle's name and contact information Jack had sent. Robert Martin Boyle III.

Sarah looked up from her eggs and bacon, holding a fork in one hand and a bagel in the other. "Why do men do that? Keep naming their kids after themselves?" she said.

"I'm going over there. I've decided. I'm just going to go up and knock on the door."

"It doesn't sound like a very good idea to me," Sarah said. "Take me."

I didn't answer.

"I'm serious," she said. "This guy, if he really is involved in all of this, is probably dangerous. I think you should see if you can get the police to go."

"I already asked Vargas about it early on. If I can believe anything he says to be true, he claims they already went on two separate occasions. He also said it didn't appear anyone was there. There wasn't any warrant or anything. And the last time I asked, Vargas said that they really don't have any evidence to petition a judge for one now."

"Well, it doesn't sound like he's going to make another trip over there for you."

"I doubt it. The worst part of all of this is Lazzy. I feel like the longer this goes on, the deeper the trouble for getting Lazzy back. I can barely sleep at night thinking about him. He must be scared out of his mind by now," I said.

"I can see how hard this has been on you. And I know you're not going to let this drop until you go check out this Martin guy's place. Even still, it seems pretty dangerous."

"How about this? What if I call Jack and ask him to go with us? It's Saturday. I bet he's not working today," I said.

An hour later, the three of us drove toward Martin's apartment, I looked out the window of the car, taking it all in. Sarah rode up front with Jack. I think it was the first time I'd ever been in the back seat of my own car.

"So, let's go over this one more time: We knock. If Martin comes to the door, great. If not, we leave. No poking around. That's when people get shot for trespassing." Jack turned and looked directly at me

"No poking," I said.

A moment later, we pulled up along the curb in front of a row of small houses lining Glenburn Avenue.

"I thought he lived in an apartment," I said.

"I think it said 'rental,' so I'm guessing all of these are rentals. Maybe," Jack said.

The three of us got out of the car. As Jack closed his door, I noticed the holster under his jacket.

"You carrying?" I asked.

"Yeah, I have my concealed carry permit. I'm an excellent shot, I might add. My mom taught me. It was one of our favorite things to do. Go target shooting together." He pointed up the street. "It's up here, about a block. I don't want him to see us coming, not that it will help any. We're looking for 656."

As we walked up toward the small stoop in front, the windows of the house all looked dark. Jack rang the doorbell. Then knocked. We waited a few minutes; he knocked again. Nothing. I know I promised not to poke, but I walked over to the first window and looked inside. The place looked empty. There were no signs of dirty dishes on tables or clothes having been tossed on furniture. In fact, it didn't especially look like anyone lived there at all. I looked over to Jack and Sarah standing on the front walk, both with their hands on their hips.

"I know, I know," I put my arms up in surrender and started walking toward them through the leaves.

"Excuse me," someone called out. "Hold up there a minute." A balding man in a flannel shirt and blue jeans walked toward us. He held a paper in his hand.

"Are you friends of Martin's?" he asked.

"Uh, not really. I work with him," I said.

"Well, when he comes in on Monday, can you give this to him?"

"What is it?"

"His eviction notice. He's three months late on rent. I try to give people the benefit of the doubt, but I'm not Daddy Warbucks, either. I need the money, just like everybody else. Sorry. Terry Simmons. I own the place. I own these four right here," he said, pointing.

"Nice to meet you, Terry. But Martin hasn't been to work all week. That's the reason we were dropping by, to see what was going on," I said.

"Oh, well then," he said, putting the paper in his front chest pocket. "I'd say the guy's skipped out on all of us.

"It looks that way," Jack said. "Uh, listen, Mr. Simmons. If you happen to see him, would you mind giving me a call?" Jack handed him his business card with the Columbus police logo.

"You're the police?

"It's an unofficial visit," Jack smiled.

"I surely will. And if you see him, tell him his landlord wants his rent."

"Deal," Jack said, waving. We started to walk back to the car.

"What now?" Sarah asked.

Jack smiled again. "Now we hold up Rory's end of the deal. Now, we go get lunch. She's buying."

At Benson's Bistro, a little place on the south side of town, we ordered burgers and fries.

"So, I hate to bring it up again, but what are you going to do now, Rory?" Sarah turned her head sideways.

"Well, there's bound to be an FBI investigation. Thank God no one got killed. I think the final total I heard on the news last night was that 11 people were injured."

"Will CAR close down then while all this is going on?" Sarah asked.

"Yeah. They officially closed down our facility right after the bombing. The CEO sent out an email. All non-essential workers are supposed to stay home until notified. But the essential workers still have to go in. That leaves a lot of us still working because of the animals."

Sarah shook her head, "I didn't even think about all that. How are your animals doing?"

"I'm worried about them, honestly. I really wish CAR had alternative places to house all of them. But they don't. Not on such short notice. The Indianapolis Zoo said they could take some of the birds, but there's no point in it, really. As far as Della and Gloria go, they're pretty much a mess. They don't like anything to be out of their normal routine. And they certainly don't understand any of this. At least, I don't think they do. But regardless, both of them have been shutting down with all the disruptions. I mean, our research is totally stopped at this point, so we aren't doing all their daily lessons and exercises. They're used to being busy all day. So we're completely regressing in terms of their mental well-being," I said. Jack and Sarah had both been good listeners, sitting there attentively while I explained everything.

As our lunch neared its end, Jack said he would keep his eyes and ears open at work and let me know of any news. We dropped him off at his house and started heading back toward our homes when I noticed my gas gauge was getting low. I asked Sarah if she would mind if we went uptown a little ways so I could fill my tank. Just as I was finished pumping, a car passed on Marr Road, moving along at a good clip. I could have sworn Martin Boyle was in the passenger seat. I jumped back into my car, fired up the engine, and started following the dark sedan, maybe an Audi, maybe a Toyota.

I weaved in and out of traffic, trying to catch up. We were headed north, and I thought I had the car in sight. But as we approached the top edge of town, I could no longer see it. It must have turned, maybe, onto Rocky Ford. I doubled back, heading west on Rocky Ford, but there was no sign of Boyle's car. But I realized we were incredibly close to all the old warehouses.

"I want to cut over to the warehouse district," I said.

"Go, go. You're driving great if I keep my eyes closed," Sarah had one hand on the dashboard. I thought she was overreacting. We were in my little Honda Insight. How fast could I have been going? After ten minutes or so of scurrying through the streets, we gave up. I'd lost Boyle. If, in fact, that really had been him. I could feel both the frustration and uncertainty rising in me.

I started prattling to Sarah. "I sort of figured that, somehow, Martin might not be connected to this anymore. I mean, I didn't know what to expect as far as what we'd find at his house. But once we saw it empty … Well, it made me think he skipped town and that he never really had any part in this to begin with. Like he had nothing to do with Lazzy's disappearance. Three months behind on rent and everything. But now? Seeing him like that? And driving toward the warehouse district. Now, all of a sudden, I think he might be connected again," I said.

"I think you don't know what to think because you don't have anything to go on. I wish I could help," Sarah said.

I sat in the driver's seat, looking at the traffic signal. The red light. Everything, right at that moment, felt like it was at a standstill. Stopped. I wished Sarah could help, too. I wished someone could help. Then the light turned green.

Chapter Thirteen

They say there is safety in numbers. They also say that two heads are better than one. And if both of those things are true, what about four heads? I decided to invite Maggie, Jack, and Sarah over to my house. I wanted everyone to meet everyone else, my little band of close friends, old and new. And who better to help me try to see a new strategy for finding Lazzy than the three of them? They all seemed to be more than willing when we spoke one-on-one. Yet, all these individual conversations felt like four different paths spinning in different directions. The revelation came at that traffic light.

I asked Sarah to help me cook. We roasted a whole chicken with baked sweet potatoes, corn casserole, and a nice homey coleslaw. With biscuits. And butter. I set the table as Sarah finished with the final preparations in the kitchen. Just as I placed the last fork, the doorbell rang. There stood Jack and Maggie, both prompt at five o'clock sharp. I smiled when I saw each of them holding a bottle of wine.

"Did you two ride together?"

"No. But I brought white, she brought red. We've got all the bases covered," Jack said, holding up his bottle.

"Excellent. Come in. Magdalena Porter, this is Jack Everton. Jack. Maggie." They both walked in, slipping off their coats and handing them over to me.

"Let's start in the living room," I said, though the two of them had already started toward the kitchen to set down their bottles of wine. Sarah stood looking in an open oven.

"I think you both know Sarah."

"Yes, we do," she said, waving a pot holder in the air.

We stood around the kitchen as Jack uncorked both bottles of wine. The conversation moved freely, as I knew it would, mostly with Jack and Maggie exchanging their background stories of where they worked and lived.

"So you are in animal communications, like Rory?" Jack asked.

"I am. I mostly teach these days. Up at Butler University."

"Maggie's being modest right now. She's been one of the pioneers. The greats. I mean, this woman has answered her phone, and the likes of Jane Goodall have been on the other end of the line, just calling to chat. That's how crazy smart she is in all of this," I said.

Maggie waved her hand in the air, reluctant to speak. "Jane and I have worked together over the years. Her work has been focused on animal behavior in the wild; how animals, chimpanzees, communicate naturally with one another. My work, however, has been centered on bridging the gap between animals and humans. Not just primates, but any species that see fit to have a word with us," she said, crossing her arms and leaning back on the counter.

"So? What's the verdict?" Jack spread some cheese on a cracker, all the while watching Maggie.

"My verdict? I'm not sure I have a verdict yet. But I'm leaning in the direction that animals are every bit as smart as humans. But in a different way. For years, we've been judging them on our methods of communication. How we, humans, form thoughts and ideas, and more pointedly, how we convey those thoughts to one another. We try to impose our language on them, and with that, we 'judge' them by that standard."

"I'm not sure I follow completely," Jack said.

"Well, for instance, we say dolphins are one of the most intelligent animals. But we base this on the fact that dolphins can understand more human words than, say, a frog. Same with certain primates, who can assimilate human sign language. On the other end of the spectrum, certain animals are classified as being dumb. When, in reality, they are simply following their species' behavioral rules. Like pandas. Or sloths. Another great example is ants."

"If you want to hear more, you better come sit at the dining-room table," I said.

Maggie and Jack took their seats as Sarah and I brought the food to the table. We all handed around the platters and bowls, filling our plates. Everyone ooohed and awwed over the meal, staying fairly quiet otherwise.

"So, I promise not to keep badgering you all night, but why, then, are some animals so much better at speaking our language?" Jack asked.

Maggie glanced at me, and I smiled back at her. I think she was worried about taking up too much of the conversation, but I found her fascinating every time she spoke. It seemed I was always learning something new from her, even though we'd known one another since I was a little girl.

"Well, there are really several different distinctions when it comes to this. For instance, animals that are able to talk like humans are categorized as vocal learners. They hear sounds and learn how to imitate them. Humans are good at this. But other good vocal learners are animals like parrots and certain songbirds. Dolphins and beluga whales are also good at this. Ravens. Crows. Orangutans. The list goes on.

"The region of their brains that allows them to imitate speech is called the forebrain. I won't go full into all of this, but the brain circuits in the forebrain help animals to learn new sounds. And from there, those signals tell their vocal tract muscles to produce those same sounds. Hence, the talking parrots. But certain animals don't have those particular brain circuits."

My phone buzzed in my pocket. I reached down and silenced it. A moment later, it chimed again. Once it signaled a third time, I decided I better have a look. Something could have been going wrong at the lab. I reached down and opened it in my lap.

I had another text message. Once again, it came from an unknown sender. This time, a photo of Lazzy holding up a copy of today's newspaper. A *USA Today*. Below the photo was the message: *Stop the work. Stop what you're doing. Or pay the consequences.* Sarah, Maggie, and Jack were all staring at me silently.

"What's going on?" Jack said.

I handed him my phone.

"Can I use your computer?" he asked. I retrieved my Macbook Pro and set it on the table. He flipped it open and began typing away at the speed of sound, moving back and forth between my phone and the laptop. After a few moments, he looked up.

"It looks like it's coming from the same area as before, Rory. I can't narrow things down any, though. I can only trace the signal to a nearby tower."

I was pacing the floor. "I don't get it. The message. At this point, we aren't doing anything groundbreaking. Not as far as I can tell, at least. I mean, Lazzy was worlds ahead of Della and Gloria as far as word recognition goes. And tasks. But we were just starting—and I mean just starting—with concepts. With abstract thought. Everything we've done so far has been done before by countless others. We're just laying the groundwork." I rubbed my temples, trying to avert the headache that was looming.

Maggie pulled her chair around the table next to mine. Jack continued typing away.

She patted my chair. "Come sit for a minute, Ror," she said.

I did as she asked, taking a big sip of wine before I sat down. Maggie cleared her throat.

"Think hard for a minute. About Lazzy. Here's what I'm thinking about all of this, especially now that you got this text. Someone in the lab or in your company saw something. Either they are working for another company, which is likely, or another government, which is a maybe. But they saw something. It had to be Lazzy. Did he say something extraordinary to you? Did he perform some sort of task that totally surprised you? Anything that might have happened, and you made a big deal about it to the others?"

I thought about her question long and hard. "Nothing, Maggie. Honestly, I can't think of a single thing."

"Okay, let's try this. You tape all your sessions, right? All your training exercises?"

"Yes, they're on file in the lab. It's all set up automatically."

I explained how we use iPads to control almost everything we do there—from the filming of the sessions to taking notes to capturing photos. Everything.

"But with the cameras, all I have to do is log in, and it starts a new session. The recording begins and ends when the training session ends, and I log out."

"Who has access to these tapes?"

"I do," Jack broke in, smiling, looking up from the computer.

"We need to start watching them. Backward," Maggie said. "From the day Lazzy was taken. We need to look for something he did that might be of interest. Something a competitor might want to pursue. And obviously, something they want you to stop doing."

Sarah spoke. "What I want to know is why they texted Rory like this. With the photos, the videos?"

"They want to scare Rory, that's why," Jack answered. He turned his attention directly toward me. "They know how much Lazzy means to Rory, so they are playing with her emotions," Jack said.

For a moment, everyone paused, looking lost. Maggie cleared her throat. "How about this? Let's eat this fabulous dinner that you made. And after, one of us can start watching the videos and get to the rest of this."

"I don't know about you all, but I'm pretty hungry," Jack said. "I'll eat fast and take the first shift of watching the recordings."

"It should probably be Rory or me who watch the tapes. We'll be more likely to see the thing that might be the key," Maggie said.

"In that case, I'll do the dishes," Jack said.

"I'll dry," Sarah added.

Chapter Fourteen

We took a brief pause and tried to enjoy the food, but the whole while my mind was distracted by the thought of watching the recordings. These sessions were of no use to the police, as the cameras were pointed at a small corner of the lab where we had our working table set up for the bonobos and the researchers. The kidnapper most likely would not have gone out of their way to walk into this secluded location.

Documenting these sessions had been a stipulation of our contract. Every minute our team worked on communication exercises had been recorded since the beginning of our funding. But we rarely reviewed the tapes unless we had a specific need. In most cases, we all kept our own notes, which we then used in collaboration for our weekly reports. It was strict company policy that nothing from CAR left the property. Not the files. No materials. Not even our notes.

Maggie and I moved to the far end of the dining-room table with my laptop while Jack and Sarah cleared the plates and started on the dishes. We watched for nearly an hour without pause, both of us sharing one Airpod each so we could listen to the audio at the same time. It all looked liked standard procedure. Clip after clip of us teaching signing signals to the bonobos and having simple conversations. Occasionally, we would work in descriptor words, like colors and shapes. Most of the segments were of Andy and me, with fewer of Martin.

But then, we noticed Martin pulling a small satchel out from under his lab coat. He got up from his stool and positioned his back in front of the camera. He stood, hunched over the table like this, working on something out of view. After a few moments, he sat back down. I could tell by the body language of the bonobos that they didn't like what had gone on. Della and Gloria had pushed their chairs back slightly, and Lazzy was no longer sitting right on his chair but squatted atop the seat. At that moment, I walked into the room. Almost exactly. I told them the session had run a little over and that the bonobos were due for their dinner time. We led them out of the room, and Martin stopped the taping session.

"What was that?" Maggie asked.

"I have absolutely no idea."

"It looked like some small case, maybe leather. Hard telling. Can Jack do anything with this? Blow it up or anything?" she said.

"Unless he can install some kind of x-ray vision to see through Martin's body, we're never going to know what went on there." I rubbed my temples, suddenly feeling sick.

"All three of them looked upset. Did you see that?"

"Do you think he gave them a shot?" I asked.

"Maybe. But of what?"

During Martin's training sessions, he would almost always position himself in front of the camera, blocking the view. At least for a short while, nearly every time. He rarely followed the lesson plans he was assigned. And all three bonobos seemed to react with apprehension toward him. I kicked myself for not seeing it in the lab.

Maggie guessed how I was feeling about it. "Don't you go and pile on a bunch of that deep-seated Catholic guilt on yourself," she said. "I know you are beating yourself up over all of this."

I took a breath because, inside, I could barely contain my worry over the prospects for Lazzy.

"I can't help it. I feel like I should have been able to protect him somehow. And watching the recordings hasn't helped us much. I mean, we know for sure that Martin is in on things. But we still don't know why they took Lazzy and not one of the others. We haven't seen Lazzy do anything other than perform expected results."

"We have a lot of footage to go, though."

Jack and Sarah came in and sat at the table with us, having finished in the kitchen. They'd spent as much time talking as they had cleaning the dishes and putting them all away.

"How's it going?" Jack asked.

"Well, it's clear in the tapes that Martin's up to no good. But we still haven't found anything that might help us in finding Lazzy. In fact, I'm not sure they are going to let us find Lazzy."

"You don't know that, Rory." Sarah nudged my arm and gave me a supportive nod.

"I'm just looking at this realistically. He's been gone for days now. There hasn't been a single word about ransom. The only instruction they've given us is to stop working. And even though the lab is closed now, we know that things are going to start back up sooner or later. Corporate will press through with our contract agreement. They'll still want results. Besides, I wasn't going to say anything tonight, but I just got word today. We're getting a new bonobo tomorrow. Apparently, they're writing Lazzy off as a loss. I'm guessing they don't want to put any more research dollars into a lost cause."

I tried hard not to start crying, but I couldn't help it. Maggie pulled her chair closer and wrapped her arms around me. I felt embarrassed, and angry, and sad, all at the same time. I took a moment, then pulled away, wiping my tears.

"Sorry," I said. "I think I just need to get some rest. Do you guys mind if we call it a night?"

"Sure, Ror. It's getting late, anyhow. We'll start back in on this tomorrow," Sarah said, "and I'm sorry. I wasn't making light of the situation. I guess I just don't know how to help."

I smiled and told her it was okay. The three of them gathered their things and their coats and headed out the door. The house and all its quietness felt good somehow.

I took the laptop into the living room, fixed a bourbon on the rocks, and started to work through the rest of the recordings. About an hour in, I noticed something during one of Andy's sessions. It was a counting activity with blocks. He would ask one of the bonobos how many blocks, and they were supposed to sign the answer. We taught them numbers by showing pictures of three blocks and then signing the word "three." And so on.

In the session, Andy showed Della four blocks. She, after a long pause, signed the word "four." But off to the side, Lazzy had his arms over his head; he held up two fingers with one hand. Then he raised it twice. Next, he hit the table two times. He repeated this. All the while, Andy was focused on Della, waiting for her answer, and didn't notice Lazzy's gestures. Lazzy was using several methods of counting, signals we had not yet taught him. He'd figured out something outside of our training. What he was doing was not just learned behavior. He was coming up with counting concepts of his own. Not only that, but it looked like he was trying to give Della the answer. I knew right away that had to be it. He'd recognized signals. I could only think that, somehow, Lazzy had seen us doing these things and incorporated them into his own way of counting. Adding, multiplying. And trying to share. This transcended any level of learning that I had personally seen. I picked up my phone and called Maggie.

The new bonobo arrived first thing the next day. I made a point to get to work a few hours early, to get as much done as possible before the arrival, for it would surely take the better part of the day to acclimate the new animal.

Apparently, it was coming from a company somewhere in China. When they wheeled the bonobo in, the handler informed me it was a juvenile male named Boris. I walked over to his cart, his little portable cage on wheels, and said hello. He mostly looked tired.

"I'm going to unlock your door now, Boris. Then I am going to show you your brand-new room, okay?"

I got down on my knees and opened the door. Boris took my hand immediately. He was much smaller than Della and Gloria, and he put his arms around my neck, wanting me to pick him up. Boris was at a manageable weight, so I was able to lift him. Prior to his arrival, I felt very worried that I'd resist the new bonobo. In my heart, I did not want a replacement for Lazzy. No one could replace Lazzy. I'd tried all morning to get my head straight and to try to be neutral with this new member of the team instead of begrudging him. Yet, as soon as Boris squeezed my neck and gave me a peck on the cheek, my heart melted. He pulled back and put both hands around my face, looking me straight in the eyes. As they say: he had me at hello.

"Well, aren't you a little sweetheart?" I said.

Boris patted my face and then went back to hugging me.

"Let's see about your new room."

I opened the cage and sat him down inside. Gloria and Della were both in their cages, looking on. Gloria was in the space closest to Boris's cage.

"Gloria, this is Boris. He's come to live with us, to work with us," I signed and spoke.

"No Lazzy," she signed.

"That's right, Gloria. He's not Lazzy. I'm hoping Lazzy will be back soon. Then there will be four of us. Okay?"

"Where Lazzy?"

I latched Boris's door, walked over to the bars on his side of the cage, and sat down.

"I don't know, buddy. I just don't know."

Boris moved a couple of feet closer, but kept a little distance. Just then, Gloria struck out with her arm through the bar. She opened her mouth wide, making a hissing noise, and hit the cage with the inside of her hand. Boris scampered to a far corner.

"Gloria, that's enough," I said. "Boris wants to be your friend. Like Lazzy. Like Della. Boris is nice," I continued saying and signing.

For the moment, I lowered the drop curtain between the two cages. At the very least, it would give Gloria some time to smell and get used to Boris. I walked over and checked on Della, who didn't seem as affected by things. In the wild, bonobo females are highly social and form alliances with other females. It doesn't matter if they are related or not. They work together to command the stronger males in their group. They like to establish strong social networks. I wasn't sure if this might be the cause or if it was the fact that Gloria missed Lazzy, and she had become the one resenting this new arrival, not me.

Hannah and Brad had been standing at the counter watching. They were our essential employees for the day, in charge of feeding and cleaning.

"Well, that stinks," Brad said, chewing on his pen top.

"They'll calm down. We just need to give it a few days. I may have maintenance come in and rearrange the cages. I might put Della in the middle for a while."

"Do you think that's a good idea?" Hannah asked.

"I do. It'll give Gloria a chance to watch Boris from afar. And I'm guessing Della will be fine with Boris, so Gloria will be able to see that too. I'm not that worried at this point," I said.

"Anything more on Lazzy?" Hannah asked.

"I haven't heard a single thing. I'm heading back down to the police station this afternoon to see what Vargas has been up to. If anything."

I started to walk toward my office but stopped. "I know we're in shutdown mode, but I'd like you both to give Della and Gloria a little more attention. Maybe go over a few vocabulary lessons. I don't care who takes who, but let's just keep them stimulated a little bit today."

They both nodded, and Brad gave me a little salute.

"At ease," I said. "At ease."

Chapter Fifteen

I am ambidextrous. I can write with both hands. Eat. Anything, really. A lot of people show surprise or make a comment when they meet someone who is ambidextrous. Or left-handed. I think it is because we live in such a dominant right-hand society. I mean, for all my childhood life, adults tried to "correct" my left-handed side.

Like when I was eight and started playing Little League Softball. The first year, I'd walk up to the plate and go one way one time; the next time up, I'd switch over to the other side of the plate. The coach would always run out there and take me by my shoulders, moving me to the right-handed side of the tee. It took a while before he would figure out that I could hit the ball either way and that it was actually a good thing.

I think being able to use both hands equally has helped me with a lot of things over the years. Playing an instrument, for one thing. Like in band class during my grade-school years, it was easy to move both my right and left hands along the keys of the clarinet. Other kids struggled with their left hands, mostly. Don't ask me to play the clarinet these days. All of that ended by the time I was 12.

But what I'm getting at now, with sign language, and a lot of other things, it is easier.

I think being ambidextrous is my one advantage physically. Everything else about me is ordinary and typical. I'm average for my height and weight. I try to stay fit physically. But I've got just an average body.

On the intelligence scale, I'm pretty middle of the road too. My colleagues always say how smart I am, but truthfully, I think I'm typical. The good grades always came because I worked for them. Although, to my credit, I was second in my graduating class at IU. Mostly, though, I'm just a run-of-the-mill, middle-of-the-road kind of gal. I get a lot of people who say, "Don't I know you from somewhere?" I'm sure the reason is because I look average, like the girl at the donut counter or the woman who handed you the deposit slip at the bank.

Regardless of all of that, I think my ambidextrous ability is one of the reasons I felt drawn to Lazzy. Lazzy uses both hands interchangeably too. I first read this report by Bill Hopkins a few years back. He was an Agnes Scott College primate researcher and biopsychologist. Smart guy. Anyway, he was one of the first to establish that humans tend to be right-handed, worked over by societal implications. He found that the percentage for chimps is more level-handed. With humans, about 90 percent of us are right-handed. I don't think he studied bonobos. Anyway, his chimpanzee research showed that movements requiring skilled coordination were often done with their right hands. But if they performed things like simply reaching for some object or any unskilled movement, the chimps would use either hand. I always used Dr. Hopkins's test. He would have the chimps try to fish peanut butter out of the end of a plastic pipe, a complex movement. Most would use their right hands, but Lazzy would go back and forth between left and right. Our ambidextrous bonobo.

On my first day with Boris, I offered him the pipe test. Oddly enough, he used both hands in his work, trading back and forth until he had every drop of peanut butter. And when he was done, he pointed to the end of the pipe and handed it back to me—a clear sign of his comprehension that I was the one who'd jammed the peanut butter down there in the first place. I gave him another pipe full. I liked him already.

I wanted to get the testing in before taking my trip to visit the Columbus Police Department again. Even though Vargas hadn't been helpful to that point, I felt the need, at the very least, to check in to see if there was any news at all.

As I drove downtown, I thought of my interaction with Boris. I noticed, right then, that my left hand rested on the steering wheel. It was a thing with me. I always tried to make a connection between myself or my own behaviors and my subjects. It ran pretty consistently in me, this need to explore any little thing that might link us, that might open the door for unrestricted communication. My dad used to say to me frequently, "Consider all the possibilities." So I tried.

It's quite a phrase, really. So much of the time, we go through our days mindlessly, flipping from one repetitive task to the next. We rarely notice what is going on around us in each moment because it all seems so familiar, this repetition. Sarah, dear Sarah. She meditates and does yoga. She's a little bit Zen about things and will always tell me to "Stay in the moment. Be present in the moment." I tell her that is exactly what science is. It is really the same thing my dad told me all those years ago. Consider all the possibilities. Take notice. Look around. Be aware.

I thought about all of this as it related to Lazzy. Something was bothering me, nudging me from deep inside, and I couldn't quite put my finger on it. I'd missed something. I hadn't noticed something important. I simply was not considering all the possibilities. Eyes wide open. Be mindful, I told myself.

I parked in the furthest row away from the building simply to do a little bit of walking as I made my way to the headquarters. There didn't seem to be much activity out there, which was mostly par for the course. Inside, I found Vargas sitting at his desk.

"Hello, Detective. Is now a good time?" I asked.

"There's never a good time, Ms. Greene. How can I help you?"

I sat down in the visitor's chair and looked directly at him.

"I'd like to know how your investigation is going into finding Lazzy. Do you have any leads? Is there anyone searching the warehouse district, as I asked? Have you attempted to find Martin Boyle?"

Vargas pushed back his chair and opened the top drawer of his desk. He retrieved a plastic tub of TUMS, shook a few out, and tossed them into his mouth, crunching loudly.

"So far, we don't have any leads. And we can't just go traipsing through those warehouses without a warrant for each one. No judge is going to authorize anything like that. I sent a patrol car over there a couple of days ago, and the officer didn't see anything suspicious. We'll keep patrolling the area every few days or so."

I tried to remain calm. "And what about Martin? Have you found him yet?"

"Nope, sure haven't. The guy just dropped out of sight." He tilted his head slightly, looking up at the ceiling.

"Look, Detective. I know Lazzy is just some dumb animal to you. But I can assure you he is not. For that matter, neither are any of the animals that are here sharing the planet with us."

"Oh, you're not one of those PETA people, are you?" he scoffed.

I felt the anger rising into my neck and cheeks, certain I was turning red. I took a long breath. "I am not a member of PETA, although they've been known to do some good work. But right now, they aren't of any concern here. I don't even know why we are talking about them." I stopped and looked at him for a long moment before leaning in closer to his desk. "Detective Vargas. Glenn. I need your help. I really and truly need you to help me figure this out. I have to find Lazzy. And, honestly? I'm not sure I can do it without you." I sat back in my chair and waited. As I watched him, Vargas took on an entirely different look. His face changed, the way he held his mouth, and the furrow of his brow seemed to soften. He looked around the room and looked again. Finally, he leaned over his desk and began to speak in a low tone. I could barely hear him.

"Look, lady. Here's the thing. Let's just say I'm doing all I can do right now. Okay? And," he paused, looking around again, "I don't want there to be any kind of trouble around here. I don't want to see anyone trip and get hurt. So, it might be a good idea for you to just take a step back, okay? Just let your company handle things. That's the way they want it, and so should you. Despite all our little encounters here, you seem like a real nice lady. So, please, just let the people who are handling things handle them."

I didn't know what to say. I looked him right in the eye without speaking, and he gave me a long nod.

"Perhaps it would be best if I just saw you out, Dr. Greene." He stood, raising his hand toward the door.

"No need. I know the way. Thank you."

As I drove back to the lab, I reran his little speech over and over in my head. But the message was plain to see. He told me, in so many words, to back off. And I'm pretty sure I got the notion that CAR was somehow pushing this. But how and by whom? I needed to talk with someone about this, but if I truly were in danger because of my own investigations, I didn't want anyone else getting hurt as a result. Not Sarah. Not Maggie. Not Jack. Not any of my coworkers either, like Andy, or Brad, or Hannah. They were all so close around me. I started entertaining the idea of disengaging everyone else from the search.

My mind was churning and going in a thousand different directions. But then I thought about Maggie once again. With her being up in Indianapolis, whoever was behind this would be less likely to notice her involvement. Whoever they were. I pulled into the parking lot at CAR and dialed her number.

~

The place in little Franklin, Indiana, was tucked a few blocks down from the McDonald's, a mom-and-pop place that specialized in overstuffed sandwiches with funny names. I sat at a booth in the corner, waiting for Maggie, who was always right on time. But, on that evening, she was running late. I'd ordered two beers and was a quarter of the way through mine when she walked in the door. I flagged her over.

"Well, your invitation was a pleasant surprise. Sorry I'm late. One of my students needed to see me about his term paper," she said.

"I'm not quite sure how pleasant it's going to be," I said.

"Why? What's going on?"

"I had a meeting with Vargas. Things didn't go so well."

"You should have just told me to meet you back at the police station again. Maybe he needs more pressure."

I shook my head and began telling her about his warning for me to back off. I also explained his demeanor, which transformed him into almost looking scared for me. She sat in the booth listening, turning the glass of beer in slow circles in front of her. The waitress came to our table just as Maggie started to answer.

"What can I get for you ladies this evening?"

"Are you eating, Rory, because I'm starving?" Maggie said.

I waved her on and glanced back over the menu.

"I'll have the Shipwreck," Maggie said, "with fries."

"May I have the Toolbox? And a small salad. Bleu cheese on the side."

After the waitress left, I started back in on the conversation.

"So, what do you think about Vargas? I mean, he flat out told me to leave all this alone, or I might get hurt," I said.

Maggie folded the napkin in front of her, and spread it out flat, then folded it again.

"Rory, we have to talk about something. I was hoping I'd never have to tell you, but it seems like the time has finally presented itself, and there's no way around it."

I sat up a little straighter in the booth.

"Of course, you remember our first meeting, that time down in Kentucky when your parents invited me back to your campsite for dinner that next night."

"Sure I do."

"Well, after you went to sleep, and your mother too, your father and I stayed up late into the night, talking about my work. And his work. Even though your father's field of study wasn't in animal communications, he'd reached some pretty significant milestones on his own."

"I know he worked with Oliver a lot. I saw him. I also know he was focused on nonverbal cues," I said, shaking my head. I couldn't understand the graveness in Maggie's tone.

"You know the novel, *Hitchhiker's Guide to the Galaxy*, by Douglas Adams? He gives us the idea that humans are ranked as the third-smartest species on the planet, despite our own popular belief that we're the ones who dominate the animal kingdom when it comes to smarts. Adams says mice are first. Then dolphins. Then us."

"Yeah, well. It's good fiction."

"Yeah, well. Maybe so. Maybe not. Your father held the belief that many animals are more intelligent than humans when it comes to communication skills. Mice, dolphins, yes, and yes. But a host of other animals, including those bonobos sitting in your lab right now."

"Certainly, he couldn't have made any credible advances in his theories about animal communications," I said.

"But he did, Rory. He did. He took a totally different approach to his theory. He based everything on his chemistry and physics background. He built some excellent hypotheses about motion on an anatomical level."

It was about that time that the waitress brought our food to the table. She didn't put my salad dressing on the side, as I had asked.

I had to chuckle, wondering about the power of my own communication skills.

"So. My point to all of this was this. Resonance. All things in our universe are constantly in motion. Your father and I theorized that resonance is at the heart of everything in existence. But, taking it one step further, we suggested that it's also at the core of animal consciousness. Animals are innately in tune with this resonance. These molecular vibrations. And they utilize these frequencies to communicate." Maggie stopped to take a bite of her sandwich.

"Okay, so you are suggesting that, say, my bonobos, or even animals in general, are talking back and forth to one another through resonance?"

"Yes. That and spontaneous organization. Did Lazzy ever just get up and hand Della a toy for no reason? Or share a bite of banana with Gloria? Do any of them seem to get upset, or happy, or whatever, while they're just sitting there? They are probably, most probably, responding to a communication signal from one of the other monkeys. Gloria said to Lazzy, 'Hey, give me a bite of that banana.' And so on," Maggie said, looking at her watch.

"Do you have to go?" I asked.

"No, not yet."

"Good, because you were going to tell me something. And I'm guessing that big ball drop wasn't about the movement of atoms. You were going to say something about Dad."

"There's no good way to say it other than just to put it out there." She set her sandwich down on her plate and wiped her hands with the napkin.

"Rory, I think you should know. Your father didn't die of a heart attack. At least, not naturally. Your dad was murdered."

Chapter Sixteen

The drive back to Columbus was dark and cold. The autumn winds blew bursts of leaves across the highway. Never before had darkness fallen so hard to the ground. Stark. Empty. Bleak. That is how it looked outside. And that is how I felt inside. I didn't know what to do with the story Maggie told me. I didn't know what to think or how to react. Scared? Angry? Deceived? I noticed my grip on the wheel, my knuckles white.

Mostly, I felt vacant.

My phone, lying on the passenger seat, vibrated again. The third time since I left the restaurant. Maggie. I didn't want to talk with her now. I couldn't. My dad had been dead 27 years, and she finally decided to tell me all of this? Maggie was my best friend. All these years. Or maybe she was more like that older sister everyone hopes to have, the one who shares every confidence. Maybe she was more like a mother to me. Regardless of the label, I thought, in my heart of hearts, that I could trust her. But somehow, this news, after all that time, betrayed that confidence. What else had she hidden? What else would she hide in the future? I just knew as I sat there at that table, listening to the rest of her story, my entire perception of life was being altered by her every word.

The phone went off again. I picked it up, feeling ready to hurl it out the window, but there on the display was Jack's name. I took a deep breath and answered.

"Hey, Jack. What's happening?"

"Lots. I've tried to call you a couple of times. I've got good news. Well, yes. Good news."

"I could use some good news right now," I said.

"I think I might know where Lazzy is."

"Oh my God! Tell me where. I'm in my car right now." I was frantic, trying hard to pay attention to the road.

"Slow down, Ror. You're not going there by yourself. And certainly not without a plan. Why don't you meet me at my house? I'll give Sarah and Maggie a call, too, and see if they can come by. Okay?"

"Not Maggie."

"Why not? Is everything okay?" he asked.

"Yeah, uh. It's all fine. I just left her, though, and she was heading back to Indy. She, uh, said she had a late meeting with a student, so. Yeah. Just don't bother her right now. I can call her later."

"Okay. Well, come on over. I'll call Sarah. Good?"

"Good."

I hung up, and my head felt like it was nearly spinning off my neck. From the lowest low to the highest high, in nothing flat. I tried to put every thought out of my mind and focus on driving my car. I pulled up to Jack's house about 15 minutes later. I ran to the front porch, nearly falling up the steps. Jack was waiting at the front door, smiling.

"In a hurry?" He pushed open the storm door.

"I was hoping no one saw that," I said.

"Big Brother is always watching," Jack led me into the kitchen. Sarah, already there, sipped on a beer.

"Well? My car's still warm. Let's go," I said.

"Slow down, Rory. I said I think I might know where Lazzy is. Well, I'm fairly certain I know where he is."

"Then what are we waiting for?"

"We need to be careful, that's what. Not only for us but for Lazzy too. These guys are dangerous. They blew up your building. Did you forget that?"

I inhaled deeply. "Okay. So, what do we do? Is there any sort of plan yet? How did you find him?" I was talking a mile a minute.

Jack broke in. "So, I contacted a friend of mine. A guy from one of our poker games. He used to be a detective for Boston PD a few years back, but he and his wife moved out here to retire, supposedly. Anyway, he works part-time now for a security company. They mostly do concerts up in Indy, sporting events, those sorts of things. Anyway. He owes me some money, so I traded it for a favor. I had him stake out Martin's place round the clock for a couple of days."

"Wow, Jack. Thank you," I said, touched.

He smiled and shook his head, trying to dismiss the attention.

"So Kip, that's his name, Kip Jones, has been there for maybe half a day when Martin shows up, driving near his house through the back alley. He parked about a block away and then entered through the back door. He didn't stay for long, maybe ten minutes, and then left again. Kip followed him north of town but not to the warehouse district. There's an old strip mall right near there. It is mostly abandoned, except for a couple of lower-end businesses. That's where Martin went and where he has been ever since."

"Well, is it just Martin? Heck, we can take Martin."

"We don't know. I don't know. Kip and I are going to check it out. He went to gather some supplies, and then he's coming this way to pick me up. Rory, listen. We are going to watch it for a little while. We'll see if we can see Lazzy and who else might be there. And in the end, it might just be best to call the police."

"No. No Vargas. I don't think we can trust him."

"Okay. For now, no police. But let Kip and I go over there and feel things out. He knows what he's doing. We'll probably be watching the place overnight, and Kip will be staying there tomorrow too. Unless something should happen."

~

It had been my way for quite some time to try to be in control of situations, to take charge of things. I mean, I think it is human nature for people to want things to go their own way. So, yes, the truth is that I like to be in control of things. On the other hand, I wouldn't say I've been bossy in my life. I suppose the reason for this is because of my sister Ruthy. She was bossy. And I never wanted to be like her in any way.

I thought about all of this as I paced my living-room floor with Sarah looking on. I like to hold some responsibility for the direction of things, but I knew right then that I was completely helpless in the situation at hand.

"You really ought to try to get some sleep. What the hell am I saying? *I* should really try to get some sleep," Sarah plopped her head down on the couch pillow. "But I'm not leaving you while all this is going on."

"You can go home. I'll be alright. Or, if you want, the guest room is made up. Go crash in there," I said.

"How about if I just nod off right here for a few minutes," she said.

She already looked half asleep. A moment later, I heard her breathing change. Just like that, lights out. I went to get a blanket to cover her. Sarah. I spend more time with her than anyone outside of work. We're together all the time and know each other better than most husbands know their wives. Her favorite color is blue. She played basketball when she was a kid and wanted to be a Harlem Globetrotter when she grew up—specifically the old-school Meadowlark Lemon. Her favorite dish is Carbonara, and she'll puke if she rides anything that spins.

She looked so peaceful lying there, like she didn't have a care in the world. But in reality, she had plenty of cares in the world. Sarah was a vice president in administrative lending for the Midwest Division of Accura World Bank. She never complained about her job, but she'd often say things like she felt sorry for the little guy or she wished the underdog would come out on top every once in a while. She never went into details about her work much, only to say that she felt a lot of pressure at times. It didn't show. She was always quick to smile and to see the bright side of things. I liked that about her because, many times, I felt like I was the exact opposite in that way. Like right then, sitting and waiting on a call from Jack.

Immediately, I fell into the mindset that something had gone completely wrong. But when Jack left on the stakeout with Kip, he didn't mention one word about calling anytime soon. I put my phone down on the coffee table and picked up a novel I'd just started, *Cloud Cuckoo Land* by Anthony Doerr. It was a hefty book, and I'd just cracked it open. Twenty-five minutes later, Sarah popped up off the pillow like a rocket taking off.

"I fell asleep, I think," she said.

I laughed. "Not that long. You've only been out for about half an hour, tops."

"What'd I miss?"

"This is it." I held up my book. "Don't you have to go to work in the morning? Why don't you call it a night?"

"No way. You're staying up; I'm staying up." She rubbed her eyes with one hand.

"In that case, can I tell you something?"

"All ears," she said.

"So, Vargas told me to keep my nose out of things. I wanted to talk with Maggie about it. Well, while I'm giving her the details, she breaks in and says she has something to tell me. And then she proceeds to tell …" I stopped.

"I'm listening," Sarah reached over, touching my forearm lightly. "Go on, Ror."

"She proceeds to tell me that my dad was murdered. That he didn't really die of a heart attack. Somebody poisoned him to make it look that way. At least, that's what Maggie thinks."

"What the hell?"

"I know," I said.

"Who did it?"

"Well, that's the thing. Maggie thought it might be the Russians or the Chinese. She felt fairly certain it was one or the other. Apparently, my dad had figured out some things in animal communications, things they were working on. They didn't want him to share that information. So they killed him. Again, this is all according to Maggie. It all seems just a little incredible to me."

"I'm sorry, but I'm a little lost here. I don't mean to be rude, but does Maggie have any proof? I thought your dad worked in the hospital lab here in Siler. Like, didn't he just run tests and analyze blood and urine samples? Isn't that what you said?"

"That's what he did. I mean, that was the thing that brought home a paycheck every week. That's all we ever thought he did," I nodded. "But, according to Maggie, he worked in communications research on his own. Of course, I always knew he had a fascination with animals. He used to spend hours with Oliver. And I knew the two of them would talk." I made little quotation marks with my fingers. "Maggie said he started to figure out some significant details about their communications and began documenting these. From there, he expanded out to the animals around our house. Again. All according to Maggie."

"What the heck did she mean by animals around your house? It wasn't like there were a bunch of sloths hanging from your trees," Sarah shook her head.

I laughed. "I wish," I said. "No. But Dad was in our backyard a lot. And at the park. And the pound. I'd go out there, and he'd be sitting on our back steps with a squirrel on his knee, feeding it peanuts. Or other times, there'd be four or five birds pecking around on the ground, right at his feet. As soon as I'd show up, everything would scatter. He'd also go to the animal shelter and tell them he was looking to adopt a dog. He'd sit with them in their little pet greeting rooms and do his experiments."

"Did he use drugs on them or something? He could've gotten in huge trouble for that."

"No, no drugs," I said. "Nothing like that. His experiments were all about," I hesitated.

"All about what?"

"I'm not sure I should tell you for a couple of reasons. For one thing, if someone, by some stretch of the imagination, is really killing people over this, I'm not sure I'd want you to know. And secondly, it is hard to explain. We'd be here all night."

Sarah got up and went to the kitchen. She came back in with a couple of cans of Diet Coke, popping them open and placing one in front of me before sitting back down on the couch.

"I got all night. Besides, I've already been running around playing detective with you. I might as well be all in," she said.

I went on to tell her all about the "Resonance Theory" and spontaneous self-organization and how it starts on the most basic level. That we, and everything else on Earth, are made up of atoms.

"So, in those atoms, the protons, and neutrons, and electrons are moving around like crazy. They are vibrating at a unique rate in each atom. From that premise, he took things a step further and kept expanding outward to our entire bodies. Snails are vibrating along the same rate. Ostriches. Dogs. Bonobos."

I explained how all matter is in motion on an atomic level, including all humans and all animals. She listened carefully, attentively. When I was through, she continued to nod, as she had the whole way through my dissertation.

"When someone says, 'You catch my vibe?' it really isn't that far off," I said.

"It makes perfect sense to me. Granted, I'm not a scientist. But, yeah. It makes sense," she said. "But how did that get your dad killed? That part I don't understand."

"I'm not sure I understand it either. Back then, the hospital was owned by Rhoeta Global Research. Maggie said that Dad wrote up his findings in a formal paper and submitted it to the research board at the parent company. And they seemed interested. They told him they were going to put his findings under special review. According to Maggie, it was a couple of days later, and the board called Dad in to expand on his findings. All of that happened about two weeks before he was found dead in his car."

"And what makes Maggie think he was killed?"

"My dad, apparently. A few days before he died, Dad called Maggie and told her he had been followed a couple of times. He also said his office at work had been turned over, as well as his office at home. I don't remember anything about someone breaking into our house. But I was ten, you know? I need to call my mom and ask her about all of this. Anyway, Maggie felt pretty sure it was poison."

Sarah scooted forward in her chair. "I'm not trying to discredit Maggie or anything, but why is she bringing this up now?"

"Because of what Vargas said to me about watching my back. Maggie thinks it's related to what happened to my dad in 1995. She explained to me that at the end of 1991, the dissolution of the Soviet Union occurred. Russia claimed they were liquidating military aspects of the Cold War. There were summits held with the United States. First with Bush senior, then with Clinton. In reality, they were doing the opposite of breaking apart their military. In truth, they felt vulnerable, like a superpower that had faded. So they focused on building their military covertly. In all sorts of different ways. And one of those branches of their reconstruction was training animals to perform military tasks. At least, that's the theory."

Sarah crunched her Diet Coke can, setting it down on the coffee table. "So, I'm assuming the U.S. was doing the same."

"Exactly. My dad, Maggie, and a few others were being watched, or even called on, for their advancements in animal communications."

"How'd the government know," she asked.

I cocked my head and made a face.

After a brief pause, Sarah looked over at me. “Damn,” she said.

“I’ll double dog damn it,” I nodded.

We sat there for a few moments in the quiet, taking it all in.

Chapter Seventeen

After eating a huge breakfast, I made my way over to the lab early, texting Jack to let him know where I was, just in case they'd learned anything. About six hours later, my phone buzzed. A message from Jack to meet him at Burls, an old car-repair garage on the west side of town. I hadn't planned on taking a lunch break, but this was the perfect opportunity. I checked out of work and headed to Burls without question. When I arrived, only two cars were parked on the side. One was Jack's. The building looked completely dark and abandoned. I knew they'd gone out of business a couple of months before because I used to take my car there for its oil change. I decided to go around back so I'd be less conspicuous, and knocked on the door on the alleyway side.

A man I didn't recognize opened it.

"Rory?" he said.

"Yes, I'm Rory."

"C'mon in." The man was tall and lanky and looked vaguely familiar. He walked in long strides down the hallway and opened a door on his left. "In here," he said. I was apprehensive, wondering if I'd just walked into some sort of trap. But then I heard Jack's voice. "We're in here, Rory."

And there, at the far end of the room, Lazzy sat in a chair next to a desk. Sitting on a chair in one corner was Jack.

"Lazzy!" I opened my arms—crying, smiling—trying hard to contain myself. But instead, I cried harder. "Lazzy? It's me. Ror. Your pal. Rory," I signed and spoke.

Lazzy gave me a vacant stare and then looked away.

"He's been a bit to himself, Rory. I probably should have warned you," Jack said, standing up.

"How long has he been like this?" I asked.

"Ever since we got to him. I've been keeping my distance, but he doesn't seem to want anything to do with anyone," Jack said.

The man who showed me into the building interrupted. "Jack, I'm going to take off now unless you need something else. Lock it up when you go, okay?"

"Thanks, Burl," Jack gave a short wave of his hand.

Jack offered me the chair. I pulled it across the room in front of Lazzy.

"Lazzy sick?" I signed.

He looked back at me, then away again.

"Lazzy mad?" I signed.

He turned around in his chair, facing the side wall, letting out a "humph" with his breath.

I never dreamed our reunion would go this way. Deep inside, I'd sort of given up hope that we would get Lazzy back alive. And in those times when I would allow myself to imagine that we did get him back, I always envisioned him running to me, hugging me. I never thought, not even once, that our meeting would be like this. From the moment I first met this young ape, we had an uncanny connection. And now there was nothing.

I stood up and walked over to the door where Jack stood.

"So, what happened? Tell me everything," I said.

"Well, Kip and I went to that strip mall in separate cars. We found Martin's car there. Kip staked out the front, and I was in the back. We had two-way radios, using off-channels, just in case. We were there all night and felt sure Martin was the only one inside.

We didn't see any other cars in the vicinity. Not only that; we could see into the business through the front. It's all floor-to-ceiling windows across the street side. You can see the interior hallway clearly. Anyway, Kip spotted Martin a couple of times in the storefront on the far end. Just briefly. But no one else. What I'm trying to say is he appeared to be alone, and we felt pretty confident about it. Kip and I spent a lot of time trying to decide if we should muscle in or not. Both of us were armed, but we didn't want anyone getting hurt, especially not Lazzy, if, in fact, Lazzy was in there. Then our luck broke. Martin came out of the door, got in his car, and drove away. My guess is he was going to get something to eat. So Kip and I moved. I picked the lock, and we were in. We found Lazzy in a small cage, just sitting there in some dark office. I grabbed his hand, and out we went. Then I texted you. That was it. It went off easy."

I threw my arms around Jack and hugged him for a long time.

"Thank you. Thank you, thank you, thank you," I said.

I looked over at Lazzy. He touched his hand to his chin and moved it downward. The sign language meaning for "thank you" as he continued to stare at the wall.

Chapter Eighteen

It is no secret that animals show signs of emotion. I've found so much of it fascinating to learn. Like the countless studies proving that animals can also experience depression and anxiety. Scientists cite the premise that animals, mostly mammals, and humans share the same basic wiring in their brains for emotions. A classic example came from the United States Marine Mammal Program. They mostly used dolphins and beluga whales in their missions. But there was a division created solely to train sea lions. The military taught the sea lions to detect enemy divers. Once the military-ranked sea lion spotted an enemy diver, it would quickly swim to him or her and attach a tracking device (designed like a handcuff) to one of the enemy's limbs. They had also been trained to locate and recover military hardware at sea. The sea lion division suffered many setbacks along the way. Several of their sea lions quit eating, slept for long periods of time and became lethargic. Some displayed obsessive behaviors, like butting their heads against their underwater cages. Both veterinarians and psychologists were brought in to assess the animals, and all agreed that the sea lions were suffering from depression.

I thought of this as I sat next to Lazzy, watching him. I was trying to decide how much I should push him to interact with me or if I should just give him some space. Maggie would have been the one to advise me, but I couldn't bring myself to call her just yet. I was mad at myself for feeling this way, but I couldn't help it.

I got up for a moment to walk and think, pacing around the room. Just then, the door opened, which startled me beyond reason. Kip smiled as he peered through the door. He walked in carrying a large grocery bag, as well as a cardboard tray with three cups inside.

"Provisions," he said, smiling. "Coffees, black. Sorry, I didn't know how you took it, Rory. And some food and other items for the four of us." He pulled out a bunch of bananas and handed them to me, along with a small carton of milk. I squeezed his arm as he handed the bananas to me.

"Hey, Lazzy. Look what we have, buddy. Kip brought us some goodies. Want to split a banana with me? Or do you want one all your own?"

He glanced over at me briefly and returned to his far-off stare.

"Shit," I said under my breath. Jack walked over and stood in front of me for a moment. He glanced over at Lazzy and then finally returned his attention to me.

"I know you're the expert here, but it might not help things any if he sees you getting upset. Maybe we should just back off a little."

Jack was right.

I walked back to Lazzy's corner. "Here you go, Laz," I said, peeling the banana and setting it down next to him on the desk. "Dig in." I turned and walked back to Kip and Jack. They had already started rifling through the groceries, which sat on a table nearer the door. "Oh, my favorite. Nutter Butters. Oh, and Lay's chips. I love those too. Kip, this is a junk fest in here," Jack laughed.

"There's nutrition in there too. Some deli sandwiches at the bottom. And fruit. And maybe some Doritos and Swedish Fish," he winked.

The three of us sat on the floor near the middle of the room, close enough to Lazzy, but also far enough to give him space. My eyes didn't leave him, not even once. He had one arm propped up on his knee, and his hand covered the right side of his face. Every so often, he'd lift his hand and peak over, looking toward us. I tried to act like I wasn't noticing. After a few moments, I tried again.

"You want a bite of my turkey sandwich? Or some chips?" I spread out a paper towel, tore a piece from my sandwich, and grabbed a handful of potato chips. I took the makeshift plate over to Lazzy and stood by his chair. I tore his banana into bites and opened the milk carton. "Why don't you try eating a little bit, bud? I bet you're hungry. You look famished. In fact, when Gloria sees you, she might laugh because you are skinny. We probably shouldn't let Gloria laugh at you."

Lazzy looked at me, then the food, then back to the wall.

"Just a bite," I said.

He let out a sigh, reached over, picked up one of the banana pieces, and began chewing it slowly.

"Thanks," I said. "Do you want me to leave you alone? Or do you think we should eat lunch together?" He turned his head toward the wall once again, so I went back over to Jack and Kip.

"This is scaring the hell out of me," I said under my breath.

Jack put his hand on my shoulder and squeezed it gently. Then he leaned over, whispering, "We can tell. I know this is stressing you out, but it seems like Lazzy can tell, too. Try to relax a little bit. If you can. It might help."

"I know you're right," I said, looking down at the floor. For the first time since we'd been there, I started noticing our surroundings. I'd been so excited, happy, worried, to see Lazzy that I didn't even pay attention to the place. Everything was dirty. The floor, the walls. The place screamed "dark and dingy" from top to bottom. Not only were we sitting in some back office at a car garage, but the place had also been closed for quite some time.

"We have to get him out of here. And me too," I said rather suddenly. Lazzy had a thing about being clean.

Both Jack and Kip looked at me with concerned expressions.

“Rory, that might not be such a good idea. The people who took Lazzy are going to be looking for him, so it is probably best to lay low for a while,” Jack said.

“Then we lay low someplace nice. I don’t know. A hotel, maybe? Or do you guys have some sort of a safe house? Anything like that?”

They both chuckled. “Sorry to disappoint. We’re not the FBI. We don’t have a witness protection program going anywhere,” Kip said, all the while grinning.

“I’m thinking you’d probably get some attention, hauling a bonobo into a hotel room.” Jack shook his head.

“Hold that thought. I’m way over on my lunch break. I’m just going to step out in the hallway and call in sick for the rest of the day. I’ll be right back,” I said.

By the time I stepped back into the office, Kip and Jack were packing up the groceries we’d scattered about and cleaning up our little pile of trash.

“What’s happening?”

“What do you think about going to my house? We can pull the car right into my garage, and no one will see Lazzy. Plus, not many people know that you and I are friends, right? I’ve got lots of sick time piled up. I’ll come down with some sort of bug for a few days. Lazzy and I will just be a couple of bachelors, hanging out, watching football, drinking beers. Right, Laz?”

“No beer for Lazzy.”

“Check.”

“Are you sure, Jack? I was planning on taking a few days too.”

“Stay at my place. I have lots of extra rooms,” Jack offered.

I looked over toward Lazzy, who seemed to be completely oblivious to our conversation.

“Hey, is that okay with you, buddy?” I asked and signed.

He didn’t answer. So we took him by his hands and put him in Jack’s SUV. And off we went.

~

As we walked through Jack's garage door leading into the kitchen, Lazzy seemed somewhat more aware and interested in his surroundings. A Rubik's Cube sat on one of the shelves in the kitchen, along with an assortment of other wooden puzzle toys and brain teasers, like the triangle thing with all the plastic golf tees in the holes. Lazzy picked up the Rubik's Cube and twisted it around, making a little "oooh" noise when any block of color would line up. We had one just like it back at the lab. He continued to hold it in his hand, down at his side, as he walked around looking.

"You break it, you buy it, Laz, old pal," Jack said, smiling, leaning against the kitchen counter. With any other subject at the lab, I might be quite nervous about some sort of violent backlash. But Lazzy had been docile and peaceful from the very first day with us. He never showed signs of aggression. In fact, it was quite the contrary. He'd go out of his way to keep peace with anyone and everyone.

Jack searched around the grocery bag he'd just carried in and pulled the bananas back out.

"How about a snack," he said, tearing one off and holding it out. Lazzy walked over slowly, took the banana from Jack, and cradled it between his arm and his chest, along with the Rubik's Cube. He walked into the dining room, glancing around, then into the living room. He put both of his items on the coffee table and walked over toward the TV screen mounted on the wall.

"You liked when we watched videos back at the lab, didn't you?" I said.

Lazzy turned his head, looking my way briefly.

"I don't think he's ever seen real TV shows. We always watch training videos at work, things that have been approved by our contract and are built into their program," I added.

Jack grabbed the remote from the side table and flipped it on. Dr. Phil's big bald head appeared on the screen, saying he'd been at the rodeo before or some such thing. Lazzy eked out another "oooh" and stood watching. Jack turned the channel. *Divorce Court*, a man and a woman arguing over the way the husband mowed the lawn. Then another channel. *Gunsmoke*. Two guys stood on some dusty old saloon town street, pistols pointed at one another, getting ready to shoot as their horses looked on. Lazzy let out a piercing yell and smacked the top of his head with one hand, then the other. Jack flipped the station again. Big Bird talking to the Cookie Monster about counting cookies. The number for the day was 11. Lazzy plopped down on the floor and crossed his legs, eyes transfixed on the screen.

"You like this, Laz?" I asked. No answer. He appeared to be mesmerized by the magic of *Sesame Street*. Jack motioned his head toward the kitchen, and I followed.

"Looks like you were right. I think his surroundings are already making a difference," Jack said.

"I hope so." I tiptoed into the dining room and peeked around the corner. Lazzy hadn't moved an inch. I stepped back in to talk to Jack. "Hey, I think I'm going to run by my house and pick up a few things for Laz. Maybe grab some food and some clothes."

"Just pack it up heavy. We don't want anyone noticing your staying here. The less we go in and out right now, the better," he said.

It didn't take me long to gather my things. At Jack's insistence, I parked my car in one of the additional spots in the three-car garage. As I walked into the house, I noticed right away that things had gotten extremely quiet. I crept into the dining room, then around to the living room. Jack and Lazzy were sitting together on the couch. Jack held a large picture book in his lap, and Lazzie looked on. I chuckled, and they spotted me.

Jack held up the book. "It's one of my favorites. Dr. Seuss," he said. "My folks kept a bunch of my old books from when I was a kid."

Lazzy grabbed the book by the corner and pulled it back down into position, tapping his hand on the page while Jack gave me a look, raising his eyebrows. He continued reading. I started fixing a healthy dinner after bingeing on snack food all day at the garage. All the while, Jack and Lazzy stayed on the couch, going from one book to the next, mostly Dr. Seuss, *Curious George*, and a handful of others. I thought it was sweet that Jack had kept such an extensive collection of children's books. I continued to be amazed by the funny nuances of Jack's personality, not to mention his talents and skills.

I checked on them occasionally, but I wasn't worried about leaving Lazzy with Jack, or anyone else for that matter. Even still, I kept an eye on them as I prepared the meal.

When I finally called them for dinner, Jack came into the kitchen, looking a little sheepish.

"He signed something to me, but I didn't understand. But I did get this much. He's not coming in here."

"What do you mean? Does he want you to keep reading?" I asked.

"That's not it, Rory. I hate to say this, but I don't think he wants to come in here with you."

I felt a pit in my stomach. Jack continued.

"He pointed in here and shook his head no."

"Okay. Well, clearly he's mad at me."

Jack reached over and snatched a piece of steamed cauliflower from the vegetable dish I made.

As hard as it was for me to do, I decided to give Lazzy some space. I fixed Jack a plate and another plate with fruit, nuts, greens, and some honey. Jack tucked Lazzy's milk bottle under his arm and carried the plates back into the living room. I flipped on the small TV in the kitchen and sat at the table there, eating alone.

The six o'clock news had just started, with the third story into the newscast talking about the bombing at the lab. The reporter said a person of interest had been brought in for questioning, but no charges had been filed at the time. I reached for my phone and called Vargas, expecting his voicemail, which is exactly what I got.

"Detective, this is Dr. Greene. I just saw on the news that you've brought someone in about the bombing, and I'm wondering who it might be. If you could return my call, at this number. Thank you."

I wanted to tell Jack but decided to leave it for later. I bet Lazzy's kidnappers were seething. I imagined Martin Boyle standing in front of his employers, whoever they were, and having to answer to them about losing Lazzy. Yes, we'd have to be careful to stay hidden. That was a given. Yet, more than anything, I thought about what they might do next. If they could bomb a building, the retribution for our actions could be substantial.

I felt like I needed to warn the people at work. And I'd have to do it in such a way so they didn't know I had Lazzy. Hannah may have been right: there could be a mole in the system. I hadn't called in sick yet for the next day at work.

Then it hit me. I needed to go back home for the night, stay there, and go to work as always in the morning. I'd keep my routine the same as always. That way, if there really were some sort of operative at CAR, or even someone watching my house or me, I wouldn't be alerting them to our recent activities.

I popped my head around the corner into the living room. Immediately, I felt a wave of jealousy upon seeing Jack and Lazzy enjoying their food and each other's company. I tried not to show it on my face as I motioned for Jack to tell him about my plan.

Chapter Nineteen

"Hey, Mom. It's Rory. How you doing?"

I hadn't talked to my mom since the day of the bombing. We exchanged several calls right after it happened. It took a lot to convince her that I was safe and unharmed.

"Oh, hi, sweetie. I'm just fine. Are you doing okay? Are things going okay at your work?" I could tell she was glad that I'd called her again.

"Everything's fine here, Mom. Things seemed to have calmed down at the lab, and I've been doing good too. What about you? Everything okay at the house? Do you need anything?"

"I'm glad that you called, dear. I was going to wait to tell both you and your sister at the same time, but Ruthy happened to call last night. Isn't that something?"

"Tell us what, Mom?"

"I'm thinking of moving."

"Moving? Where to?"

"Well, do you remember the Gerhardts? Louise and John?"

"Sure, Mom. They lived right next door to us," I said, thinking about how Mrs. Gerhardt used to give Ruthy and me cookies on the side.

"Well, of course you know them. They moved down to Florida. They followed the Dillmans, who went down about a year ago. I like them too, but not as much as Louise and John. But that's neither here nor there. The point is, they all seem to love it, and they've been trying to get me to move down there. It's near Fort Myers."

"I think that's a great idea. Excellent. Like into a condo sort of thing?" I asked.

"Yes, they have all different sizes and styles there. Oh, honey, I'm so glad you like the idea. Your sister told me I was out of my mind for thinking about moving down there."

"That's just Ruth, Mom. It's a great idea. It sounds perfect for you."

"So, what about you? Are you doing okay with everything that's been going on?" she asked.

"Well, I've been staying pretty busy with work things lately."

"I bet you have. I was just telling Louise and John about everything that's been happening up there. I still can't believe there was a bombing. Do you need anything, Rory?"

"No, Mom. Things are okay. We're still cleaning up from the mess. But everyone in my department is fine." I paused for a moment, trying to think of a good lead into my next question. There just didn't seem to be a good transition, so I pressed ahead.

"Hey, I've' been thinking a lot about Dad lately. About him dying. It sounds like a funny thing to ask, but did you ever think about getting an autopsy?"

"There wasn't any reason. They said he had a heart attack, and that was that. You remember."

"Yeah, I know. I just … well, he seemed awfully young. And he was so fit. It just seems like a heart attack was unlikely for a guy like him, you know?"

"Well, they can happen to anyone at any time. That's what the coroner said, at least."

"Yeah, I suppose. I was also wondering if you still have any of his stuff. I took most of what was in his office, but I wondered if you kept anything."

"Oh, dear. It's been so long ago. I think there might be a few boxes up in the attic. But I haven't been up there for years. I don't think it's a good idea for me to go up that ladder when I'm here by myself. I never trusted it to begin with. I'll tell you what: why don't you come over sometime soon and have a look up there? Maybe you can help me clear out some of the other junk that's up there while you're here. I need to do it anyway, especially if I'm really going to move. I'll make you a pot of potato soup."

Siler wasn't that far, and I felt a little guilty about not visiting my mom more often than I did. The town sits near the Illinois border, almost in a straight line east of Columbus. It only takes about two hours to drive there on a good day. I said I'd come over on the following Sunday.

Once I hung up the phone, I wasn't sure why I'd wanted to ask her about the autopsy. I mean, I knew the answer. I guess I wanted to get a feel of things from her end to see if she had any apprehensions about Dad's cause of death. In the end, it sounded like she felt assured he died from a massive coronary.

After our talk, I decided to watch a few more of the videotapes from the lab. That is when the text came through. A number I did not recognize, once again.

Three words: *You are dead.*

I decided not to bother Jack again. Or Vargas. Instead, I went up to my bedroom and took a revolver from the bottom drawer of my dresser, along with the box of bullets. Jack had given me the gun a couple of days before, along with some lessons on safety. He took me to a local firing range and gave me a quick shooting lesson. Other than that, I'd never held a gun before in my life. I sat on my bed, loading six bullets into the chamber. I then placed the loaded gun, pointing away from me, on my nightstand. That night, I did not sleep.

~

I don't normally frequent the few Starbucks we have in town, but I stopped at the one closest to work and ordered a triple espresso shot, along with a venti black coffee. By the time I got to work, I felt the caffeine jitters taking over my body, especially since I hadn't gotten any sleep. I kept breathing deeply as I walked back to my office, trying my best to focus. As soon as I turned the key and unlocked my office door, the lights cut out in the building. Everything was ultra quiet. After a few seconds, the backup generator system kicked in. A series of groans could be heard throughout the hallways. It meant we all had to get back to work but under adverse conditions. I laughed a little at all the verbalizations. Like a choir, on cue.

My office remained dark. It must not have been a priority when they mapped out the backup electricity grid. I grabbed my things and headed for the main lab area. Andy sat at the counter working, while Hannah and Brad were both in the cages doing their routine morning clean-ups. I slid a stool up next to Andy, wanting so desperately to tell him that Lazzy was safe. But I resisted, knowing the insider might be anyone, even though Andy seemed to love the bonobos and the work every bit as much as I did.

He slid a paper in front of me, a graph he had created showing the progress of the three bonobos. Of course, Boris had no data as of then, but Della and Gloria were mapped out clearly. They each showed strengths in different areas, but overall, Della appeared to be slightly ahead of things.

Then we heard the loud noise—a major jolt causing all the lights to black out immediately. Everything fell to a hush throughout the building. After a second or two, different voices could be heard, mostly lamenting the situation of all-out darkness. Things like "What the heck is this?" and "Now what?"

I called out to our immediate group. "Just stay put, people. Something probably shorted in the generator. Just stay where you are. They'll give us instructions in a minute or two."

Andy and I sat there, talking quietly about the data he had

shown me a few moments before. The next thing I remember was the flash of light, along with the loud pop. Then, three more. Andy toppled off his stool to the ground, and I followed him down. I could hear other movements, the door maybe, or a cage door, shuffling, movement. Footsteps, I thought. How far away? I slid closer to Andy when I heard it: the gurgling. The heavy breath.

"Andy?" I could barely make him out, even though he lay on the floor right next to me. It would take a few seconds for me to see the blood running down his neck. He'd been shot in the neck. At least, that is what it looked like, his life pumping out of him with every beat of his heart. I stripped off my lab coat and began pressing on the wound in his neck.

I tried to take notice of the rest of the room, wondering if anyone else had been shot. I heard the bonobos in their cages. And I detected a murmur of voices, but couldn't make out who. I also thought I heard the slight sound of moaning.

"Hang on, Andy. Don't you even think about leaving me. Do you hear me, Andy? Hold on," I whispered into his ear. Then I knew. I could just tell. He was gone. Just like that.

I could still hear movement in the room, unsure of who or what. I let go of Andy and slid back all the way to the wall where our walk-in cooler was located. Quietly, I pulled down on the latch and crawled into the cooler, silently closing the door behind me. Quickly, I found a stack of boxes, fruit boxes, most likely. I slid under the back shelf and pulled the boxes in front of me. I waited, still able to smell the blood from Andy's wound all over my hands and clothes.

Someone opened fire in our lab. We were the targets this time. Why? Who? My mind raced. My heart pounded; I felt sick to my stomach. Suddenly, the door was kicked open. A bright light shined around the room. I knew I was dead. But then I heard that one word, yelled loudly.

"Clear."

Chapter Twenty

"Don't shoot. Please don't shoot," I whispered. The light flashed around the room again. I slowly pushed the boxes aside, and raised my hands slowly, where they could be seen. Then louder, "Don't shoot. I'm Dr. Victoria Greene."

The security officer rushed over to me, pointing his rifle, barking orders.

"Hands in the air where I can see them. Don't move. Don't move. Hands in the air. Backup!"

I didn't know if he wanted me to back up, but then I grasped he was calling for help, calling for backup. I stayed motionless. Another officer rushed in, shouting the same things. He quickly came over, pulling me out of the cooler. In one swift motion, he threw me down to the floor, pulling my hands behind me, cuffing me, all the while yelling not to move. Apparently, in that moment, my identification badge didn't matter to them.

More light filled the room as more security guards and police officers entered the scene. It allowed me to see I was largely covered in blood. Andy's blood. I started to cry but cleared my throat. "I'm Dr. Victoria Greene. I work here. This is my lab."

"Quiet," the officer said. He led me out into the main work area. I saw that Brad was cuffed, too, kneeling in the center of the lab. Hannah lay on the floor, a pool of blood next to her, another officer by her side, working on her. I panicked about the bonobos but spotted them right away. All three were huddled down, holding themselves, each one in a corner of their own cages, mostly under their beds. All three were highly verbal at that moment. I couldn't blame them. I wanted to scream too. Within 30 minutes, probably less, they took off our handcuffs, but continued to hold us. Brad was incensed at being detained, but I was grateful for the officers.

What horrified me was Andy's body, still on the floor, gazing up at the ceiling. There would be no moving him until the forensic people could pick apart the scene, one thread, one drop of blood, at a time. I looked around the room in disbelief. Two paramedics rushed through the door, pushing a gurney. Within moments, Hannah was wheeled out of the lab. Brad and I would be there for hours more. Vargas moved around the room along with a string of other officers, including Detective Linda Patterson and the captain of police, Eugene Huffman. Even the mayor of Columbus, Gary Turner, showed up, poking his head in the doorway but not coming in. At that point, everything continued in a state of ordered chaos. While Brad and I had been set free from our handcuffs, we were required to sit and wait in a corner of the room while a flurry of other activities ensued.

How many others had been victims elsewhere? How many lab areas had been attacked, or was it just ours? Did they have someone in custody, or was there a chance this person was still on the loose somewhere in the building? Were we in danger? Question after question rushed through my mind. More than anything, I wanted to attend to the bonobos. Finally, after what seemed like an unreasonable amount of time sitting and waiting, I'd had enough.

"Detective Vargas," I called out. Brad gave me a look of surprise. Vargas, on the other hand, did not waver from what he was doing. Instead, he held up a hand in my direction.

"Detective Vargas, please!" I yelled so that everyone in the room could hear. Vargas looked at me and then up at the ceiling before dragging himself over in my direction.

"What is it, Miss Greene?"

"Are Brad and I free to go? We need to attend to the animals."

"Not so fast. The female vic was in one of the cages when she was shot, so we need to process that area."

"The female vic is Hannah Shultz. And this is Brad Reynolds, our laboratory assistant. And as far as that cage goes, I'd imagine your forensics people would rather not have some animal go running all over the evidence," I said.

Vargas looked over at the cage. "Wait right here." He walked over to two people collecting blood samples on the floor and returned a moment later.

"Fine, you can take those monkeys out of here. But in that first cage, watch where you step."

Brad and I led our three subjects into another holding area with cages two floors down from ours. It felt like we were in a zombie movie. We didn't see another single person while on our way there. Once we got the three bonobos settled in, I went down two more floors to get some food and milk for them. Again, no one to see there either. Then it hit me. Everyone had been evacuated from the building. I also surmised the only shooter activity had been on our floor. By the time I returned to the bonobos, I could tell Brad wanted to go. Understandably. I told him to check online about status reports for work, but I wasn't sure that he'd ever come back to CAR.

My main task was to care for the bonobos. Surprisingly, all three sat and ate, all near where I sat, in their respective cages. Four cages had been arranged there in a quadrangle formation, so we all stayed near the center where the corners connected. I felt oddly calm and decided to take a photo of them to mark the moment. When I retrieved the phone from my pocket, I saw I had eleven missed calls. Three from Jack, four from Sarah, and four from my mom. I typically switch off the ringer whenever I go to work, especially if I am in the general lab area, so my phone had been silenced since early morning. I called Sarah first.

"God, are you okay?"

"I'm fine. I'm okay. I'm sorry I didn't call sooner. The police kept us in the lab for questioning way too long."

"What happened? Are you sure you're alright?" she asked. Her voice sounded strained.

"Somebody came into our lab and started shooting. Sarah, they killed Andy. Andy. I was right there. Right beside him. And they shot Hannah. I don't know how she is. They took her away, unconscious."

"Oh my God. I'm so sorry. Have they caught the shooter? Is someone in custody?"

"I don't know. I have no idea."

"Do you want me to come down there?"

"I doubt they'd let you in. No. I'm okay right now. I'm taking care of things, taking care of the bonobos right now. It was terrible for them too."

We talked for a few more minutes. I could hear the helplessness in her voice. But I tried to assure her that there was nothing she could do. Next, I called my mom. Our conversation went much the same way. "I just can't help but wonder why this is happening. Someone wants our program to stop. They want the experiments and the trials to stop. I don't understand what could be so detrimental about our findings. If any. It just doesn't make sense."

I couldn't help myself. I had to ask her about Maggie's conversation with me.

"Mom. This probably isn't the best time. But there's something I have to ask you. You know, when we were on the phone the other day, I asked about why Dad didn't have an autopsy?"

"Yes, dear. There was no reason for one. I told you."

"But what if there were a reason? What if Dad didn't really die of a heart attack?"

She went quiet.

"Mom?"

"Why would you even think such nonsense, Rory? Your father had a heart attack. It's as plain as that."

"That's not what Maggie thinks, Mom. She seems to think someone killed Dad. Poisoned him."

"Damn that woman," she said.

"So it's true?"

"Of course it isn't true. Rory? Rory? I'm having trouble hearing you, dear. Are you still there?"

The phone went dead. I hit redial right away, and it jumped right to her voicemail. I tried two more times and left a message after the third.

I turned my attention back to the bonobos. They all sat there, finishing up their fruit and their bottles. Boris, the growing young boy, was completely done with both. I went around and cleaned up their dishes and then went about the task of finding some blankets and pillows for them. I needed to call Jack but decided it would have to wait until I got the bonobos settled and cared for.

CAR kept a large room with clean blankets, pillows, towels, and those sorts of things down on the second floor. When the elevator doors opened, I was met by Aubrey Keegan.

"Rory. I was just asking about you upstairs. Are you alright?"

"Not really. I'm not injured, though. Not physically," I said.

"Yes. The police gave me a summary." She glanced down at her watch. "Where are your animals?"

"I had to move them. I have them in some holding cages in the chimpanzee research lab in Dr. Ballard's area. But I need to find out what our contingency plan is. What's the plan for scheduling? I mean, for all the animals?" I asked.

"We're on Emergency Schedule A. So, just the bare shell of essential workers on that schedule. We've sent out global messaging to everyone, so the staffing is set to begin immediately. Do you need help finding someone else?" Aubrey asked, looking down at her watch again.

“I didn’t mean to hold you up. So, I’ll be around,” I said. I started walking down to the clean laundry room.

“Rory,” she called after me.

“We may need you here in the next few days, just so you know,” she said.

“I’ll be around.”

Chapter Twenty-One

By the time I left work, I felt completely exhausted. Not only physically, but mentally, even spiritually. I mostly wanted to collapse somewhere. But I knew I had to get back to Jack's house and help with Lazzy.

We'd talked on the phone earlier, and he told me that Lazzy seemed to be adjusting well. Eating, playing, and even signing, which Jack did not fully understand.

"He keeps making a circle by his left shoulder, near his heart," Jack said.

"That means please."

"He also keeps raising his hand to his mouth, like in one motion."

"And that's thank you. Lazzy has good manners."

An hour later, I was sitting in Jack's kitchen with Lazzy. All three of us sat at the table, each with a bottle. Jack and I had Heinekens. Lazzy, milk. He kept looking at me from the corner of his eye. Lazzy. Not Jack.

"Hey, Laz. I've missed you, buddy," I said.

He kept drinking, looking forward, but every so often, he'd give me another glimpse. Jack and I had decided not to talk about the shooting in front of him. We were trying to keep up the conversation, focusing on sports, the weather, anything not to talk about the horrendous events of the past few hours.

"Did you hear Mariah Carey is trying to get some Queen of Christmas title copyrighted or something?" Jack asked.

I nearly spit out my beer at his attempt. "You don't look like the kind of guy who keeps Mariah Carey on his playlist."

"Oh God, I'm not. Truthfully, she is way too diva for me. Have you ever seen her in an interview?"

"Actually, just the other day. She was on the news about the whole deal. It was a trademark she applied for, by the way. The trademark office rejected her application," I said.

"Score one for the nerds. Divas, zip," Jack laughed.

Just then, Lazzy started slapping the table, then his knee, laughing. He held his stomach, rocking back in his chair, head thrust back, mimicking a big laugh.

"You think that's funny, buddy?" Jack asked.

Lazzy hit the table a few more times, rocking his head forward. He was being hilarious.

"You're not a fan of Mariah Carey then either, Laz?" I asked, smiling.

He looked over at me, halting all his antics. He sat still, just staring at me. Staring. Suddenly, he lunged at me. In that instant, I held open my arms reflexively, not knowing what to expect. Jack jumped up as Lazzy thrust forward, throwing his arms around my neck. He squeezed me hard. He buried his face in my neck, holding me tight. The weight and the force of him nearly knocked me backward in the chair, but I managed to stay upright, returning his hug. He wrapped himself around me, and we sat there for a long time while he continued to hold me. Eventually, he backed himself off slightly so he could sign something.

"Why?"

"I don't know why, Lazzy. I don't know why that bad man took you. But I'm so happy we got you back. You're safe now."

He looked at me for a while, again not moving.

"Why Rory not stop."

"I didn't know. I didn't know they were taking you. If I had known anything, I would have stopped them. I promise. But as soon as I found out you were gone, I looked and looked and looked for you. And I wasn't going to stop until I found you. I love you, Lazzy. Lazzy is my friend. I love you."

His eyes moved back and forth, connecting with mine. Then, again, suddenly, he threw himself into another hug. I wouldn't let go until he did. Jack stood there watching, and I swear I thought I saw a tear in his eye. Jack. Not Lazzy.

After we put Lazzy to bed, we flipped on the late-night news. The story of the shooting was top-billing on all the local stations. The report gave us nothing we didn't already know. "One dead, one in critical but stable condition. Shooter still at large. Police investigating the motive." Blah, blah. Jack's boss called him earlier, asking him to come in as soon as possible. Forensics were running all their tests, but there was an enormous amount of video that had to be processed.

"I really need to go to the station. And I'm guessing you'll have to go back in to work too? But one of us is going to have to stay with Lazzy. Someone needs to stay with him," Jack said.

"This is a problem. I'm going to have to get someone. But they'll need to have had some experience. I mean, Lazzy is the best. He's the most intelligent animal I've ever worked with. And he is so docile, even for a bonobo. Despite all of that, it really needs to be someone with training."

"What about Maggie?" Jack asked.

"Not Maggie. I just can't do it right now. I hate to say it, but I'm not sure I can trust her. I just have a completely uneasy feeling where she is concerned. After what she told me about my dad. So, no. I don't want her knowing Lazzy is here."

Jack leaned forward on the couch, looking at me. "You know, Ror, eventually, you're going to have to talk to her."

"I know. Just not now."

"Well, then who else?" he asked.

We sat the quietly, thinking.

"Hey, what about your mom? Didn't you say she used to help in the early days when your dad was working with animals? In their college days? And, throughout their marriage, she was around all his research. She probably knows more than you think."

"You know, my mom might be a good idea. I hadn't even considered her, but it's a thought."

The next morning, I didn't have to be at work until late. I called the office to speak with Dr. Barber to make sure that everything was okay. He had already cut his vacation short and returned to work the morning before the shooting. When he answered my call, he voiced his concern for me and sounded sympathetic about everything that had happened. He also said he wished I could take as much time as I needed, given the circumstances. But they needed me there that day to help work out the care routines, not only for our bonobos but for other animals in the facility.

The next phone call was to my mom. After hearing my brief explanation, she seemed eager to help. She said she'd pack a light bag, jump right in her car, and be at Jack's in a couple of hours. She must have been driving like a mad woman, because she got there in exactly two hours. We stood in the living room exchanging greetings.

"You don't know how much this means to me, Mom. Thank you. Would you be willing to stay over tonight? Jack has a couple more extra bedrooms upstairs."

She tapped her mini-suitcase on wheels. "I came prepared," she said.

"Mom, let's sit down for a minute." We sat side by side on the couch. I went over all the logistics and safety protocols in caring for Lazzy. My mom listened attentively.

"I have to make this very clear to you. About your being here. You can't tell anyone. Not your friends, not Ruthy. Not Maggie. No one. We have to keep this completely quiet. Did you happen to mention it to anybody before you got here? I know how you like to get on the phone when you are in your car."

"Not a soul, dear. I listened to one of those podcasts on the way over. Have you ever listened to a podcast, Rory? They are the most amazing things. The one I just heard was about true crime. It's called *Strange Matters*. It's so interesting." She went on for the next few minutes, listing all the different series she was into. Finally, she came up for a breath of air, and I broke in, hoping to turn the conversation and get her settled.

I showed her around the house, to her room, and then finally introduced Lazzy, who'd been in his room napping. I explained, again, all she needed to do with him, for him, around him, and told her to call me if she needed anything. I told her to use caution around him even though Lazzy had never shown any type of aggression. Jack also had security cameras throughout his house. He gave me the login so that I could look in on Mom and Lazzy at any time. Just when I finished explaining things, Lazzy walked up to her with a block and a Rubik's Cube in his hands.

"Looks like you might be doing some puzzle-solving this afternoon," I smiled. "Lazzy, I have to go in to work for a little while. You be good for my mom, okay, and I'll see you later. I love you."

He walked over and threw his arms around my waist, hugging me again. My heart filled with joy. "I'll miss you, buddy. But I'll be back in just a little bit."

As I closed the door, I took a deep breath, hoping they'd be alright. A few seconds later, I checked the cameras on my phone. They were sitting at the kitchen table. Lazzy twisted the Rubik's Cube. And Mom smiled on.

~

Thanks to my mom, I selected a podcast about animals called *Zoo Logic*. The entire drive in, I listened to one Dr. Grey Stafford talk to a trainer who works with chimpanzees in the movies. The topic interested me so much that I hadn't even paid much attention to the driving. That's probably why I didn't see the emotional turmoil coming. As I got out of my car and started walking into the building, I realized I was terrified. I broke out in a hard sweat, my breathing got fast, and I could feel my heartbeat increasing. My body pounded all over. I stopped in the main lobby, leaning my back against the wall, and stood still. I didn't feel like doing much else.

"Hey, Doc. You okay?"

I looked over to my left, and there stood Morris Mott, the head of security. As always, he looked like strength personified. And at the top was his warm smile.

"Dr. Greene? Is everything alright?"

"Hi, Morris. Yeah, I'm okay, I think. I guess I'm feeling a little overwhelmed after yesterday. I just need a minute."

"Why don't you come back here and sit down? I'll get you a cup of coffee or tea."

I trailed him through the lobby, our muted reflections following along on the marbled walls. We walked around the security checkpoint area and down a short hallway into the guards' room just off the main lobby. One wall contained a bank of black-and-white screens, all cycling through various footage from the building. Two guards sat at a long desk in front of the screens, watching. Beyond that was a lounge area with comfortable chairs and a coffee table. A snack area lined another wall. Further on appeared to be the entrance to some sort of locker room or changing area. Morris motioned to one of the chairs. "What can I get you? Coffee? Tea? A soda? Anything you like," he said.

"How about a diet something?"

He came back with a Diet Coke and a Snickers bar.

"Everybody needs a Snickers when they're stressing out," he laughed. "I've seen the commercials," he said, nodding. "Betty White, God rest her soul."

"Thank you. Sorry about this. I just didn't realize I'd get so panicked when I came in."

"I was here in the lobby when it happened, but I read the full report about the shooting. I'm really sorry you had to go through all of that. It's only natural you'd be on edge today."

"I guess you're right. Are there many people in the building at this point?"

"Essentials. And administration. That's about it. Food deliveries came today, and they had trouble finding people who knew where things went. But I think they got it figured out."

"That's good, I suppose."

We sat for a second, not saying anything, a moment of awkward silence. I opened the Diet Coke.

"Have you heard anything, Morris? Anything about who did this?"

"Not a word. The police came in yesterday and wanted all the tapes. I say tapes. Old habit. You know what I mean. Everything is digital now. But, before they got here, I scrubbed through the hallway cameras on your floor a little bit. Looks to me like a single shooter. Probably male. But it is hard telling. They were completely dressed in black, hoodie, mask. You know," he said.

"Yeah."

"We've got this placed locked down tight, Dr. Greene. You don't have to worry about being here today. We have three times the number of guards working than we normally do. A full staff here at central, and then the rest are patrolling, inside and out. I feel pretty good about today. Besides, the police still have people here, a couple of patrolmen out front, at least."

"That's good to know. So, Morris, back to the person on the tape. Anything else about them? Like their walk or anything?"

"Well, I was thinking about that. I'm sure the police will do it, but I wanted to compare this guy to the guy who stole your bonovy. You know, watch them side by side to see if they look alike."

I didn't want to correct him on the bonobo thing, because mostly, I wanted to show appreciation for his detective work. "That's a great idea. I hope they will. If not, I'll be sure to make sure they do." I took a couple more sips of the soda and then stood up. Morris got up right along with me. "I've taken too much of your time. Thanks for everything. I feel better already. Is it okay if I take the Snickers with me? I may need it in a couple of hours," I smiled, holding it up and tucking it into my jacket.

Morris nodded and smiled. "Well, it was good to see you again," he said, holding his arm out toward the door. I started walking that way.

"Uh, Dr. Greene? Umm. There's one more thing," he said. "It's been bothering me. About both of these incidents. I can't figure how this person got in. All the exterior doors are locked tight, and they're on emergency exit alarms. So, if someone goes through one of those, we know about it. We get a signal right here if one goes off. Or if it doesn't have power. So, nobody comes in or out of those doors without us knowing it. Whoever did this, both times, had to come in through our security check at the front entrance. And I can tell you, without question, no one dressed like that came in this way."

I listened to him carefully and thought for a moment. "What about windows?"

"No, ma'am. Security windows. These babies only open a couple of inches. Not nearly wide enough for a person to fit through."

"How about the delivery entrance?"

"We monitor that with cameras too. But when someone wheels in here with a delivery, there's a checkpoint by the service elevator. They have to go through the same screening down there as they do right here in the lobby."

"I see."

"Yeah. So I don't get how they came in, and I'm not bringing all of this up just to cover my own back. But it doesn't make sense. Unless, of course, they came through, and we didn't notice anything different about them," he said.

"So, are you saying what I think you're saying?"

He spoke softly, leaning forward. "This had to be someone who was supposed to be here. Both times." Morris looked around and over his shoulder. "And we certainly would have noticed if Boyle came in yesterday. So, I don't think it was him."

I felt dizzy, knowing this, knowing what I'd suspected.

"Maybe we're not as safe as we think we are today," I said.

He shook his head. "I'll send up two guards to your floor full-time today."

Chapter Twenty-Two

I felt sick to my stomach as I passed the main lab door, cordoned off with yellow warning tape along with a sign boldly posted: *DO NOT ENTER. CRIME SCENE.* I wasn't about to enter, but I couldn't help but to look in briefly, noticing the blood stains on the floor. The reality of Andy being dead hit me. It is hard to explain the feeling that comes along when someone dies. The reality of it pours over you like wet cement. It feels heavy, and foreign, and restrictive. Andy, dead.

I moved down the hallway to my office, completely dark but with the door wide open. I couldn't remember how I left it the day before. I flipped on the light. There, sitting in one of the chairs by my desk, was Brad, his lab coat over his head.

"Brad? Are you alright?"

He turned and looked my way, pulling his lab coat down and righting himself in the chair. He started to stand up.

"Don't get up. You're fine. Stay there as long as you need to," I said.

"I'm sorry, Rory. I haven't slept. I was at the hospital all night, though I'm not sure why. Hannah's in ICU, and they wouldn't let me in to see her. You probably already know, but her parents flew in overnight, so they are with her now."

"Thanks. Yes, I heard. Brad, listen, I'm so sorry about all of this."

"Did you know Hannah and I went out on a couple of dates? Of course, you don't know that. We were keeping it secret. Since they have that stupid company policy about people dating. Anyway, I like her a lot. She's smart. And she's funny."

"She has so many good qualities. You two make a great couple, I'm sure. I'm so sorry she got hurt," I said.

"I am too. I should've stopped the guy. But I froze."

"It's probably a good thing you stayed exactly where you were. Or you could've been hurt too."

"Better me than Hannah. Or Andy. I bet you anything Martin was the shooter. That little bastard. God. I never did like him." Brad shook his head and pinched the bridge of his nose with one hand.

"The police are looking into it."

"Yeah, good luck with that. Freakin' Dumb and Dumber running that show."

"Well, hopefully, they'll find something. What are you doing here anyway? You should go home and get some rest."

"I'm only here because I have to be. They put us on Schedule A, and I'm on that list. I'm just getting ready to go feed everyone," he said. "Sorry, I crashed your office. I just felt like I had to go someplace and be alone for a minute."

"It's fine, Brad. You can come in here whenever you need to."

He got up and started to walk out the door but stopped and turned back toward me. "I'm going to find that piece of shit before he does any more damage. I mean it."

"Brad." I stood up. "Don't do anything stupid. We need to let the police handle this."

"Since Lazzy went missing, we've been bombed and shot at. I'd say they aren't handling this at all."

"Even still, don't do anything you're going to regret later."

"Yeah, maybe. We'll see."

He shook his head and gave the wall a slap with one hand as he walked out the door.

~

The day went by painfully slowly. I mostly stayed with the bonobos all day, doing an array of different activities from the regular agenda. I wanted them to feel like things were normal, like the routine hadn't been disrupted. And, who knows, maybe they weren't as traumatized by the shooting as we humans were. Maybe they didn't understand. I got clearance to enter the main lab for the purpose of getting their personal things out of their cages—their favorite blankets, toys, books, and so on. Several weeks ago, I gave Della a handheld mirror, and she loved it. By the next day, the other two wanted mirrors of their own. When Boris joined us, I gave him a mirror on his first day. It has been fun to watch their responses. Most of the time, they make faces at themselves or simply just sit and stare.

By the end of the day, I felt exhausted. The weight of being in the building fell hard on me and, truthfully, I think it fell hard on the few of us who were there. I barely saw anyone throughout the day. When I would bump into another CAR employee, no smiles lit any faces. Understandably. We didn't want to be there—none of us. But the animals had to be cared for. And in other lab departments there were processes that had to be monitored and continued.

The lunchroom was so quiet you could hear the whirring of the vending machines and the eerie clanking of silverware on plates without any dinner conversation going with it. We were all jumpy. How could we not be on edge? I stayed well past the arrival of the next shift to ensure the evening crews were settled and in place, making sure they knew of all the temporary locations of the animals. I passed several guards and a couple of police officers as I exited the building. Getting into my car and locking the door never felt so good.

I drove directly to Jack's house, and, upon arrival, I found Mom and Lazzy sitting at the kitchen table, eating sugar cookies and playing cards.

"Hello, dear. Come join us?"

"Mom! What did I tell you about giving Lazzy sweets? Lazzy! How many cookies have you eaten?"

He slumped down in his chair as the corners of his mouth turned upward.

"Don't you pull that handsome smile on me, young man. You know better than to eat all those cookies."

"Oh, Rory. You leave that poor boy alone. If you're going to yell at anyone, yell at me. I wanted to show him how to bake. So we made sugar cookies. Try one, dear, they're delicious. I got the softness just right."

I had to laugh. Lazzy had both his hands on his head, semi-covering his eyes, and it seemed as if he was trying not to grin but doing it anyway. I picked up a cookie and took a bite.

"You're right. Delicious. But that's enough for now. You need to eat some nuts and fruit for dinner." I worked at putting away the cookies and fixing Lazzy a small plate of his regular food. I figured he couldn't be too hungry and was probably maxed out on sugar. I was surprised he wasn't tearing around the room, jumping on the furniture.

"Is Jack home yet? I asked.

"Yes. He got back about an hour ago. Maybe longer. He went for a run and now he's in the shower. He said something about just ordering pizzas for dinner, so I didn't fix anything. Well, except for the cookies. But that was long before he got here. Jack liked the cookies, by the way." Mom put her nose upward in the air.

"I'm sure he did. I'll call in the pizza. What do you want?"

Just then, Jack walked into the kitchen, brushing through the top of his hair with one hand.

"Let's get Mama Mazza's. How about one cheese, one everything?" Jack pulled his phone out, dialing. We all approved. When he got off the call, he turned to my mom.

"Corine, I need to talk with Rory for a minute. Do you mind if we go into my office area?"

"Not at all. You kids have fun," Mom said as she flitted her hand in the air.

I followed Jack into his computer mecca. "Sit down right there while I cue this up," he said.

On the screen right in front of me was a tape of the hallway outside our lab. A few seconds in, a person walked down the hall toward the door, a handgun in one hand and some type of assault weapon on his back, with the strap going crossways over his body.

"He's got two guns," I said.

"Two that we can see," Jack returned. He leaned over and hit a button. The screen went black.

"I'm sorry," he said. "You know, I've been scanning this footage all day, and I'm completely desensitized by all of this. I have to be for the job. If you don't want to watch, I understand."

"Well, the footage stops in the hallway. We only have the research monitoring cameras in the lab. So, I'm okay to watch this. Thanks for asking."

He leaned over again, pushing the play button. The person moved further down the hallway, looking around and then back again before approaching the door. They then entered with the handgun pointing forward. I could see flashes from inside the lab. Moments later, he emerged, running down the hallway to the elevators. From there, he exited at the stairwell. Again, his manner of dress covered him from head to toe, including a hoodie and a mask, all black. The outfit was identical to that of the person who stole Lazzy.

"Okay," I said, turning to Jack.

"Now this." He pushed another button, and the reel of the person pushing the large cart played. He went back and forth between the two, side by side, playing them on a loop.

"See?" he asked. "Not the same person. Not even close. The person pushing the cart is a bit taller. Also a tad heavier, in the upper body especially. See? And look at the way they walk. The gait is completely different. Same with the stride. The first person has longer steps, even though he's pushing that cart with an eighty-pound ape inside."

"You're right."

"Yeah. Two different people. The FBI was all over this today," Jack took a step back, stretching his back as he straightened himself.

"The FBI?" I asked.

"They've now been down here three times. Twice after the bombing, and then again today."

"I didn't know that. Well, that's good, right? Maybe they'll get Vargas moving."

"He was a total terror at work today. He doesn't like when people pull rank on him, and these two definitely are running the show now," Jack said.

"I just wonder why they didn't question any of us in the lab. They never asked me anything."

"Oh, trust me, they will. These two agents are textbook FBI guys. Like they walked right out of some TV show. They are all business."

"Two men then?"

"Yep. And not a wrinkle on either one of their suits. I swear, they must never sit down. Somebody probably drives their car down from Indy, and they run alongside."

"You're hilarious."

"But seriously, they were all over the tapes today. And your one boss was in. The woman, Dr. Keegan. Man, she's not too uptight, is she?" he laughed.

"Just a smidge."

"She might be the reason they haven't talked to anybody else. She seemed to be pretty dictatorial about the lab, saying things like the research is highly classified and that you underlings shouldn't be asked questions about what you do."

"Sounds like her."

"At any rate, I just wanted to show this to you. I don't know. This really changes things. I mean, we know Martin stole Lazzy, and we figured he probably wasn't working alone. But now we know more than one person is involved. Which brings me to this. And you're probably not going to like it. But now that the FBI is involved, don't you think it might be a good idea to turn Lazzy over to them? Or at least let them know that we have him. I think we have to, Rory. It would really help the case."

Jack's suggestion made me feel queasy. I couldn't think of losing Lazzy again, and for some reason, turning him over to the FBI seemed like it would be too much for him to handle. I sat quietly for a moment thinking, looking at the monitors, all frozen in time with the image of someone wheeling him out in the covered cart.

"I know you're probably right. But. Let's just leave it for a little while, okay? Can I think some more on this?"

"Sure. Sure. That's fine. Take your time. And speaking of which, your mom is going to wonder what happened to us," he motioned to the door.

We walked back out into the kitchen, and Lazzy and my mother acted like they didn't even know we were gone. Lazzy straightened the little deck of cards in front of him as Mom placed one face up on the table. "Your turn."

Lazzy pulled a card out of his hand. Mom turned it over, a king of spades, to her three of clubs.

"That's yours," she said.

"What are you guys playing?" I asked.

"War. Lazzy's winning right now."

"Don't teach him any bad habits, Mom."

A few minutes later, the pizzas showed up. We shared a nice dinner, the four of us sitting around the kitchen table, talking about things like the best pizza we'd ever had, the best bananas we'd ever eaten (for Lazzy's interest), the Colts' chances of ever getting to the Superbowl again. The last time they won was in 2007 when they beat the Bears. Before that, it happened in 1971 with a win over the Dallas Cowboys. Johnny Unitas was the quarterback that year, and Mom said she had a crush on him. She was a walking encyclopedia when it came to the Indianapolis Colts.

"Your father hated football. Come to think of it, he didn't like too many sports at all. So I had to watch on my own. Well, you girls always watched."

"I remember you going to a game or two every year, didn't you?"

"Yes, a friend had season tickets, so I'd get to go every so often. I loved going to those games. Memorial Stadium. And then the Dome." Her voice drifted off, and so did her thoughts. The expression on her face even changed as she looked away, off into another time and another place.

"Well, that's pretty cool, Corine. It seems like you enjoyed it," Jack said.

"Oh, I loved those times. I really did."

Lazzy reached over, patted her hand, and made the symbol for love, the hand signal with two fingers down. He wasn't great at it, but I knew what he meant.

Yes. I knew what he meant.

Chapter Twenty-Three

After much discussion on the topic with both Jack and my mom, long after Lazzy had been put to bed, I agreed it would be best to let the authorities know we had Lazzy. We all felt like the FBI could be trusted despite what was going on within the confines of Columbus. I had no idea who I could or could not trust at work or in the police department. Yet the FBI seemed to be out of the circle of things, whatever that circle might be.

The next morning, Jack phoned me at my office with the contact information of the two agents assigned to the case. Agents Kerry Neal and Trevor Bishop. I once knew a guy in high school named Kerry, and he might have been the weirdest guy in our entire class. So, when I had to decide which FBI agent to call, I used Trevor Bishop's number. It always interests me when we humans make needless associations based on past experiences, which is exactly what I did with these two Kerrys. I wondered if animals did the same thing.

"Bishop here."

"Agent Bishop. Good morning. You don't know me. I'm Dr. Victoria Greene from the CAR Labs in Columbus, Indiana. From what I understand, you've been assigned to our case."

"That's correct, Dr. Greene. How can I help you?"

"Well, this is a bit awkward for me to say, but I'll just come right out with it. I have Lazzy."

"I'm sorry? I'm not sure I understand what you're saying."

"I have Lazzy. The bonobo who was initially kidnapped. I have him. With me right now."

"Let me make sure I have this straight. You are confessing to the crime of stealing the CAR animal from the CAR laboratory facilities?"

"Oh, no. No. I didn't kidnap him from CAR. No. I'm sorry. I … well … I managed to find the kidnapper and take Lazzy back. I did some investigating of my own. And, through a stroke of luck, I was able to locate him. Then it was just a matter of my stealing him back from the abductor. Martin Boyle. That's who took him initially. From the lab. From CAR."

"Dr. Greene, I'm putting you on speakerphone so that my partner can hear you."

"That's fine."

"Okay, please say again."

I retold the story to both agents, telling them as many details as I could remember. Of course, I didn't want to involve Jack, or Sarah, or my mom. So I made it sound like I was completely on my own in this. I told them I suspected Boyle and visited his house. And then I staked it out, tailed him. I gave them the location of the strip mall and the exact times I was there.

"Dr. Greene, stay right where you are, and we'll send some officers to your location to retrieve the animal. We'll also need you to come in for questioning. We're working out of police headquarters there in Columbus, so we'll have the officers bring you back with them."

"Well, I don't think that's quite how it's going to go," I said. "I'm sure you've put a trace on this call by now or that you're working on it. And I'll tell you straight out. I'm at CAR right now, sitting in my office, to save you the trouble. But Lazzy isn't here. And I'm not planning on telling you where he is anytime soon."

There was a brief silence on the phone. I could hear them whispering. I continued. "Here's the thing, officers. I don't trust our police department, and I don't trust most of the people I work with right now. Detective Vargas has done very little to advance this investigation. That is why I began working on things on my own. Also, I am fairly certain that whoever is behind this is somehow involved here at CAR. The way the shooter and the bomber had to get into our building indicates to me that it had to be someone who works here. Or who has access."

"I see."

"So the main reason I'm calling you is to make it official that I told you about me finding Lazzy and also who his abductor was. Martin Boyle. I don't know how any of this is going to play out, but I wanted to have some sort of record of this, for Lazzy's safety, for my safety, and for legal purposes," I said.

"How do we know you didn't kidnap him to begin with?"

"Well, I guess you don't. But it wouldn't make much sense for me to pick up the phone and tell you that I have him, now would it? There'd be nothing for me to gain by this except for trouble. Look, I'm the head of our lab section, the one in charge of running our experiments. I have been responsible for the care of all the animals within our department. So I can assure you, beyond a reason of a doubt, that Lazzy is being well cared for; he's happy, and he is safe."

"I understand your apprehension in this matter, but we really need to get the animal back into custody," one of them said.

"Sorry. Look, you know where I am. So, thanks. That's all I have for now."

I hung up the phone. I knew it would take them less than an hour to get here from Indy. In fact, I'm pretty certain they were en route as we talked on the phone. I'd guessed they'd either arrest me or strongly suggest that I go with them for questioning. And fear gripped me as I sat at my desk, phone in hand. I hoped beyond hope I'd made the right decision.

I dialed Jack. "Done," I said and hung up.

Our plan was to move Lazzy and my mom to Sarah's house. For the time being. I knew from here on out the FBI would be on my tail, so our plan got more elaborate.

Agents Bishop and Neal showed up at CAR as predicted. Jack's description could not have been more accurate. They looked like someone had ironed them from head to toe. Not a hair out of place, not a wrinkle in either suit and as clean-shaven as they come.

"I'm Agent Bishop. This is Agent Neal, FBI," Bishop said as they held out their badges. "Is there someplace we can talk?"

I led them down the hall to my office.

They got right to the matter of things as soon as we entered. "Dr. Greene, we are going to have to arrest you for kidnapping and possession of stolen property in the matter of the bonobo."

"You've got to be kidding," I said.

"We don't kid, ma'am," Agent Neal said.

"No. I imagine you do not."

"If you tell us where you are holding the animal, things will go a lot easier for you."

"And how is that?" I was not feeling very compliant at that moment. Mostly, through all of the discussions with Jack about this decision to be sitting there with the FBI, a part of me had hoped that I would never be arrested when I told them I had Lazzy. As I spoke with the agents, my nerves of pre-planned steel filled with anxiety. I didn't want to go to jail.

"That's just the way it works. The judge hearing your case will look much more favorably on you if you are cooperative," Neal spoke again.

"Well, I'm not telling you where Lazzy is. So do what you have to do."

And that they did. Agent Bishop placed cuffs on me, draped my coat around my shoulders, and led me out of the lab while all eyes watched. We said little else to one another. My hopes for the FBI to come in and make this whole investigation triumphant turned on me.

An hour later, I was sitting downtown in a holding cell at the Bartholomew County Jail. Thankfully, I had the cell to myself. The facility can hold 86 inmates. I know because I asked. The area where they took me was mostly unpopulated, save for a couple of other women. Luckily for me, my arrest came early in the day, before the court session. The Honorable Judge Ronald Jones heard my preliminaries and set the bail at $5,000. My one phone call went to my mom, who came and bailed me out by five o'clock in the afternoon. Not my best day. But at least I was walking out of there.

She drove me to the lab, and I picked up my car. I told her to drive around town for a while, stop at a grocery store, get gasoline, and drive a little more, trying to ensure no one was following her.

"Drive around the same block, three or four times in a row, slowly. Keep checking your rearview mirror, okay?"

"Honey, I've seen the movies. I know how to lose a tail if I need to." She patted me on the shoulder as we sat in the parking lot of the lab. I laughed. My mother the female version of Vin Diesel.

"Oh, do you, now? And do you have a lot of people tailing you these days?"

"Stop it. You're being smart. I'm just saying I know how it is done," she nodded her head, looking forward, indignation on her face.

"I'm sorry. You're right. It's just that it's been a bad day. And I don't want them to know where we're keeping Lazzy. I just couldn't stand it if they took him from me."

"I know, dear. I understand. And I'm not angry with you. But I can handle this, okay?"

"Thanks, Mom. I love you." I leaned over and gave her a hug before continuing.

"Okay, so. I'll be there later. We'll follow the plan. I'll go to my house first, get cleaned up, and get some things for overnight. And we're using the garages, in and out, remember. So."

"Got it."

"Then I'll go to Jack's. Change into his disguise, and I'll go over to Sarah's in his car in a couple of hours or so. She and I will switch, and Sarah will wear the disguise back out and take Jack's car back to his house later. She'll spend the night over there. And you and I at Sarah's. Okay?"

"Okay. Got it. Good luck."

"Good luck yourself. Tell Lazzy I'll be there later. And, Mom? Thanks."

I knew we wouldn't be able to keep this scenario up more than once or twice before the FBI would catch on. But for now, I didn't notice them following me when I drove home. I took a little tour around Columbus before going to Jack's, and I'm fairly certain no one was with me there either. Same, on my way to Sarah's. I thought for sure they would have someone watching me, my house, my movements, but it didn't appear to be the case. I suppose stealing an ape didn't warrant an FBI round-the-clock presence. Perhaps we'd gone to all this trouble for nothing.

When I settled in at Sarah's house, Lazzy and I were sharing a room. I was glad for it. The room had two twin beds, freshly made, and a small table with two wooden chairs in the corner. It was like it had been tailored for a woman harboring her young bonobo.

Lazzy and I sat at the table, playing with the Rubik's Cube and a wooden block puzzle.

He set the cube down on the table and put his hands in his lap, staring at me.

"What is it, Lazzy?" I asked.

"Home," he signed.

"You want to go home? Don't you like it here?"

He made his signs for Gloria and Della.

"You miss Gloria and Della?"

"Home," he signed again.

I opened my arms, and he slid out of his chair, standing by me, hugging me. I rested my head on his, trying to hold back my tears.

"I know this has been so hard on you. I'm so sorry. I'm going to try my hardest to get you home soon. I will try, try, try."

He stood there, not moving, just keeping his arms around me. At that moment, I wanted to shout at the world, to anyone who ever thought that animals are just dumb animals. I wanted to yell at all those people who think animals are unfeeling creatures and that humans can treat them any way they please. I wanted to stand at the highest height and yell, "Look at this. Can't you see?"

Lazzy backed up just a half foot or so and signed to me.

"Lazzy sad."

Chapter Twenty-Four

I'm pretty talented when it comes to stonewalling. I took a deep breath and continued talking. "It's been happening for a long time. And many times, it is a horrible travesty against them," I said. "I'm serious. I mean, take a minute to think about it. It didn't happen just one single time, but all throughout history, all around the world."

Agent Neal looked up at the ceiling, leaning back in his chair.

"Okay, for example. Take the Soviet war in Afghanistan. The one that happened during the late 1970s through the eighties. The Sunni Mujahideen fighters used camel 'suicide bombers' against Soviet occupying forces. They'd hide explosives in the camels' packs and then send them into the areas where the Soviet troops were," I continued. "Of course, I don't have to tell you the outcome. It's obvious. And horrible."

Agent Bishop shook his head, notepad in hand, staring at me.

"Oh, we're guilty of this in the United States too. Actually, most countries in the world use animals as military operatives. There's an entire industry, a huge business. I know that is the underlying motive for our studies here. Why else would the government be giving us a huge grant for animal communications?"

Bishop continued to stare. Neal sat in the other chair, nodding slightly.

"This is all very interesting, Dr. Greene, but if we could get back to the original question," Neal said, nodding larger and more pronounced.

"Oh. Sure." I paused for a few seconds. "Just remind me what it was."

"We're here to find out exactly when it was you took Lazzy. And, once again, where he is located at this moment."

"Yes. That's right. Lazzy. You know, we're studying bonobos in my lab, which are highly fascinating animals. But. In several other departments at CAR, we're conducting the same research on birds. Which reminds me of another story. Did I tell you about World War II? Animal military operations were in use all over the place during that war, with all kinds of different animals. One thing they tried was to put pigeons in their missiles. There was this guy, an American behaviorist named B.F. Skinner. He devised this big plan to train pigeons to ride in missiles and then guide those torpedoes to enemy ships. They called it Project Pigeon. Catchy, huh? Well, it never did work out, and cost a lot of pigeons their lives. But the U.S. government tried it again after the war. I think around 1948 to somewhere in the early 1950s. They called that one Project Orcon. Kind of a last-ditch effort to try the theory again. Turns out, pigeons can navigate themselves when they're flying around here and there, but they're not so great at driving torpedoes." I folded my hands on the table.

"Dr. Greene. Please."

"Oh, I got a million of them. It's kind of a hobby of mine, reading about past animal experiments. Although, nine times out of ten, I end up getting completely hacked off by what some so-called scientists did to animals in the name of discovery."

Agent Bishop stood up and walked behind his chair. He pushed it under the table and walked a couple of steps away, his back turned. He rubbed his neck with one hand.

"I'm going to go get a water. Kerry, do you want something? Dr. Greene?"

Agent Neal shook his head. He dropped his notepad and pen on the table.

"I'd love a Diet Coke," I said. I fished a couple of dollar bills out of my pocket and pushed them across the table. "It's on me, Agent Bishop. Really. It's the least I can do."

Bishop looked at Neal, dipped his head to one side, and reluctantly took the money.

"I'll be right back," he said.

"The machines are just out the door to your right, then down the hall, and then right around the corner. I've been there a few times," I said, waving a little salute, then immediately wishing I hadn't.

Agent Kerry Neal gave me a long, hard stare.

"Look, Doctor. We really are just trying to help here. CAR wants their animal back. We need to process him for evidence. And if what you say is true, that this Martin Boyle is the one who stole him, then you are impeding the progress of our investigation."

"I'm sorry. I just don't see how Lazzy can help you find Boyle. You need to be going to that strip mall and his house and turning things upside-down in those places. Lazzy's been away from Boyle for four days now. He's not going to have a bit of anything on him that will lead you anywhere."

"Well, in that case, I think we are done here. You're wasting our time."

"We're stopping before the refreshments get here? I think you better wait on Agent Bishop to see how he feels about the whole matter," I smiled.

Just then, Agent Bishop came back through the door. He placed the can of Diet Coke in front of me and went and stood in the corner with his bottle of water.

"Let's wrap this, Trevor. She's not talking," Neal said.

They looked at one another for a moment, then Agent Bishop dipped his head again and moved toward the table. He leaned over, setting his water down softly, then placing both hands on the table.

"I can stay here all day. In fact, I kind of like your stories. I mean. Who knew? Agent Neal, I can take over from here. We have the cameras rolling, so there's no need for two of us to be here."

He pulled out his chair and took a seat. "Fire away," he said.

All of a sudden, I didn't want Agent Neal to leave, cameras rolling or not. We'd started this session first thing in the morning. Now, barely an hour in, I didn't feel like backing down.

"Here's another one from World War II. Believe it or not, Japan used insects as weapons. The Japanese loaded up their airplanes with fleas and flies that were infected with cholera and plague. Then they flew over China and sprayed those fleas and flies over heavily populated areas. They'd put them in bombs too. Historians believe that these flea bombs resulted in around 440,000 Chinese deaths. Granted, I'm not sure that fleas have the same sentient awareness as, say, chimpanzees, or dogs, or pigeons do. But still."

"Look, Trevor. We're wasting our time here. We need to check back on some of those leads we started on. Let's get out of here," Agent Neal said. Agent Bishop nodded reluctantly.

"Dr. Greene. Remember the conditions of your bail. Don't leave town. You're free to go for now," Neal said, getting up and walking out the door. Bishop followed without looking back.

Feeling mildly triumphant, I wanted to see if Jack was in his office but decided against it. There was no need to draw unwanted attention to the fact that he and I were friends. I gathered my things and headed back to work.

When I arrived, I found a note on my keyboard to see Dr. Keegan immediately. I decided to take the stairs up to her office. I needed the exercise for one, but going to see Keegan always made me nervous. She was never gracious toward anyone. Especially me. When I reached her office, Keegan's receptionist told me to sit down and wait. There were only three chairs in the waiting room lined up against one of the pale tan walls. I took the closest one. I stared at the clock on the facing wall, an analog thing, a standard office issue. Black on white. It made me wonder about Keegan.

During my junior year in college, I took an elective class about the "Psychology of Creating Effective Workspaces." We covered all sorts of topics, from color design to window placement, Feng Shui to design mistakes. One of the "ten commandments" in effective designing was "Never put a clock in a waiting room." And there I sat, staring at one, the second hand slowly marching its way across the clock face. Leave it to Keegan. Once again, she was asserting her power over any minion that might be waiting for her. I laughed out loud without realizing it until the receptionist dropped her paperwork on her desk and looked my way. "Sorry," I said.

About 20 minutes later, the same receptionist picked up the handset on her phone, nodding and speaking quietly. She then hung up and looked over at me. "Dr. Keegan will see you now."

I knocked lightly before going in.

"Close the door behind you, Dr. Greene," she said. "Sit."

I took my place in the chair closest to the door. On purpose.

"I'll get right to it. There is the matter of your arrest in connection with the disappearance of Lazzy. I took it to an emergency meeting of the board this morning. I won't lie to you. I asked them to approve your termination, but it was voted down six to one. Innocent until proven guilty and all that righteous nonsense. However, they did approve of putting you on leave until the outcome of your trial. We can't have you poking around here, bombing more bathrooms, and stealing more animals," she said, looking at me over her glasses. "Do you have anything to say for yourself? Anything that you'd like to go on the record?"

I sat there for a moment, silent. I guess I should have expected this, but just like my arrest, I hadn't completely anticipated this particular outcome.

"Well, I guess nothing I can say will make a difference. I mean, this sounds like a done deal," I said. I noticed I was wringing my hands, so I dropped them down, placing my palms firmly on my lap.

Keegan laughed. "You're right about that. Frankly, just between you and me? I don't feel one bit sorry for you. In fact, this makes me happy. That higher-than-thou attitude has finally caught up with you, Dr. Greene, and now you're headed out the door for good."

Her voice oozed with bitterness and contention. She'd always been icy towards me. From day one. And I hadn't done anything to merit it. If anything, I went in the other direction, trying my best to be cordial and friendly toward her. Regardless, I knew better than to respond with a sharp tongue, though it was truly what I wanted to do. I took a moment, took a breath, and finally spoke.

"I hope you're wrong. I feel like I have a lot of good work to do here," I said, standing and heading toward the door.

"I didn't dismiss you, Dr. Greene."

I didn't turn around. I slowly opened the door and walked out, hoping that it wasn't for the last time.

Chapter Twenty-Five

Whales sing their beautiful songs. Wolves howl out in many tones and for many reasons. We've all heard frogs croaking from their hidden places. Ducks quack. Dolphins click. Elephants sound off their built-in trumpets. Birds chirp. Bees buzz. All of them, with all their voices, successfully interact and communicate with the world in which they live. Their world. Our world.

After leaving Keegan's office, I went directly to the cages where Gloria, Della, and Boris were staying. I walked in front of Della's cage, the center one, and sat on the floor right outside her door. I told them at great length every detail about what happened, starting with the day Lazzy was taken. I continued explaining all the details right up until the moment I walked out of Keegan's office. I didn't sign. I just sat on the floor and talked. Della sat near the bars next to me, and both of the others came over, getting as close as they could in their cages. When I was done telling the story, I explained to them I had to leave. I was being forced to leave. Kicked out of the troop. And I didn't want to go.

First, I stepped into Della's cage. I signed "I love you" and gave her a hug. I then went to Gloria and to Boris and did the same thing. As I walked out of the room, I turned one more time to look at them. All three were standing at their doors, hands on the bars. I tried hard not to cry.

I didn't pack up my office. I simply straightened the few things on my desk, filed all my paperwork, locked my cabinets and my closet, and gave everything the once over. I had one plant on my desk, a small fuzzy cactus that Andy had given me about four months ago. He said I needed something green in there. I tucked the small pot under my arm, grabbed my coat and my bag, and locked my office door behind me. I left the building, not saying anything to anyone. I didn't feel like talking about what had happened. I just wanted to leave it behind me without giving ten explanations to the ten different people I should have said goodbye to. I supposed there'd be time for that later.

Once in my car, I started driving. I had no destination in mind. I just drove. I didn't want to tell my mom, or Sarah, or Jack, or anyone else for that matter. I didn't have anything to say. I was numb.

I could not have asked for a grayer day to echo my feelings. And to exaggerate the point, the sky filled itself with the heaviest dull clouds it could gather. Rain started falling three minutes into my drive.

"Perfect," I said.

I found myself in downtown Columbus, winding up and down the streets. And that's when I saw the sign in neon blue. *The Every Answer Bar.*

"Well, if that isn't what I need right now, I don't know what is."

I found a parking spot on the street and pumped a few dimes in the meter right out front. I pulled open the heavy wooden door of the bar and walked inside. The place was mostly empty, which didn't surprise me, given the time of day. Still too early for most folks to be knocking back a drink or two. One man sat near the end of the bar, hunched over a newspaper, a mug of beer in front of him. A man and a woman took up one of the booths, snuggling on the same side, looking like they were madly in love. One other guy in a fine-fitting suit sat at a table in the back.

I popped up on one of the stools at the bar, grabbing a bar napkin from the stack near me.

"How's it going," the bartender came over a moment or two after I sat down.

"It's going."

"What can I get you?"

"What are you good at?" I asked.

The man, probably in his late twenties, rubbed his hand through his hair, winking and smiling.

"You name it, I'm good at it," he said, pushing another napkin in front of me.

Great, I thought. I wanted to get hammered, and I picked a place with a narcissistic bartender.

"Alrighty then. Let me have a Kamikaze, in that case," I said. It seemed appropriate.

A moment later, the cocktail sat in front of me. I reached down, pulled a notebook from my bag, and placed it on the bar, then took out my best pen and uncapped it. I stared at the blank page, the little blue lines just begging for some words. I was begging for some words.

WHAT DO I DO NOW? I wrote in bold letters.

I glanced down to the end of the bar. The guy was still hunched over his newspaper, and as far as I could tell, he hadn't turned the page, or even moved an inch. The couple in the booth across the room were necking like a couple of high-school kids. My notebook sat in front of me, still asking the same question. The guy at the end of the bar still wasn't moving. I realized right then, neither was I.

It hit me in that moment. I knew better than to look for answers at the bottom of a bottle. I reached into my bag and grabbed a ten-dollar bill. Carefully, I pushed it and my full drink forward. As I grabbed the door handle, I heard the bartender call out after me. "Hey. Something wrong with your drink? You coming back?"

As I stepped onto the sidewalk, the rain intensified, drenching my clothes and my face. But somehow, surprisingly, I felt rejuvenated. Instead of accepting my "dismissal" from work as the end of something, I saw it as an opportunity to start asking questions.

I called Sarah first as I drove toward her house. I made certain that I wasn't being followed by any law enforcement. I drove one crazy, zigzag route, keeping my eyes fixed on my rearview mirror.

"Accura World Bank. Sarah Simms speaking. How may I help you?"

"Sarah. It's me. Hey. Guess what happened to me today?"

"I'm afraid to, honestly," she said.

"They let me go at work. I'm on administrative leave. The board is going to vote on my future employment once my court case is done," I said.

"You don't sound upset. In fact, you sound a little chirpy."

"Well, I'm not happy about it, that's for sure. But it made me realize that the only thing I can do about it is to find out who's behind all of this. I'm heading back to your house now. I'm going to tell my mom she can head home."

"How do you think that will go?"

"Oh, she loves me, loves us. And I know she likes being around here. But she'd rather be home. I'm pretty sure of that."

"Hey, Ror. I hate to be short, but I have someone coming in here in a few minutes for an assessment. Was there something you needed right now?"

"I'm sorry. No, no. I was just going to see if you'd brainstorm with me for a little while."

"How about tonight? Okay? Right after work."

"Perfect. And, Sarah? Thanks."

Once again, I felt a closeness with Sarah like none other. She was always so good to me.

I hung up the phone, almost back to her house, when Maggie suddenly appeared in my mind. I hadn't talked to her since the night she told me about my dad. I knew she was giving me space, and it was high time I called her. The phone call went to her voicemail.

"Maggie, it's Rory. Hey. I just wanted to call and tell you that I was sorry I got so upset. It just came as such a shock to me, and with everything that's going on, well, I guess thinking that my dad might have been murdered just put me over the top. So … uhm … I'm sorry, and I hope you'll give me a call. I got fired today, sort of. So. Yeah. Okay. Well, I guess that's all for now. Talk to you soon."

I'd pulled into the driveway at Sarah's just as I finished leaving my message. I didn't have the garage door opener with me, and I thought better of parking my car there in plain sight. I drove around the other side of the block and left it under a tree a good half-mile away. When I got to Sarah's, I knocked on the front door. A minute later, I saw the blinds move in the front window. I chuckled as the door opened, knowing that my mom probably didn't trust the peephole in the door.

"You're soaking wet," my mom said as I walked in.

Lazzy stood right behind her in the entryway. I knelt, and he walked over, giving me a hug. "I missed you, Laz," I said. "I missed you both."

"What are you doing here so early? Did you come home for lunch?"

"I wish. No. I got let go today. Put on administrative leave until after my court case. For stealing Lazzy," I said. I looked over at him as he walked toward the kitchen.

"They let you go?"

"It'll be okay, Mom. Honest. Once this whole thing gets straightened out, everything will be fine."

"Who fired you?"

"Dr. Keegan. She acted like she enjoyed the whole thing, actually."

"She probably did enjoy it. Excuse my language, but what a bitch," Mom barked, turning toward the kitchen. "Lazzy, what are you doing?"

I couldn't remember the last time I heard my mom swear.

"You act like you know her, Mom. Have you ever met Keegan?"

"Lazzy, dear. What do you have there?" Mom said again, stepping toward the kitchen.

I could see Lazzy sitting, simply peeling a banana. "Mom, he's fine. He's just getting a snack," I said. "So, did you hear me? You sounded like you know Keegan. Do you?"

She hesitated momentarily, looked back toward the kitchen, and then turned to me again.

"Oh, sort of. Way back when that whole old crazy group of scientists knew each other. You know, your dad. Maggie. Dr. Aponte and Halverson. That one odd woman, Naomi, I think. Her last name was Peachey. And Dr. Breeden. The whole group. They all used to know each other. It was the whole southern Indiana crowd, mostly IU."

"And Keegan?"

"Yeah, she was in there too. Even though they had different areas of study, they used to hold their geeky science meetings, and Christmas parties, that sort of thing."

Mom turned and walked to the kitchen, mumbling something as she went. I followed her in there, still quite certain that Lazzy was doing just fine. He sat at the table, pulling the strings from his banana almost obsessively.

"He is so funny about that. Lazzy hates those strings on his bananas. I can't stand them on mine, either. Here, Lazzy, do you want me to do that for you, honey?" she leaned over the table, asking him.

She started clearing a couple of things from the kitchen table, the salt and pepper shakers, a butter knife, and a couple of napkins. I could tell by the way she was holding herself, the way she was plucking things off the table, that she was upset.

"Well, the good thing to come from being fired is that I can stay with Lazzy now during the days. And that means you can head back home anytime you want to. You're probably missing all your social clubs and things. And then there's your bridge club. How often do you guys play?"

"Three days a week. Monday, Wednesday, and Friday. But Virginia is really starting to get on my nerves. She's on everybody's nerves, really."

"Well, that's a shame. Can somebody say something to her? About whatever it is she's doing?"

"She's constantly telling us all how to play. I don't know. Maybe. Maybe Bob can say something to her," she said, looking off. Still, I could tell she was a million miles away at that moment.

She started wiping off the table. I walked over, closer to the table, and leaned both hands on it, looking at her. "What's going on, Mom?"

She stopped what she was doing, looked up at me with a piercing stare, and walked to the sink. "It's nothing. Now leave it, Victoria."

She called me Victoria. At that point, I knew it had to be something serious, but I also knew I'd better quit asking any more questions. "This rain's really something today. It's that cold, fall rain, the kind that really cuts right through you," I said.

My mom made her way toward the living room and headed for the stairs. I could hear her footsteps as she climbed them and eventually closed the door to her bedroom upstairs. I couldn't imagine what had upset her so much about our discussion. Was it really about me getting let go from work? Or something else? I wasn't about to call Keegan and ask her, but Maggie, on the other hand, might be able to fill me in.

Lazzy and I sat on the living-room floor, playing with a set of wooden blocks. We'd build something tall and then knock it down. I'm pretty sure Lazzy would repeat that over and over for as long as anyone would play with him. For me? There was nothing I'd rather be doing than spending time with Laz.

About 45 minutes later, Mom came clunking down the stairs, suitcase wheeling behind her. She put it down by the front door.

"Well, I'd like to stay and say my goodbyes to your friends, but I think I'd rather get on the road so I don't have to do any driving in the dark. Not that I'm having any trouble or anything. It's just much easier to drive in the daytime."

I stood up and walked over. Lazzy remained sitting with his blocks.

"Okay. Gosh. I guess I didn't think you'd be leaving already," I said, rocking back on my heels.

"Well, I suppose you were right. I do miss being at home. Not only all my activities but just being in my own house."

"Mom. I'm sorry about earlier. I didn't mean to upset you."

"Oh, that was nothing, dear. I'm not upset in the least. I just think I'm a little tired today, and I get a little cranky sometimes. There's absolutely nothing wrong," she said, grabbing the handle of her suitcase.

I stepped over to her and gave her a long hug. She hugged me back, though I could tell she was ready to leave.

"Thanks for all you did for us, Mom. For helping out with Lazzy, coming all this way. You were a real lifesaver. Thank you."

"It was nothing. Tell Jack and Sarah I said goodbye. Give them hugs. Goodbye, Lazzy. I hope I see you again soon," she winked.

I grabbed the handle of her suitcase to carry it out for her, but she assured me that she was perfectly capable on her own. And out the door she went. I stood on the porch and watched her walk to her car, watched her drive off down the street in the wrong direction. She figured it out by the first turn and righted her course, heading back toward the highway. It made me chuckle lightly, but as she moved out of sight, I realized she had taken all her thoughts and memories with her. She also took my unanswered questions along with all the rest of her secrets.

Chapter Twenty-Six

Sarah and I fixed a pot of chicken and noodles. In addition, we made a banana and berry pizza, the kind that any bonobo would like. The three of us sat at the kitchen table, enjoying our labors. Lazzy seemed especially happy. But the two humans enjoyed it all too.

Sarah and I fell into eating silence for a while. I had told her earlier about the conversation with my mom. Like me, Sarah did not know what to make of it. I'd gone over it again and again, and I still couldn't imagine why Mom got so upset over my asking about Keegan.

We were nearing the end of dinner when I got a text from Maggie.

Maggie: *You fixing me breakfast tomorrow morning?*

Me: *Sounds great. What time?*

Maggie: *See you by 8.*

"I just got a text from Maggie. I'm fixing her breakfast tomorrow if that's okay. At eight. You are more than welcome to eat with us," I said, "in your own kitchen …"

"Mi casa tu casa."

We finished dinner. I cleaned the kitchen while Sarah and Lazzy watched TV in the living room. As I peeped around the corner to look in on them, it made me happy to see Lazzy doing so well. Not only did it seem like he had adjusted to living this way, but he also hadn't been showing any signs of residual trauma from the kidnapping. I was glad for that too.

The next morning, Maggie arrived early. Always early. We buzzed around the kitchen, fixing eggs, bacon, bagels, and cream cheese. It was good to see her, as we hadn't spoken since our last discourse at the restaurant. We hugged when she arrived, but we didn't breach the topic, as breakfast was in the midst of coming together. When we finally sat down, we didn't waste any time getting to our discussion. It always went that way with Maggie.

"So, are you still mad at me?" Maggie asked.

"No, I'm not. I'm sorry about all of that. It just came as such a surprise. You caught me off guard."

"I just thought you needed to know."

"Well, I didn't think so at the time, but now I think you are right," I said.

"Oh?"

"Maybe. One of the reasons I called you was because of this conversation I just had with my mom."

"About your dad's death?" Maggie dipped her bagel in her yolks. Always early and always a dipper. I think she loved eggs more than I did, if that is possible.

"No. It's kind of a long story, but basically, we were talking about Keegan putting me on administrative leave. Mom acted like she knew her. When I asked her to tell me more about Keegan, she got all defensive and quiet. I mean, she completely shut me down. Just like that, she put an end to the whole conversation."

Maggie focused on her plate, stacking some bacon and egg on half of a bagel. She seemed transfixed.

"No comment?" I asked.

She continued to work on her sandwich for a moment, then set it down completely, taking her napkin from her lap. She started wiping her hands. Thoroughly. As if to stall, I thought.

"What a group that was. That whole quirky bunch. We all knew each other. Well, actually, we knew of each other. Most of us came from IU, but there were a few others from different places. But I think all of us went to school in Indiana. It doesn't matter. For the most part, we'd just get together to talk. About things that were happening with all of us, like our advances and findings. Or, in some cases, our troubles. We'd share information about grants we'd heard of. Those sorts of things. We were a mixed bunch. Some biologists. Some chemists or physicists. A couple of astronomy people. A couple of times a year, we'd throw a party. Once during the summer, a big barbeque deal at some park somewhere. And the other at Christmas, with a White Elephant and such. Sort of like a friendly support network."

"That all sounds pretty great. So why in the world would Mom have gotten so upset about that? I mean, what the heck?"

Maggie dropped her hands in her lap, staring down at her plate. I could tell something pressed heavily on her, and she didn't know what to do with it. I could not imagine what great big thing about this group would weigh so excessively, first on my mom and then on Maggie. My mind started trying to connect the dots. Any dots. Keegan seemed to be a key in all of it. What could this group have possibly done that was so diabolical? Finally, I reached over to Maggie and gently touched her arm. She looked up at me.

"You know, you've been like a second mom to me. All these years. I mean, after Dad died, you helped me more than anyone else in this whole world. Mom struggled just to keep herself together. But you. There you were. Good old Maggie came right in and scooped me up. Took me places. Taught me things. Listened to me. You filled a huge gap in my life. Heck, I guess you've been like a second mother and a father. Not to mention a best friend," I smiled lightly. She smiled a bit, too. "So right now I'm asking you to tell me the truth. I can tell this is something you don't want to talk about. Not you. Not my mom. But I need to know. At least, I think I do." I took my hand from her arm and grabbed my fork, just sitting, waiting.

Maggie shook her head for a second. "Rory, I can't. I'm sorry. I just can't."

I paused, trying to calm myself. I could feel myself getting upset again, a combination of worry and helplessness. "What am I supposed to say? What am I supposed to do with all of this? Mom won't talk about it. You won't talk about it. So I'm stuck. Wondering. Not knowing. And, truthfully, I'm upset about the whole thing. I mean, why won't you tell me? I'm 38 years old. I'm not some kid, Maggie. Don't you think I'm old enough to hear whatever it is you're keeping from me? How bad could it be? Really." I picked up my plate and walked to the sink, scraping my food into the disposal and flipping it on, filling the kitchen with the loud noise of the motor. A minute later, I hit the switch again. Silence.

"Come sit back down," Maggie said.

I walked over and took my seat.

"Honest to God, Rory. It isn't my place. This shouldn't be coming from me, okay? I love you like you are my very own, but this is something your mom should be telling you."

I paused for a couple of minutes, trying to decide what to say. "Mom isn't going to tell me."

"I know she won't. So, for that reason, I don't think I should either." Maggie started rubbing her temples as if to fend off some impending headache, the result of keeping a deep, dark secret. She went on another long explanation as to why she shouldn't tell me about whatever this thing was. She didn't know where it would go. Or what would happen. It was complicated, a lot involved, blah, blah, blah. Then she brought Mom back into it again. Maggie said that if she ever did tell me about all of this, it would have to be our secret. She wasn't sure that I should ever let my mom know that I knew about this. The more Maggie went on, the more I wanted to hear the truth. No amount of wiggling was going to keep me from it at that point.

"So, what? I'm just supposed to forget about all of this? Seriously, Mags, I can handle it. Just put it out there and let me decide what to do."

"You don't understand, Rory. It would absolutely change everything."

"Tell me. I'll decide what it changes and what it doesn't."

"You have no idea," she sighed, looking away.

Maggie pushed her chair back from the table. She leaned her elbows on her knees, folded her hands, and stared down at the floor. I couldn't see her face. Finally, she drew in a deep breath and looked up at me. She started to speak quietly, stoically, calmly.

"The science group. We'd meet. For years, we met. I told you how we'd have those parties. Everybody's husbands and wives and families would come. This was a long time ago. Long before you. Most of us were pretty close. Good friends. Sometimes we'd hang out and meet outside the group. Well, one year, at a Christmas party, it seemed like everybody got just a little too hammered. Music was playing, people were dancing. There were a lot of people there. Having fun. Everybody was tossing back drinks on hyperdrive for some reason. Anyway, Keegan's husband, Teddy ... well ... he ... he was right in there with it, too."

Maggie stopped talking. She reached over for her coffee cup, which had to be empty or cold. I got up and went to the counter, grabbed the pot, and refilled her cup. I sat back down, paying her full attention. She thanked me, took a sip, and continued.

"So, Teddy Keegan. He ... uh ... he asked your mom to dance. A lot of people were dancing. Different people together, no big deal. It was Christmas. The song was a fast one, I don't know which. But then it ended pretty quickly and went to a slow song."

"Oh my God. Mom had an affair with Keegan's husband?" I blurted out.

Maggie nodded her head to one side, tilting it down toward her shoulder. She continued. "That's not all of it, Rory. You're right. They had an affair. But here's the thing. About a year later, your mom was pregnant. Pregnant with you," she said.

I sat breathlessly.

"Charlie, your dad, asked me to meet him one afternoon, and that's when he told me that the baby wasn't his."

An overwhelming heat filled my body all at once, rushing all over me, spiraling up toward my head, my face. I started sweating. Suddenly, I felt sick. I ran for the bathroom, just off the kitchen, and lost my breakfast. I stayed there, sitting on the floor of that small half-bathroom, my back to the only open wall, trying to catch my breath. I threw up again.

"Rory? You okay? Why don't you come out of there? Rory?"

I didn't want to leave that bathroom. Not ever. The great Dr. Charles Edward Greene, communicator with animals, wizard of science, and king among men, was not my father. The man I'd admired and adored. The man who I'd shaped my life after. Not my dad. Maggie was right. This did change everything.

"You've been in there an awful long time," she called through the door again. "Lazzy just woke up and came in here. In the kitchen. He's looking for you," she said.

I opened the door and walked out, sitting back down at the kitchen table. I took a drink of water, and it tasted good, rinsing the taste from my mouth. Maggie walked back over, pulling her chair next to mine. She sat down. Lazzy already had his place at the table, eating grapes.

"I don't even know what to say," I began. I held my head in my hands, my elbows propped on the table.

"I tried to warn you."

"Yeah, you did, didn't you? Was my mom ever going to tell me? Hell. Who else knows? Does Ruthy know? Jesus. What a fool I am."

A million thoughts flashed through my mind. I couldn't keep myself straight.

Maggie patted my back. "Who else knows? Well, I know. Of course, your mom knows. The Keegans, obviously. I guess from there, I don't know who else knows. I mean, I can't imagine either couple telling many more people about it," Maggie said, drawing on the kitchen table with her finger.

"Keegan. Jesus. No wonder she hates me," I said. "How long were Mom and this Teddy guy sleeping together?"

"It went on for a couple of years. It was a rough time for your parents. Truthfully? I don't know how your dad did it. He must've really loved your mother because he gave her plenty of room with this."

"I just can't believe what I'm hearing. So, what did my dad do?"

"Well," Maggie exhaled heavily before she went on. "They decided to try to work things out. But he caught the two of them together again. Your dad finally gave her an ultimatum. It was either Teddy or him. He told your mom he would raise you like his own daughter, but she had to end the affair. Once and for all."

"So, after all that, what? Mom just dumped Teddy?" I asked.

"I hate to tell you this, but I wasn't sure what she was going to do. Your dad was a mess. And then Teddy got killed in a car crash. He lost control on that curvy stretch of highway just south of Bloomington. Hit a tree. Head on."

I closed my eyes. I couldn't hear another word. I leaned over, my head bent down, my eyes closed. I just wanted to shut everything out. I felt nothing at that moment, which was the strange thing, only that I wanted to get away. I wanted to be gone. And as long as I kept my eyes closed, I couldn't see any of this strange world I was suddenly in. I had just become the daughter of some man I'd never met. Teddy Keegan. Was that his real name? Was it Theodore? Where was he from? What did he do? Everything seemed to be crumbling around me. Spinning. Like I had been dropped down into a deep nothing. Just then, I felt a hand on my shoulder. I slowly opened my eyes, expecting it to be Maggie reassuring me once again. But there, standing beside me, was Lazzy. He showed his teeth in a wide smile and grabbed my head with both hands. He kissed me right on my forehead, making it grand with his theatrics. Then he reached across the table, grabbed his half-eaten banana, and handed it to me.

"You are a sweetheart, Laz. God, you're sweet. I sure do love you," I said as I gave him a big hug. He grabbed my hand, pulling me out of the chair toward the living room, wagging his finger at Maggie as we walked. Once there, he patted a cushion on the couch for me to sit, then handed me his favorite book, *Red Fish, Blue Fish*. We sat there for a good hour as I read the lines over and over as he pointed at pictures and pointed again.

Maggie stood watching us, leaning against the doorway. I looked up at her and shook my head.

"I'm sorry," she said.

"Not as sorry as I am.

"Black fish, Blue fish, Old fish, New fish."

Old fish, new fish.

Chapter Twenty-Seven

I wanted to know every detail about Teddy Keegan. Maggie and I continued to talk at great length that day. She didn't have any classes, no appointments, and had blocked off the day to spend with me. We talked about the affair for nearly the entire day. We stayed on the topic for a long time. Looking back on that conversation, I have to say that Maggie was great. She answered every single one of my questions the best she could. She listened, she supported, she comforted and, most of all, she was there, not judging me in any way for the things I was thinking and feeling.

My emotions ran the gamut. Mostly, I felt anger toward my mother and, truth be told, I didn't lose that anger. Maggie suggested I seek some counseling. Sooner rather than later. And it was a good idea because my mind felt like a bed of hot rocks when it came to all of this.

After lunch, I decided to drive to my house, still ever cautious of being followed by the FBI. There were no signs of them. When I got home, I went directly up to the spare room where I'd stored all the things I'd saved from my dad's office. I grabbed a couple of his old boxes and took them back to Sarah's house. I started going through every piece of paper and object in those containers, bit by bit. This undertaking had been long overdue, but it seemed especially important then. The first two boxes were filled with inconsequential items, things like expenditures, and random notes about the house and its maintenance. There were a couple of ledgers and my dad's budgets for a few years. Most of it went in the recycle bin. These particular things of my dad were no longer needed in this world, I deemed. And, so, the paper they were written on would be reborn into something useful for someone else. Some people decide to burn old memories as a way of letting go. I thought it would be better to give them a new life.

Lazzy had fallen fast asleep, and Maggie sat on the couch grading papers.

"Did you find what you were looking for?" she asked.

"I don't know what I'm looking for. You know, I've kept all this stuff of my dad's for almost 30 years now. And I've never seemed to find the right time to go through all of this. Back when he died, Mom just wanted to throw it all out," I breathed out one exasperated laugh. "No wonder, huh?"

Maggie shrugged her shoulders.

"At any rate, now seems like the time. Dad was always writing. He'd get done spending time with Oliver in one of their little sessions, and then he'd pull out one of his little composition notebooks and start writing away. It appears he wrote everything in these composition notebooks. I mean, I'm finding everything from house notes to budget items. It must have been some kind of habitual need. And these composition books were his favorite."

Maggie laughed. "They are very stylish but not worth a damn. The paper always pulls out of those bindings if you use them at all," she said.

"Yeah." I held one up from the recycle pile and pulled a section of the paper out. "Like this."

I got up off the floor and stretched for a minute, trying to decide what to do next.

"Are you done for now?" Maggie asked.

"I can't decide. Part of me wants to run back over to my house and get some more boxes, but the other part feels like I've had enough for one day."

"Why don't you give it a rest, Rory? Do something fun for a little bit."

"You're probably right," I said. I gathered up the two boxes and carried them out to the garage, placing them near the recycle bin. While I was out there, I looked out the window and down the street. I had noticed a black sedan parked there earlier. It had since pulled away, and I felt a bit of relief. I walked back through the kitchen, grabbed a couple of beers and some peanuts, and headed back for the living room. I took the large chair next to the couch.

"Mind if I flip on the TV?" I asked, handing Maggie one of the bottles.

She nodded. I hit the remote, and the five o'clock news appeared.

"The investigation continues in the double homicide at the CAR Research Facility in Columbus, Indiana. The second victim, Hannah Shultz, died earlier today. She'd been in intensive care since the shooting. Also dead is Andy Turner, who died at the scene. Both were employees of CAR. The police do not have any suspects at this time," the reporter said.

The news completely shook me. I would have thought someone from CAR would have called me. But I guess administrative leave really meant leaving.

"Jesus. Hannah died. I really thought she'd pull through. This is just terrible. I bet her parents are a mess right now," I said.

"It's all so sad." Maggie put her paperwork on the coffee table.

"I just can't imagine who'd be doing all this, Maggie. Honestly. Our work with the animals so far has been standard practice. Nothing groundbreaking. I'm thinking there must be a reason other than our research." I dialed Jack's number, but it went right to voicemail. I left a message for him to call me.

"You've had more than your fair share of stress today. You need to get out for a while. Why don't you see if Jack wants to take you to get something to eat? Or Sarah. Or both. Whoever it is, you need to take your mind off things for a while. I'll stay here with Laz," Maggie said, standing up and heading for the kitchen. "Do you want another beer?" she asked.

"No thanks, I'm still working on this one."

She came back in with a bottle of milk for Lazzy.

"This little boy and I will be fine here tonight, but I think you need a break."

I took Maggie's advice. I needed to get a little relief from all the stressful news. My dad. Teddy Keegan. And then Hannah. So Jack, Sarah, and I went across town to a little place called Nick's Kitchen. The setting makes you feel like you are in your own kitchen, with sturdy wooden tables and chairs and a warm fire crackling in the fireplace. We ate a long, slow dinner. Sarah and Jack did most of the talking, and I was glad for that. My mind drifted off occasionally. I felt despair over Hannah's death. And I couldn't get past the fact that my dad wasn't my birth father. It all weighed heavily. Regardless, Jack and Sarah were good for me right then. Maggie had probably texted them, saying I needed to get my mind off things, and it was sweet of them to try.

On the way home, I asked them if they'd mind stopping by my house to pick up some more boxes. Jack had driven his SUV, so there was plenty of room in the back. And I also figured I could carry a lot more material with two other people helping me. We pulled into the garage, shut the door, and made quick work of things. I grabbed an overnight bag, the day's mail, and a few games for Laz.

Jack dropped us off without coming in. I hadn't decided when I was going to tell Jack and Sarah about my dad or even if I was going to tell them at all. But with Jack heading home, it would have to wait for at least another night, either way.

Sarah continued to be completely gracious with her home. She let me stack the boxes in the corner of the dining room so that I could easily use the table to spread out and work. I wanted to get to it right away, but Maggie convinced me that I was supposed to be taking the entire night off. She left shortly thereafter, heading back to Indy. I thanked her for everything that day but was sad to see her go. At that moment, Maggie felt like my only real family connection.

Sarah and I plopped down at the TV. We popped some late-night popcorn and watched *His Girl Friday*, with Cary Grant. About midway through, we both decided we'd had enough for the day and headed to bed.

I stayed awake for quite some time, staring at the ceiling, thinking about the day. I was a Keegan. My father was Teddy Keegan. At least I wasn't blood-related to Aubrey Keegan. All that aside, I still couldn't understand how my mom could have done such a thing to my dad. In my view of things, I thought my father was about the most wonderful guy ever to walk the Earth. Granted, I was only 11 when he died. But that didn't matter. In those early years, he filled my world with his kind, gentle, compassionate manner. He never harmed anyone or anything. In fact, he showed me so much about having care and concern for the world, especially its animals.

But maybe that was part of the problem with my mom. Maybe he cared too much about the animal world and perhaps not enough about her. Or it could have been the other way around. Maybe she didn't pay him enough attention, so he turned to the animal kingdom for his connections.

I didn't know a thing. My view of him, of that life, and that time, came through the eyes of a child, through the mind of my young self and my limited vision of the world. As I lay there thinking about all this, I felt like I couldn't be sure of anything.

Chapter Twenty-Eight

"Have you watched the news this morning?" Jack's voice sounded strained.

"No. Lazzy and I are in the kitchen, working on a puzzle. We've been at it for about an hour. It's so funny how much he loves these puzzles. We haven't even had breakfast."

"Rory. The news. I heard it when I got to work. They found Martin Boyle," he said.

"That's excellent. What is he saying?"

"He's not saying anything. He's dead."

"Dead? What do you mean he's dead?"

"Dead. Shot. They found him in one of the warehouses over in the district."

"Oh my God, I can't believe this. When?"

"I'm not sure when it happened, but they found him overnight. Someone had called about a fight. It sounds like it was unrelated, just a couple of drunks mixing it up on one of the streets. But the responding officers did a sweep of the area, you know, just to check things out. That's when they found his car in one of the alleys. Then they found him."

"Are you hearing anything at work?"

"Not really. The place is buzzing. The two FBI guys showed up a little bit ago." Jack paused. "Rory, they're probably putting you way up there on their list of people to talk to," he said.

"Me? Why?"

"Because you told them he stole Lazzy. You brought up Boyle's name several times, remember?"

"Of course I remember."

"Well, it doesn't look good that way."

I knew Jack was right. The police had most likely flagged me as the chief suspect right now. Part of me just wanted to drive right down there to the station and let them grill me. I had an alibi, after all. At least until I went to bed. Regardless, I wouldn't be leaving the house anytime soon. Not while I had Lazzy with me. It would be the full day, too, as Sarah had left for work by the time Jack called.

"Lazzy, I'm going to flip on the TV, but you keep working on your puzzle," I said.

Sarah had a small television mounted on her kitchen wall. I turned it on and found the news. It took a while before they reported on Boyle again. But they didn't tell me anything new, nothing different from what Jack had said. I turned the station to cartoons for Lazzy.

Jack called again about an hour later.

"Three shots to the chest. A revolver. The slugs were .38s."

He went silent for a moment. "Rory, the gun I lent you … it's a .38."

"It's been sitting in the drawer of my nightstand," I said rather defensively.

"Okay, calm down."

I could tell by the sound of his voice he wasn't giving me the whole story. "Is there something else?"

"I just heard they're getting a warrant to search your house."

"You've got to be kidding me."

"Just steer clear for a while. Stay where you are and, whatever you do, don't go home," he said, taking a long pause before continuing. "Listen, I shouldn't even be talking to you from here. Somebody could be listening. I'll try to see you at lunch."

After hanging up, two entirely different thoughts hit me. First, I felt largely grateful that Jack and I had become such good friends. His initial willingness to help me had turned into a great friendship. But the positive feelings about Jack were quickly replaced with a wave of unrelated anger. Or an endless surge of dark despair.

The attacks at CAR had been horrendous in every way. Two people were dead, others had been injured, and who knows what would come next. To top things off, the police suspected me of committing the crimes while they were no closer to finding the true culprit. And all of this came with the realization that my father wasn't my father. Pile that on with the fact that I couldn't go home. And neither could Lazzy. The entire situation felt totally out of hand. I sat back down at the kitchen table across from Laz. He continued to work on his wood block puzzle, trying to make pieces fit together.

"That's the whole game, isn't it, Lazzy? If only I could make the pieces fit together," I said, putting my head in my hand.

He looked up at me and pushed the puzzle across the table toward me.

"No, that's not what I meant, buddy. I've got a puzzle of my own to figure out."

He nudged it again, so I reached over and took the blocks of wood.

"Maybe if we do it together," I said.

He came over, sat in the chair next to me, and started fumbling again with the parts. A couple of minutes later, he still couldn't get it, so I showed him how it worked. He smacked his forehead, and I had to laugh at him. Lazzy always displayed so much intelligence, and emotion, and heart. And comedy. In ways like smacking his forehead.

As I looked at him, I could easily see our similarities. Humans share 99 percent of the same DNA as bonobos, after all. Chimps and bonobos are our closest living relatives. It has long been known that biologically we are much more closely related to chimpanzees and bonobos than we are to gorillas. Through genetics, we've proven that we, and bonobos, have descended from a single ancestor species. One that lived around seven million years ago, a common hominid.

So it really shouldn't surprise anyone that these bonobos have the ability to learn human languages like the version of sign language we've been teaching them. And chimpanzees too.

Obviously, we aren't the first ones. The first subject in this breakthrough was a girl chimp named Washoe. She has the distinction of being the first non-human to learn to communicate via sign language and was able to do more than 350 signs. That was way back in 1967 at Central Washington University. Another great distinction? Washoe actually taught some signs to her adopted son later on. This was amazing to me. As I look back on these things, I'm grateful to the pioneers in my field. Including my dad, who was making tracks of his own.

Lazzy continued to shuffle the blocks around. A few were out of his immediate reach. He carefully picked up a fork that was lying on the table in front of him. Then, with the fork, he pulled in the blocks that were out of reach. Again, another reminder that bonobos are one of the few animals that are known to use tools.

Just like us, they have ways of figuring things out. Problem-solving. Chimpanzees and bonobos utilize self-made tools for all sorts of reasons. They've been observed to be rather ingenious in this manner. In the wild, they will use small branches to dig out termites from their mounds. They also take rocks and smash open nuts. They've fashioned back scratchers from branches. They are smart, smart little apes in so many ways.

I reached over and patted Lazzy's arm in admiration. Hilarious Lazzy. He reached over and patted my arm back.

“What should we do, Lazzy? I can’t sit around here and do nothing all day. And you’ve certainly been cramped up in here too long, too, haven’t you?”

I took a quick shower and made Lazzy stay in the bathroom during the process. Then we ate a good breakfast, did the dishes, and got ourselves ready to go. I put him in a pair of warm pants and a heavy jacket. We got in my car and headed down to the park. When we got there, both of us headed directly for the monkey bars and played there for quite a while. You know, they call them that for a good reason. While he is not a monkey, Lazzy showed off his athleticism. We went down the slide several times, played on the swings, and got on the metal merry-go-round. During our time cavorting, we received attention from several passers-by. After an hour or so of play, we loaded back into my car.

“I thought for sure someone would have called the police by now,” I said. “I mean, you have been all over the news lately.” I didn’t care either way. We were on our way to see them next. We buckled back up and got on our way, heading directly for the Columbus Police Department, which was only a few minutes away.

As we walked toward the front steps, we passed a news crew from Channel Three interviewing someone. They quickly turned the camera toward us as we went by. The reporter started yelling questions after us.

“Is that the missing monkey? Is that the kidnapped monkey there with you? Miss! Did you take that monkey from CAR?” The questions pelted on.

We hustled up the steps. I did not give them a look, but I could see that Lazzy was turning his head, interested in the commotion.

“Come on, Laz. Let’s get inside, buddy,” I said, pulling his arm just a little harder. Once we were through the doors, I headed directly for Captain Huffman’s office. As I walked through the paper-stacked desk maze of the detectives, I heard a couple of voices call out with a “Hey.” No Vargas in sight, but I could see that Huffman was sitting at his desk, the door wide open. I knocked on the door frame and walked right in.

"Holy sh ..." he said under his breath.

"Captain Huffman. Hello. I figured you'd be wanting to talk to me today. You or the FBI." I looked around the office to see if I could spot the officers. Just then, I saw Jack walking with them. I caught his eye, and he stopped dead in his tracks. The FBI guys looked at him and then over to me. They both started rushing toward the office, both with their right hands on their holsters.

"Not good," I said.

"Dr. Greene, stay right where you are, hands in the air," one of them said.

"I'm not armed," I called out loudly. "But I'm not going to let go of Lazzy. In fact, don't come near him," I said.

They slowed down their approach, glancing at one another and then back to me. Jack stood directly behind them with the most astounded look on his face. Several of the detectives had their hands on holstered guns, also looking on.

"Listen. I came down here of my own free will. I figured you guys were wanting to talk to me, so that's why I'm here. But I'm not turning Lazzy over. When we're done talking, I'm leaving here with him. You're going to have to shoot me if you want to stop me," I said. I kept Lazzy standing near to me, although he was still mostly in front of me.

"Just calm down there, Dr. Greene," Agent Neal said, holding out his left hand straight in front of him, his right hand still on his gun.

"I'm perfectly calm. I'm just setting down the rules of our engagement," I said. "Now, why don't we go somewhere we can talk? You can ask your questions about Boyle, and then we'll be on our way."

"What do you know about Boyle?" Neal asked.

"I know he's dead. I saw the morning news. So basically, the only details I know is what I heard on Channel Eight this morning."

"Alright, alright, let's go." Neal waved his hand, motioning in his direction. They started walking back from where they came, all the while keeping an eye on me. "There's an interrogation room right down here we can use."

Jack was shaking his head. He had been holding a coffee cup, and he threw it, with force, into a trash can near him. I could tell he wasn't happy about my decision to show up at the police department. At that point, I wasn't sure I had made the smartest move either. Either way, done was done.

I followed Neal and Bishop into the room. Bishop shut the door behind me while Lazzy and I sat on the nearest two chairs.

"Okay, Dr. Greene. First of all, where were you last night, between the hours of 11 p.m. and 3 a.m.?"

"At my friend's house. Sarah Simms, 924E. Fillmore Avenue. Columbus."

"The entire time?"

"That's correct."

"And can she vouch for you?"

"Well, we stayed up until about one, so yeah. After that, I went to bed in my own room," I said.

The two detectives looked at one another. Just then, I saw someone pass the interrogation room through the window. It was Jack. The detectives continued to grill me with the usual questions about my whereabouts, asking me things a couple of times over. They wanted to know when I last had contact with Boyle. All of those standard inquisition-like questions. Repetitive, trying to trip me up in some kind of a lie. Over and over again.

I put my hands in the air and interrupted them. "I'd like to reach into my bag and get Lazzy a toy. Would that be alright?" I asked. It was then I noticed the bag wasn't beside my chair where I'd left it. Sly Detective Bishop must have slid it away from the table with his foot. It now sat in the corner behind me, way out of my reach. "Go ahead and look through it. There's nothing in there of consequence. I just want to get something for Lazzy to do while we thrash all this out," I said.

Bishop picked up the bag and dropped it on the table. He proceeded to search it thoroughly, placing several items on the tabletop. The last things he pulled out were the Rubik's Cube and a bag of puzzle pieces. Bishop shrugged his shoulders, looking at me.

"The Rubik's Cube," I said. "It's his favorite."

"He knows how to work that thing? Geez, I've never been able to solve one of those," Agent Neal chuckled, folding his arms.

"Well, I don't think Lazzy's ever solved it either, in the sense that the rest of us try to solve it. But he seems to have successes of his own making."

"What do you mean?" Bishop asked.

"How we measure animal intellect always holds them up against human intellect. Yet animals think in a much different way than we do. They communicate among themselves, largely with an organized verbal system that is specific to them. Just as we do. It is a fact that they vocalize a lot of their thoughts and feelings, but they utilize much more than that when they communicate. When they think. So there are those of us who approach research by trying to measure their intellect without comparison to ours."

"I don't get it," Neal fiddled with his notepad as he listened.

"Okay, here's a good example: There was a border collie down in South Carolina. His name was Chaser. Two Wofford College researchers there taught this dog the names of more than 1,000 objects. To be exact, it took them three years to teach Chaser 1,022 words. And, with that, they compared his vocabulary to that of a three-year-old child."

"That's amazing," Neal said.

"It is, I agree. But it is a memory thing, not necessarily a communication skill. And while the dog is extremely adept at recalling what words mean what—green fuzzy guy or squeaky hotdog—the study, and all the training, didn't really widen the communication levels between dogs and us. Of course, I've been working mostly with chimpanzees, bonobos, gorillas. And they work much differently. We've isolated more than 80 different gestures that they use in communication. Probably the most interesting part is that these gestures significantly overlap with human toddlers. These signaling actions aren't taught to them. These apes devised these things on their own, between themselves, their own way of communicating. Things like clapping, hugging, stomping, raising their arms, and shaking their heads. And they often string these moves together to convey complex ideas to one another. Or to us. So you see the difference?"

Both agents stared at me for a moment and then glanced at one another. In the same motion, they turned their focus over to Lazzy, almost simultaneously.

"Does he know what we're saying right now?"

"A lot of it," I said.

Neal cleared his throat, then looked at Bishop again.

"How many fingers am I holding up?" He held out his hand, displaying three fingers, directing his question to Lazzy.

Laz glanced up from the Rubik's Cube. Then, with his right hand, he rubbed his forehead before displaying three fingers. Lazzy shook his head and went back to twisting the colored blocks.

"That was a dumb question, wasn't it?" Neal asked.

I couldn't help but smile.

"Never mind," he said, waving his hand. "What are we doing here? Let's get back to it." Neal looked a little put off. He flipped back through his notebook.

Bishop interjected. "So, from one in the morning until what time were you by yourself?"

"I slept until about six. Both Sarah and I were in the kitchen by six. Look, I'm guessing you don't have enough to arrest me. Otherwise, you would have done it by now. And unless you want to ask me again how long I slept, I don't see that we have much else to talk about here. I didn't kill Boyle. That's what I came down here to tell you. I don't own a gun. I've never owned a gun. A friend loaned me a gun recently, but it's at my house, in the bottom drawer of my nightstand. And it hasn't been fired except for the day I got a lesson at the firing range. I should probably add that I'm not that great at hitting a target," I chuckled. "So unless there's anything else, I'm going to take Lazzy and head back home. He's getting tired, and so am I."

"We can't let you take the animal, Dr. Greene," Bishop said.

I grabbed Lazzy's hand, and we started to get up. Neal stood up quickly, placing his hand on his weapon.

"Jesus, what are you going to do? Shoot me? Look, I'm the best one to be taking care of Lazzy right now. He's safe with me. And while I'm sure you are just following orders, I'm not sure the lab is the best place for him to be. Not until this thing gets solved," I said.

"He's the property of the CAR facility," Neal said, his hand still clutching the gun in his holster.

"I understand that. But for once in your FBI life, think for yourself. Martin Boyle stole Lazzy, to begin with. And now he's dead. So, what chances do you think Lazzy will have by going back to CAR? Think about it."

Bishop took a couple of steps toward Neal. At this point, I had moved Lazzy behind me. I stood, watching and waiting. Bishop leaned over and whispered something to Neal.

"Stay right there," he said. "We're stepping outside for a minute."

I couldn't see them through the window. Lazzy tugged on my sleeve. He signed, asking for some milk.

"In a little bit, Laz. As soon as we get home, I'll get you some," I said, leaning over.

Just then, Agent Neal entered the room without Bishop.

"What's going on?" I asked.

"Agent Bishop needed to make a phone call. He'll be back in just a minute."

"Then what?"

"Then he'll be back in just a minute. Why don't you take a seat while we're waiting."

I told him we preferred to stand at this point, and we edged our way to the wall next to the window. I had a better view down the hallway from there. I leaned down and zipped Lazzy's jacket.

"Just a few more minutes, buddy, okay?"

Neal stood with his back against the wall by the door, arms crossed, looking straight ahead. Of the two agents, I liked him the least. He seemed to be a little thick to me. Stiff might be a better word. He played by the book, his lines were drawn, and there was no crossing over any of those boundaries. That isn't to say that Bishop wasn't about as straight as they come, either. He just seemed to be more of a thinker. A solver. Yet, for the life of me, I couldn't imagine what they had talked about or where he had gone. Unless, of course, this turned out to be all about a restroom break. I looked down at Lazzy, who'd dropped down on the floor to sit, looking terribly restless, as he picked at his arm.

A few minutes later, the door opened, and Agent Bishop entered the room. He leaned into Neal, whispering again, and then stepped toward me.

"Dr. Greene, we can do one of two things here. We can take Lazzy from you by force and return him to the CAR facility. Or we can put you under protective custody, the both of you, for an undetermined amount of time," he said, glancing back a Neal briefly.

"How long is undetermined?"

"As it sounds, ma'am. Undetermined."

"Hours? A day. Five days? What?" I asked.

"It will be more like days. I've gained clearance so that you would be permitted to stay in your own home with one agent on duty, or we can take you both to a holding facility. It is your choice," Bishop said, nodding.

"Well, I guess I choose the least of all evils. How do you feel about Broadmoor Lane?"

"We'll both be going at this point to secure your home. Then I am going to take the first shift. Agent Neal or another officer from our branch will relieve me after 24 hours."

Bishop rode with us, and Neal followed. Once we arrived at my house, they followed me in through the front door. I'd have to make arrangements to pick up our things from Sarah's later on.

"Make yourselves at home, guys. I need to fix Lazzy something to eat," I said. We headed for the kitchen while the two agents began to make their way around the house, checking every room, including the attic and the basement. Lazzy was quite hungry, scarfing down a banana, an entire bottle of milk, along with a bowl of nuts. He asked for a second milk, which I started to give him when my phone rang.

"How're the new roommates?"

It was Jack.

"Hey. How's it going?"

"For the life of me, I will never understand you."

"What's wrong?" I asked.

"What's wrong? Holy smokes, Rory. I tell you to stay put, and what do you do? You and Lazzy march right down here. I mean, what were you thinking?"

"Well, I wasn't thinking this, that's for sure. Oh, I don't know. It all seemed perfectly clear when I decided to do all of this. I couldn't stand the thought of being pent up in someone's house, hiding indefinitely. Not only that, but Lazzy hadn't been outside for a long time, and he needs to get out sometimes. I decided that talking to the police would be the most direct way to tell them I was innocent. I mean, hiding just made me look guilty, I think."

I handed Lazzy his new bottle. There was a long, silent pause on the phone. "Are you still there?" I asked.

"Yeah, I'm here."

"So that's what I did," I added.

I could hear Jack take a long breath. "I suppose when you put it that way, it doesn't sound that bad," he said. "But now those guys will know your every move, round the clock."

"Yeah, I've been thinking about that too. That's not such a bad thing, is it? I mean, if someone out there still wants to hurt Lazzy, who better to be in my house than the FBI? Not only that, I'm sure they'll have Columbus PD cruising by every so often too."

"From what I'm hearing around here, that is the plan. So, what now? What are you going to do?"

"I suppose I'll just work on things from here. I haven't sorted out all the details with them yet, like if I'm allowed to leave. I'm guessing I'll be able to since, technically, I'm not under arrest. But for now I want to keep going through my dad's stuff. I'm hoping I'll find something there."

"I've been working on something too. I've been going through a lot of the video files from the CAR cameras, seeing if anything clicks anywhere. I made copies so I can work from home at night."

"You were allowed to make copies?" I asked.

"What do you think?" Jack laughed.

"Where are you now?"

"At lunch. At Wendy's."

"How much do you adore us, Jack? Will you bring me a single with cheese, mayo, and pickles? And for Lazzy, a plain hamburger? He deserves a treat."

"What about the FBI guys?"

"You want me to see if they want something?"

Jack laughed again. "Do you really think it's a good idea for me to come over to your house? They'll catch on pretty quick that I don't work for DoorDash."

"I think full disclosure is in order from here on out. What's it going to hurt when they find out we're friends?"

There was a long pause again. "I suppose it isn't going to matter one way or the other," he said.

~

Twenty minutes later, Jack was at my front door, Wendy's bag in hand. Agent Kerry answered the door, letting him in.

"You're Jake, aren't you? The guy from our video department down here," Kerry said.

"Jack. Jack Everton. And, yeah, I work for Columbus PD. I'm the tech guy."

"What can I do for you, Jack?"

I was standing in the living-room entrance after hearing the doorbell.

"He's bringing me lunch," I said.

"Oh, you two know each other then?" Kerry pointed both hands back and forth at us. I could tell Jack was holding back some smart comment.

"Yeah, we're friends. Come on in, Jack. Come see Laz." We walked into the kitchen. Jack dropped his jacket on the back of one of the chairs and sat down, placing the bag in the middle of the table.

"Lunch is served."

"Thank you. How much do I owe you?"

He waved his hand in the air dismissively, then leaned over the table, starting to speak in a whisper.

"I've been meaning to tell you: Vargas has called in sick two days in a row now."

"Serious?"

Jack nodded. "That guy never calls in sick."

"I noticed he wasn't at his desk when I walked through this morning. What do you think is going on?" I whispered back.

"I have no idea, but I think it's weird," Jack said, looking through the door toward the living room. He pointed, then mouthed, "Do you think he's listening?"

I shrugged just as Lazzy stood up on his chair, putting one finger to his lips like he was shushing us. Jack and I couldn't help but to laugh at him.

"Lazzy, the All-Knowing," I said.

Jack shook his head, giving Lazzy a little high-five. "I'm thinking of driving past his house just to see if his car is there."

"What for?" I asked.

"Oh, I don't know. I kind of have a funny feeling about the whole thing." He looked down at his watch. "I better get going. I need to get back to work. Vargas's house is sort of on the way back to the station. I think I might just swing a little wide and check things out."

He stood up, putting on his coat. "Don't get up. You guys enjoy your lunch. I'll call you later." And with that, Jack headed out to the front door.

Chapter Twenty-Nine

My speculations about Agent Trevor Bishop appeared to be correct. At his core, Bishop seemed to be a truly nice guy. I mentioned leaving a lot of my things over at Sarah's house, including several boxes of my dad's paperwork, things I was hoping to retrieve. Bishop immediately offered to take me there to gather my belongings, so long as we moved quickly and returned to my house straight away.

The two of us made quick work of carrying the items to his car, with Lazzy contributing in his own special way, including climbing the tree in Sarah's front yard and swinging happily from a branch or two. Bishop stopped what he was doing and watched closely as Lazzy had his fun.

Once back at the house, Bishop asked about the importance of the boxes.

"My dad kept an office at home for all his research. As a kid, I asked my mom if I could keep all of it. So, for years, most of it has been stored at her house. But now, with all the trouble that's been going on with work, I decided I'd start looking for connections. Any possible tie-ins. Not that I'm particularly expecting to find any connection in these boxes. I suppose it just seemed like a good time to go through all my dad's old notes. And whatever else might be in these files. I don't know. We'll see if anything comes of it. Plus, I'm decluttering. What's that woman's name with all the decluttering books? Marie Kondo or something? But I'm also keeping my eyes open for anything interesting."

Bishop stood by a small stack of the boxes and flipped open the lid on the top one. He rifled through the folders with one hand, his face immediately transforming into that of an explorer, an investigator.

"Seems mostly like old financial records. Paid bills, tax information. Looks like some insurance policies, home, car, medical. Doesn't appear to be any earth-shattering news in here," he smiled.

"Yeah, that's mostly what I found. Day-to-day records he kept. I think he heard that old rule about keeping everything for seven years, so he did."

I opened the box next to me and shuffled through a few of the folders inside before pulling one out. "But there are things like this. Tax return. From 1987, for crying out loud. I was three. That's the thing about going through this stuff. I know I have absolutely no use for this. None. It serves no purpose. But there is just something about it being my dad's and me wanting to hold on to it. Especially with it being from so long ago. I don't know. It is hard for me to get rid of this stuff," I said.

"I understand completely. My parents divorced when I was pretty little. Our dad took off. Never saw the hair on his chinny-chin-chin again. And then, recently, my mom died. Damn cancer. Anyway, we went to her house to clear it out, and it was hard. In fact, the three of us ended up keeping quite a bit of her stuff," he said, running his finger along the file folders.

"Three of you?"

"Yeah. I have two sisters. One older. One younger."

"Lucky you. Wedged between two girls. Were they always putting makeup on you?"

"And bows on my head. And nail polish," he laughed. "Bright red was my color." He held up his hand.

"They live around here?"

"Actually, pretty close. One sister lives in Fort Wayne, and the other up near Detroit. Ann Arbor, actually."

"What do they do?"

"The older one is married with kids. She takes care of things at home. And the younger one works for the Ann Arbor Police Department. She's a sergeant."

"Well, two cops in the family. Was your mom in law enforcement?"

"No, but the reason my parents divorced was because my father was a low-life crook. He told Mom he had a job, but the whole time, he was really going around and hitting convenience stores and small banks. Then, to top things off, he was cheating on her the whole time. So she told him he had to straighten up or leave. We never saw him again after that day." Bishop pulled out one of the chairs at the dining-room table and sat down. "Too much information?" he chuckled. "Anyway. That all might have had something to do with why we went into law enforcement."

"I'd say that's a pretty good push from where I'm standing." I paused. "It's kind of terrible when our parents don't turn out to be who we thought they were."

Bishop laughed, rubbing the bridge of his nose. Then he looked up at me. "Why? Was your dad some hitman for the mafia or something?" He smiled again.

"No, my dad was completely incredible as far as I can tell," I smiled, thinking about all that had gone on in my young life. And before. Then, without thinking, I just said it, "Turns out he really wasn't my father."

As soon as it spilled out of my mouth, I wanted to pull it back in. I couldn't believe I just blurted it out to this FBI agent, this guy I barely knew.

Bishop looked totally unaffected by my words. Perhaps because he had been in law enforcement for so long. Maybe nothing surprised him anymore. He continued to listen attentively. Of course, that made me feel like I had to explain.

"My mom had an affair. I just found out about all of this a few days ago," I said.

"That must have been hard," he said, seeming to reach out momentarily and then drawing back.

"Hard doesn't even describe it. I'm still in a bit of shock. I kind of idolized my dad, you know? I'm sure I chose this career because of him. So it really hit me right here." I put my hand to my chest.

"There's no reason to stop idolizing him, right? He didn't do anything wrong. Besides, from what you've said about him, he'll always be your dad. He's the one who raised you." Bishop reached for another file folder.

"You're absolutely right. Thank you. I need to remember that. Even though he died quite some time ago, I still miss him. And I'm always grateful for all he gave me. Which was a lot." I reached down and flipped open one of the files. "It's my mom who I'm going to have trouble forgiving. She doesn't even know that I know yet."

"Well, that right there, my friend, is a horse of a different color. But, if you want some advice from somebody you barely know, I've always found it's best when we communicate with people about things. Communication is all we've got. Without it, we are left alone wondering."

I had to smile at the irony of his statement. My life's work in communications. I'd spent my whole career trying to figure out "the wondering."

"That's good advice, which I will take. And I'll try to use it when it comes to dealing with my mom," I said.

He continued looking down at the folder, or, more to the point, a notebook tucked inside the file. He flipped back and forth through a few pages. "Who's Oliver?" he finally asked.

My interest sparked. "He was our family bird. A parrot. What did Dad say about him?"

"He's talking about agreeing on words with him. Agreeing on words. What does he mean by that?" Bishop turned another page.

"I'm not entirely sure. But when we teach an animal sign language, sometimes some of us wonder if we are just getting them to memorize words without meaning behind them. Maybe Dad was figuring out ways to communicate meanings. I don't know," I said.

"Do you want me to help you go through these?" Bishop asked.

"I never turn down help."

"Excellent. Now, here is the FBI agent in me speaking: do you have a system for this?"

"Not so much. I've just been going through them, you know, box by box. And if something has no bearing on my life whatsoever, I put it in a pile. Then I shred it. Then I recycle it. So far, the only folders I've opened have fallen into this category. I really haven't thought too far ahead about finding something that might mean something. Maybe because I don't really know what I'm looking for."

"That was my next question." He held up his index finger. "What are we looking for? You mentioned earlier that you were doing this right now because you thought something of interest might come up. Or, an outside chance that something will pop up to help with this case, right? So? What did you have in mind?"

"Like I said, I don't have any idea what either of those things might be. But all of this kind of started when I found out about my dad." I stopped for a moment. I didn't know if I was entirely sure how much more I should tell Bishop. On the other hand, maybe being open with him would help somehow, in solving the case. Eventually, I shrugged to myself and continued. "You know my boss, Dr. Keegan? Well, it was Keegan's husband that had the affair with my mom. That makes Teddy Keegan my biological father."

"Oh, shit." He paused. "Sorry. But, oh my goodness. Now that's quite a thing."

"Bet me."

"What did Keegan have to say about all of that?" Bishop asked as he closed the file and leaned on the table.

"She doesn't know that I know either. I haven't talked to anyone about this. Not really."

"What a big mess."

I nodded and began explaining the big circle of science nerds and their makeshift support network. The whole lot of them, including my dad. "So, yeah, my friend Maggie told me all this. Maggie was one of the people in the group back then. And, of course, the Keegans. And the Greenes. Maggie and my dad were really close friends. But I'm guessing the affair between my mom and Teddy Keegan is the reason Dr. Keegan hates me as much as she does. All this time I've worked with her, I've never understood why she treated me so terribly. And now I know. All because I'm her husband's illegitimate daughter."

"And you haven't talked to this Teddy Keegan either?"

"No, he died some years back, from what I understand. It's kind of a weird story."

"I'm all ears."

"Well, again, Maggie is the one who told me all of this. Anyway. After I was born, the two couples, my mom and dad, and Aubrey and Teddy Keegan, each decided to try to make their marriages work. Mom and Teddy agreed to quit seeing one another. But Dad caught Mom with Teddy again. So Dad gave her an ultimatum. Mom never had to decide because, like a week later, Teddy Keegan was driving home and crashed his car on a bend and was killed."

"Any witnesses?"

"Not that I know of. I'm pretty sure he was all by himself. Hit a tree, head on," I said.

Trevor Bishop pushed away from the table and began tipping his chair on its back two legs. He looked up at the ceiling, seeming to be totally unaware of anything around him. His eyes moved slightly, back and forth, like he was watching some tennis match in his head. I cleared my throat just a little. "You okay there, Bishop?"

He rocked back down, all four chair legs on the floor.

"I'm sorry. Sorry. I didn't mean to lean back in your chair like that."

"It's okay."

"I do that sometimes when I think," he said, standing, walking over to the big window, looking out. "I'm going to make a couple of calls real quick," he continued. "Then I think we should start digging in on your project here." He pointed to the boxes.

"Sounds good to me."

We spent the next few hours sifting through boxes. I kept waiting for Bishop to suggest some filing system, but the truth was, we weren't finding anything of consequence or merit since happening on those few notes about Oliver. Besides that, there was nothing worth keeping. We crossed over endless amounts of receipts, paid bills, statements, ledgers. Car maintenance schedules. Kids' doctor and dentist records. House mortgage payments. Again, some of those things I wanted to hang on to just because they were Dad's. But to what purpose? I decided to get rid of the most of it. I thought we might wear out the shredder, but it continued to chug along with every paper we fed its hungry teeth. We then boxed the shreddings for recycling. All of this, a mundane cycle of boring.

Several times, we took breaks, paying long attention to Lazzy. But for the most part, he stayed in front of the TV watching DVDs of *Sesame Street*, *Curious George*, and his favorite movie, *Horton Hears a Who!*

It was after six when I suggested we fix some dinner. Moments later, I got two texts, one from Sarah and another from Jack, both wanting to know what I was up to. Through a series of back-and-forth digital messages, we all decided Jack would pick up carry-out at the China Dragon. When I walked into the kitchen to clear the table, I found the entire place spotless. The table was clear, the few dishes in the sink were washed, the counters were scrubbed. Even the stainless-steel fronts on the dishwasher and the refrigerator were spotless.

I turned and stood in the doorway.

"Thanks for cleaning the kitchen. I didn't even hear you in there."

"You were busy with Lazzy, so I just tidied up a bit," Bishop said.

"You didn't have to do that. But thanks."

"Can I help you set the table?" he asked.

"No, I got it. But help yourself to something to drink. There's some beer in there, or I have a couple of bottles of liquor if you want a mixed drink or something."

"I'm on duty. I'll just get some water." He walked over to the cupboard and pulled out four glasses.

"So, how can I say this nicely? You seem a lot, uhm, a lot friendlier than Agent Neal."

"Kerry? Oh, he's not so bad once you get to know him. He's a straight arrow. You know what I mean. It's the letter of the law with him. Maybe I should say, by the book, I guess." He stopped talking and looked like he might have been blushing. Then he returned to his thoughts, saying, "I didn't mean to imply that the rest of us aren't by the book. Because we are. Well, most of us." He stopped for a moment and shook his head. "Why do I feel like I'm digging a very deep hole here? I just need to shut up."

I laughed as I finished placing the silverware around the table. "I didn't mean to put you on the spot," I said. I saw, in fact, that Bishop *was* blushing. Just about then, the door from the garage opened, and Sarah walked in.

She shouldered off her coat as she moved past the table. "Can I just throw this in the dining room?"

"Sure, just don't disturb our system," I said.

Sarah possessed the curiosity of a cat. I stood in the doorway, grinning at her. "What do you think?" I asked. "A total mess?"

"It looks like you've been busy. I noticed you came by and picked up all of your boxes. Have you found anything good?"

"Not yet," Bishop said, joining us. "But we're digging."

"Agent Trevor Bishop. Sarah Simms."

"Like the game. The Simms," Bishop said, extending his hand to shake Sarah's. "That's me. Controlled by some external guiding force as I make my way through the living space around me."

Sarah smiled, looking down at the pages on the table. "You want any help with this tonight? Dinner and dumpster diving. What more could a girl ask for?"

"Let's see what's happening after dinner. But sure. I wouldn't turn you down. Look at those stacks of boxes. I'd love to get through all of this stuff, once and for all." I heard Jack come into the kitchen.

"Soup's on," he shouted.

Throughout dinner, we didn't talk about the case. Not one word. We covered current events and spent a good deal of time talking about sports. We hit the good movie and good book conversation as well, with Bishop surprising all of us with an extensive list of fiction. He said it helped him unwind after a day of seeing bad things. Throughout the whole conversation, Lazzy stayed focused on his fruit-and-nut mix, taking special care to pick out all his favorites first.

From there, we all shuffled around the kitchen, cleaning things up after we ate, before migrating to the dining-room table. I put Lazzy on the floor with Jenga and got him started. He had a knack for keeping himself entertained.

"So, what's the system here?" Sarah asked.

I laughed out loud rather hard. "Agent Bishop asked the same thing," I said. "I don't really have a system, because all I've found so far has been a bunch of paper for the shredder and the recycling bin."

"Why don't you call me Trevor?" Bishop said, nodding slightly.

"Got it," Jack said, giving a thumbs up. "Just don't call me late for dinner," he chuckled. "Sorry, that's something my dad always says."

We'd all taken a folder off the stack in the middle of the table and began sifting through it quietly. For quite some time, we worked through one after the next, with little noise in the room, except for the whirring of the shredder.

And then a couple of low hums came from Jack. He flipped through a few pages and made the same noise. He proceeded to close the folder and hold it to his chest, looking concerned.

"What is it?" I asked.

"I'm not quite sure what to make of this." He glanced over at Bishop, then back to me. "There's something. I don't really know what to say."

"Just let me see it, Jack." I stood halfway out of my chair, reaching across the table toward him. He handed me the manilla folder and rocked his head back and forth.

I opened the file. The first three or four sheets were blank pieces of paper. The next page, handwritten, came from my mom to my dad.

> Charlie,
> I know how hard you've tried, but things have
> changed. Everything has changed. I don't think we
> can ever go back from where we came.
> I'm sorry.
> Cory

Sarah, Jack, and Bishop looked at me, all of them concerned.

"It's from my mom. To my dad." I read the letter aloud.

"What the hell, Rory?" Sarah reached over and put her hand on my shoulder.

I took a deep breath. I then sat back squarely on my chair and glanced around the table.

"I've been trying to decide if I was going to tell you guys all of this or not. But it seems like that's all I've been doing with you both lately. Unloading a bunch of crap on you, one thing after the other." I stopped and took another deep breath.

"Agent Bishop—Trevor—already knows. But. Well. Here it is. Maggie, just yesterday, told me that my mom was having an affair. A long time ago, before I was born. She was sleeping with Teddy Keegan. As in Aubrey Keegan's husband. So, yeah, my current boss's husband."

"Holy shit," Jack said, taking a sip of beer.

"There's more. A whole lot more. Teddy and Mom got pregnant. And that baby turned out to be me. So, yeah, my dad, Charlie Greene, isn't my biological dad. Teddy Keegan's my father."

"Can I say holy shit again?" Jack asked, shaking his head.

"But I didn't know Mom decided it was over with Dad. I mean, they seemed to have patched things up after I was born, somehow. I never even knew the Keegans while I was growing up. I wish this letter had a date," I said, staring down at the page.

"You better go to the next letter, Rory," Jack pointed.

Sarah turned her head swiftly toward him. "You've got to be kidding me," she said.

Jack nodded at the file I was holding.

I flipped to the next page. Blank. And another blank. Then a second letter. The handwriting didn't look familiar.

> Dear Charlie,
>
> I'll get right to the point. Nobody wants this baby.
>
> Your wife's pregnancy was a horrible accident. It

will just be a constant reminder of this terrible thing between Teddy and Cory. You need to convince her that no good can come from this. I don't want that kid around. Not around Teddy. And certainly not around me. If you're smart, you shouldn't want it around either.

Aubrey

I felt my body sinking into the dining-room chair as I thought about my father holding that same letter, reading it, trying to decide what to do. There it was, in my own hand, my life on the line. From the very beginning. My heart broke in half that night. I stared at the letter before reading it again. And then again. Finally, I looked up and around at the three friends sitting with me. Their faces said it all.

"Well, it's no wonder I haven't gotten any raises in a while," I said.

The three of them tittered nervously.

"It's okay, you guys. Clearly, Mom and Dad didn't abort me. And Aubrey Keegan didn't choke me in my crib."

Finally, Jack spoke. "There are more letters in that folder, Rory."

Bishop leaned over and put his hand under the cover of the file folder, flipping it closed in my hands. "That's probably enough for one night, don't you think?"

"That's a good idea," Sarah said, getting up. "Besides, you need to get Lazzy to bed and then yourself. It's been a long day."

Sarah and Jack both offered to stay overnight. I had another extra bedroom and, of course, the living-room couch. Enough for everyone. But I didn't feel like being on the receiving end of all that pity. Once they left, I said good night to Bishop and took Lazzy upstairs.

As I tucked him into his bed, he sat back up and put both arms around my neck, giving me a hug. I tried to back away slightly, but he only pulled me closer. Finally, he placed both of his hands on my shoulders and started shaking his head.

"What are you saying no to, Lazzy?"

He continued to shake his head, back and forth, in little sweeps.

"You don't want to go to bed? Is that it?"

More shaking. Finally, he started to sign. First, he pointed directly at me. Then he shook his head again. He repeated the entire gesture, not once, but twice.

"You don't want me to go to my room? To my bed?"

More shaking. "Sad," he signed.

"I am sad," I said. "You are right, Lazzy. But I'll get better. I promise. It's just been a hard couple of days, okay? It will be better," I signed to him.

After finally getting him to settle in for the night, I guessed I wouldn't be able to fall asleep myself. But the next thing I knew, morning had rolled around. I realized then how exhausted I must have been. As I lay there looking at the ceiling, I wasn't sure how much more news about my life I could bear.

Chapter Thirty

Bishop sat at the kitchen table, drinking coffee and reading the morning edition of *The Republic News*, Columbus's only print newspaper. Lazzy and I walked into the kitchen, each taking a chair at the table.

"Anything good?" I asked.

"Just the normal grind. Local news, sports, obituaries. There was a fire last night on Hutchins Street. No one was injured. And the animal shelter is holding a fundraiser this weekend."

"Sounds about right," I said. I grabbed a banana from the fruit bowl and handed it to Lazzy, along with an apple. He held the apple and then pushed it back across the table to me and began working on peeling his banana. I handed him a second one. He grinned big, shaking his head.

"I'm going to fix a couple of eggs. You want some?" I asked as I walked toward the stove.

"No thanks. I already ate. I brought a couple of power bars with me and had those about an hour ago." Bishop took another sip of coffee.

"Power bars? That doesn't sound like much fun."

"They're alright. These are mostly healthy, and they taste like candy bars to me. Larabars. I had a Cashew Cookie and a Peanut Butter Cookie."

"Well, at least they sound good," I said.

"I'll leave you one."

We didn't talk much more as I worked around the stove, fixing my eggs, bacon, and grits. I toasted an onion bagel, which filled the kitchen with its aroma. Finally, I sat back down with my plate and a bowl of nuts for Laz.

"Rory, I want to make copies of those letters for the investigation. Not that it'll come to anything, but at this point we are collecting data on everyone who works at CAR. We're hitting all the angles. I need your permission."

"I know you're just doing your job. It's just that this is hard for me. I've taken some pretty big punches in the last 24 hours, and it's all still sinking in. The thought of a bunch of FBI guys sifting through those letters just feels a little bit, oh, I don't know, like an invasion of my privacy or something. I mean, this is all very personal."

"I understand."

I sat for a moment, looking at Bishop. The look on his face was soft and caring. He looked authentically concerned, like he truly did understand. Finally, I answered, "Yeah, well. You have my permission to copy what you want. You'll have it sooner or later anyway."

He stood up, taking his coffee cup over to the sink. He washed it out and placed it in the dish drainer.

"I'm sorry," he said. Bishop turned and started walking back to the dining room. "Agent Neal will be here in a few hours to replace me. I'm not sure who has the next 24 hours after that."

I heard him shuffling through the papers in the dining room, most likely scanning the documents with his phone. He kept mostly quiet as he worked. After 15 minutes or so, he came back into the kitchen.

"I'll need you to sign this form. It's a release. You can just use your finger to sign your name in that box," he said, holding out his phone. I followed his instructions and handed his phone back to him. As he started to take it, I held on for just a moment.

"It's okay, Bishop. I know you're just doing what you have to do."

Having Agent Kerry Neal in the house proved to be quite different. The guy seemed like a robot to me. Even though Bishop had just spent the past 24 hours in the house, Neal required that they do a full sweep, first thing. Then he asked for the keys to my car. He walked Bishop to the door and, once it closed, it felt incredibly silent and cold.

"Can I get you anything, Agent Neal?"

He had an overnight bag on the floor, as well as a backpack.

"No, thank you. I'm all set," he said, tapping the bags with his foot.

"Let me show you where you'll be staying."

I led him upstairs and told him his sheets were in the washing machine. I'd gladly wash the bedclothes for my captors, but I wasn't about to make up their room each day they switched shifts.

The mood in the house for the next hour felt stiff. For the first time, I got the sensation that I truly was a prisoner in my own home. Neal watched me. My every move. At one point, I went into the bathroom and started texting people, just to get a break.

Me: Can't stand this guy Neal.

Sarah: What's up?

Me: Stalker. Hawkish. Prison guard.

Sarah: You're funny.

Me: Not funny.

Sarah: Get a lawyer. Get the house arrest lifted. This is ridiculous.

It hadn't hit me before then to get a lawyer because I hadn't done anything wrong. I called Jack and asked him who was good in town as far as criminal law was concerned. He gave me three names and, after dialing the office of the first one on the list, I didn't need to look any further. When I called the offices of Marshall, Price, and Curtis, I talked to the assistant of Lionel Price. I explained my circumstances and a few short details of the case and, within 30 minutes, Lionel Price himself had called me to talk about the particulars of my situation.

I gave him Vargas's name, as well as Neal and Bishop's. Over the next day, I talked a few times over the phone, either to Price or his assistant. By the third day, he had convinced a judge to order the FBI presence from my home. There had been no official arrest and she ruled that their being there was unwarranted. Mr. Price also convinced the judge to award temporary custody of Lazzy to me, given the initial details of his kidnapping from CAR and citing negligence on their part. I couldn't have been happier with Jack's selection of lawyers.

Next, I contacted Brad Reynolds and asked if he might be willing to babysit Lazzy on occasion. He jumped at the chance, saying he'd missed seeing him at the lab. Not only would it give me more leeway at home, but he would be able to get me all caught up on things happening at work. Gloria had been showing daily signs of worrying, like pacing and a stunted appetite. It made me want to get this entire matter resolved and to get back to my work and back to my friends. My primate friends.

But the truth of the matter hung like a heavy weight on my shoulders. The police did not appear to be any closer to finding the person behind all of this. I wasn't sure how it would all end or how it could get much worse. Just then, my phone rang. It was my mom. Things were about to get worse.

Chapter Thirty-One

"Hello, dear, how are you? How's everything going over there?"

"I'm okay."

"How are all my new friends? Especially that Jack? Goodness, Rory, I have to say, he's such a sweetie. And so cute. Have you thought about going out with him?"

"We're not like that, Mom. We're just friends, that's all. You know, sometimes a man and a woman can be friends. Just good friends. Without one or the other of them feeling the need to get into bed."

"Oh, your mouth, Rory. For goodness sake. I just meant that he seems like such a nice young man. And you're not getting any younger, you know."

"Got it, Mom." I couldn't believe I'd picked up the phone. As I sat, trying to figure out what I was going to say to her to end the conversation, I regretted even answering her call. I sighed.

"Is something the matter, dear? You sound a little short this afternoon."

I didn't answer immediately, still trying to gather my thoughts.

She pressed. "Is it something I said? About dating Jack? I only meant that in a supportive way. I just heard on a podcast that we're supposed to talk in supportive ways, and …"

"Mom, it isn't Jack, okay? Let's just skip it for now."

"Oh, something really is the matter. Tell me what it is. It is better to get these things off your chest."

I hesitated. This wasn't the time or the place. I wanted to talk with her in person about Dad, and Teddy Keegan, and the whole lot of it. But I couldn't be sure when I'd see her again. Maybe she was right. Maybe I needed to get things off my chest. And, just like that, there it all went.

"Teddy Keegan, Mom."

Silence fell hard on the other end of the line. I said it again. "Teddy Keegan. That's what's wrong. Sound familiar?"

"What about him?"

I felt like exploding. "What about him?! Jesus, Mom. What about him? Oh, I don't know. Let's see. Should I call him Dad or Papa? Or Father? Which one, Mom?"

"Rory."

"Don't Rory me right now, Mom. When were you going to tell me? Were you going to tell me? Ever?"

There was a long pause.

"I don't know. Probably not," she answered quietly.

"I'm 38 years old, Mom. Don't you think I have the right to know who my damn father was?"

My voice didn't sound like my own. My anger spilled out with every word. I took a brief pause.

Mom took the chance to respond. "I didn't see any sense in it," she said, growing quieter with each word.

"No sense in it? No sense? Well, that's just rich, you know? I just thought of this. Right at this very minute. Ruthy and I don't look anything alike. Forget the fact that we couldn't be more different in every way. And now I know why. Who's her father?"

"Victoria, you're being ridiculous."

"Am I, Mom? Am I? Well, let's talk about what is ridiculous, then."

I felt myself getting angrier with every word. I tried to rein myself in, but all my emotions were boiling over. I couldn't pull it back. "What's ridiculous is you cheating on Dad, having a kid out of wedlock, and then not telling that kid who her father was for her whole. Entire! Freaking! Life! That's what's ridiculous."

She didn't respond. I imagine we sat there for 30 seconds without saying a word. Finally, I spoke again. "Look. I don't know what more we can say here. I have to go."

And I hung up the phone. I sat down in a kitchen chair and drew a deep breath. I needed to calm down, as I expected her to call me right back. I counted on it, actually.

But my phone didn't ring. Nothing. A huge wave of disappointment washed over me. How dare she not call me back? It made things worse, and I knew I was growing angrier with each passing moment. I started to dial her number when another call came in. Bishop. I was in no emotional shape to talk to anyone at that moment, but I felt compelled to answer the phone, mostly because I felt like we hadn't left things on a great note.

"Hello, Agent Bishop."

"Hey, it's me. But I guess you knew that. I'm sorry," he said, all rather quickly.

"It's okay. Really. So, what's happening?" I asked.

"It's good news, as far as these things go, I suppose. There's been some new information in the case. From Intelligence. I can't tell you much, but we have clearance to release certain details."

"I understand," I said, although I wasn't sure that I did.

"Well, there's been activity lately. From Russia. On several different levels."

"I'm not sure I'm following," I said.

"Apparently, Homeland Security has been picking up on several major threats from Russia over the past few weeks. The same week all this started at CAR, the Russians had also launched data attacks on a national defense research company, Global Impact Research. They allegedly breached more than a million records during that cyber attack. There were also physical break-ins at two other labs or research companies during that same week. One in California, and one in Nevada."

"And what does all this mean to me?"

"Well, HS has markers they monitor and evaluate. Long story short, they feel like the attacks on CAR are coming from Russia. Apparently, they are deep in utilizing some sort of animal warfare capabilities that were not disclosed to us. But CAR and the other three companies are all involved in either animal communication research or alternate defense communications research."

"So they're saying Lazzy's kidnapping, the bombing, the shootings, all of that, came out of Russia?"

"That's what intel is pointing to. They've scheduled a meeting with the CEO at CAR, along with all their board members. It's happening tomorrow morning, here in Columbus."

"What kind of evidence did they find?"

"That's all classified. But I will tell you this if you promise to keep it quiet for now: they think Boyle was central. He'd been to Russia about 18 months ago. Were you aware of that?"

"Well, yeah. He went on vacation. To St. Petersburg. He showed us photos of, like, the Hermitage and the Summer Palace."

"We're hearing he also went to Moscow during that time. In fact, he was in the capital for most of his trip. Did he mention that to you?"

"No, I don't think so. But still, this all seems kind of sudden, don't you think?"

"We're still looking into Boyle's connection and who else might have been involved. If anyone. But Homeland probably knew these things were going to happen even before they happened, Rory. Most of the time, the markers are there, but they can't act without hard evidence. They can issue warnings or heighten threat levels. But in this case, being that all the companies are privately held, they probably didn't see it as a high-level threat, just localized incidents."

"This all sounds crazy to me. Russia? Attacking us?"

"There's a lot happening on the global front that most citizens are unaware of. But, mainly, I just wanted you to hear it first from me. There's one more thing. Word is going around that CAR will be lifting your suspension, given all this new evidence. But please remember, as a favor to me, all of this is off the record for now. I figured you'd be happy to know."

"That is great news, for sure. Thank you, Bishop. When do you think it will be official, as you put it?"

"My guess is they are going to give recommendations to your board. They're probably going to ask for some deep dives into the company's records too. Not that they need permission. I'm sure by now they've taken a look at everything they need to see. This is all just formalities at this point."

"I don't know what to say. I mean, thank you so much."

"We'll be wrapping up here in the next couple of weeks once we've ensured things are secure. After that, I'll head back to Indy. And then? I'll be on to something else," Bishop said. His voice sounded flat, disconnected.

"I guess that will be it then." I felt an immediate emptiness.

"I suppose so. I'm sure we'll run into each other throughout the rest of this. But just in case we don't? It was nice to meet you Dr. Greene. Rory. Truly it was."

And, a second later, the phone went silent.

Chapter Thirty-Two

I liked Agent Trevor Bishop. But due to our life circumstances, our circles, I would probably never see him again after his involvement with our case was completed. That's how our lives go sometimes. People cross our paths. Sometimes, those crossings become permanent fixtures. Other times they simply drift away. We don't notice at first. But then, after time, those connections are gone. Our lives are filled with these comings and goings. Sometimes, I wonder about the ones I missed. Those people I used to know but don't anymore.

I think back to different times. We've all had them. Sitting on the curb with your one and only best friend in the fourth grade, and being absolutely certain at that moment that you will never have a friend like that again, not in the entire world, you think. Seven years later, you find yourself riding in a car on the way to the movies with someone completely different. Your new best friend in high school. This, you think, is a person unlike anyone else in the world. You are convinced in that happy moment that you'll never, ever have a friend like this one. And then, four years later, you're at a table in the university library and happen to glance over at your best friend, whom you met in the dorm on your first day at your new college. This person is, by far, the greatest friend you've ever had. You smile.

And so we roll along.

I felt like Bishop and I could have been good friends. Great friends. We clicked, and I think we both knew it. But just like that, people drift in and out. And often we wonder what might have been.

I thought about this, hands on my steering wheel, as I drove to work. It had been a few days since that conversation with Bishop. Since then, Dr. William Barber called and asked if I could come in for a meeting with the head executives and board of CAR. We'd set up the time and, nervously, I was driving to my appointment. I tried not to focus too much on what might be ahead. Although Bishop hinted that CAR might reinstate me, in my mind, it could go either way. I knew that Keegan would not be in my corner.

As I entered the building, the security team quickly found my name on the list. I was given clearance and a visitor badge, which, for some reason, made me all the more nervous. Standing just outside the meeting-room door, I checked myself one more time before knocking and going inside.

I never imagined how completely intimidated I would feel at that moment. There, seated around a large table in the boardroom, were all nine members, including the CEO, CFO, and a handful of other C-dash-Os. I motioned to the one empty seat at the end of the table and sat down.

Without going into the details of the drawn-out meeting, the board voted and decided that I could return to work in my old position, with the contingency that Lazzy be returned to CAR immediately.

Of course, I felt completely overjoyed by the news. But I needed some clarification.

"If I may ask a question?"

"Of course, Dr. Greene. Go right ahead."

"Two people lost their lives in all of this. Strike that. Three people, when you include Boyle. Then there are the ones who were physically injured in the bombing. And that's not to mention the psychological and emotional duress that so many continue to suffer as a result of these attacks here at CAR."

"Yes, Dr. Greene. We're well aware."

"And then there are the animals. They've suffered greatly too," I added.

Nods could be seen around the table, people shuffling papers and exchanging looks.

"We are aware of that too. We now have a full-time psychiatrist on staff, and we are encouraging people to meet with Dr. Davies during their work schedule for any type of counseling they may need. All with pay, all on company time."

"That's all excellent. I'm glad to hear that's been put into place. But what is keeping the Russians, or anyone else for that matter, from committing another attack?" I asked.

The board had two main talkers who were answering all the questions, neither one I knew. Board member number two, a woman in her late fifties, answered my question.

"I guess to answer honestly, there is no guarantee that something bad will never happen again. However, Homeland Security has told us that the 'chatter' around these attacks has completely ceased. At least for now. In addition, they have placed two Homeland Security Agents at our site. As a further precaution, they have locked down our system digitally. They are monitoring us around the clock for any type of cyber attack or for any activity that might indicate a physical attack. In other words, our security has been heightened to the highest level possible. Or so we are told."

"So we're safe? The animals are safe?" I asked.

"Homeland Security has given us every indication that we are no longer in any type of danger. And if they uncover any type of further activity, they will alert us immediately."

~

Once the meeting concluded, I went home and retrieved Lazzy and all his belongings. Sarah had taken a personal day off to watch him. I felt thankful to have such a good friend in Sarah. And now Jack. When I walked into the living room, they were sitting on the couch together, doing something on her phone.

"Hey, you two, what's going on?"

"Don't mind us. We're just playing a little game of Threes. Lazzy likes the voices. The little cheers they do when we make a match." She turned up the volume on her phone to demonstrate. Lazzy slapped his forehead and fell back into the couch, grinning. He rocked back and forth, holding his belly.

"That's pretty funny, isn't it, Laz?"

He nodded his head and reached over to touch Sarah's screen.

"Hey, guess what, you guys? Lazzy gets to move back home today. Lazzy, what do you think about that? You want to go back home? Back with Gloria and Della? There's a new guy too. I think you are going to like him. His name is Boris."

Lazzy nodded again, standing up on the couch. He reached out his arms toward me. I walked over and gave him a hug. "Hey, mister. Who said you're allowed to stand on my furniture?" I laughed.

He jumped up and down, just a little, before hopping down onto the floor. His blocks were spread out across the living room, and he began collecting them, putting them back into their box.

"I think somebody is ready to go back to CAR," I said.

"So, how'd it go?"

"Good, I guess. They've given me my old job back. I'm still the supervisor of the lab. But Andy and Hannah are gone now. Their plan is to hire two new people to fill those positions. But for the time being, the lab assistants will have to step in where they can. Of course, the assistants aren't certified to do any of the testing or anything like that, so we'll be a little thin for a while."

"I'm sure they'll get some new people in soon. Other than that, how are you feeling about everything?"

I went over and sat down on the couch beside Sarah.

"Honestly? I'm nervous. I know the FBI and Homeland Security, and whoever else might be standing with the man behind the curtain, have said that we're all clear. They feel completely confident that all the crimes against us came directly from Russia. Although the official statement from the Kremlin denied any connection to any of these attacks. Nationwide. Homeland is also saying that Russia, for whatever reason, has now backed off completely, maybe due to discovery. But I don't know. It just seems weird to me. I mean, why would they drop everything? All of a sudden? Something in my gut feels off. I'm still really worried about the whole deal." I paused for a moment, looking down at Lazzy, who was totally oblivious to Sarah and me. He had got sidetracked and had begun building a tower with his blocks instead of putting them away. "I'm sure it's all fine. I'm probably just overreacting from the trauma of the shooting. But still." I sighed heavily, reflexively, without meaning to do so.

"I think you have every right to be nervous. I mean, that whole thing was crazy," Sarah said, patting my knee. "I don't blame you one bit." She stood up and started heading for the kitchen. "You want some lunch? I'll go see what you have in the fridge."

"There's not a lot in there," I called after her. "Help yourself to anything you find. I need to get Lazzy together and get him back to the lab."

It didn't take me long to pack up his belongings from his room. All the things he had at my house were items that I'd purchased for him since we rescued him from Boyle. Martin Boyle. It is true. I never really cared for the guy, but I was still having trouble seeing him as a Russian operative. I shook my head, thinking I should have noticed something. Anything.

When I got back downstairs, Lazzy and Sarah were sitting at the kitchen table. Sarah had a slice of cold pizza in her hand, and Lazzy was just finishing off some grapes and a pile of nuts.

"What do you think, Lazzy? Ready to hit the road?"

He grabbed a banana from the fruit bowl and started to peel it.

"You can finish that here, and then we have to leave," I said. "Thanks for taking the day off to watch him. Sorry for your trouble."

"Oh, I think I needed a day off. And now that you're taking Lazzy, I'll probably go home and start painting my hallway bathroom. I've been putting it off forever. So today is the day. Maybe," she said, laughing.

"Dinner later?" I asked.

"Dinner later."

When we pulled up to CAR, Lazzy sat up straight in his seat. He watched the building very carefully as I parked the car in my numbered spot. Once inside, he started waving to everyone we passed. All the guys at the security checkpoint were laughing heartily at him. I had hoped Morris would have been at the main check-in, but I didn't see any sign of him.

We stepped out the elevator on our floor and headed to the main lab. Once he saw Gloria and Della, Lazzy let go of my hand and ran toward the cages. I let all three of them out, including Boris. I moved them into the play area and couldn't help but grin from ear to ear. They seemed so completely happy to see one another. Even though things were going well, I watched them carefully, apprehensively, making sure to monitor their first reunion. By the time they had finished greeting one another with hearty hugs and questioning looks, I felt more relaxed and highly grateful. I could plainly see they were talking about something, but their language escaped me. They would hold each other's faces and look deeply into each other's eyes. They'd stroke one another and hug. Clearly, this meeting felt long overdue to all of them.

On the outside of the circle, though, was Boris. Eventually, Gloria drew him in and included him, giving an introduction of sorts to Lazzy. I watched closely to make sure there weren't any problems. Lazzy didn't give Boris much attention, one way or the other. Overall, I was happy with how things were going, so I let all of their homecoming socializing go on for quite some time. I called the maintenance team for a new cage installation. Once they completed their work, the two lab assistants and I finished setting up the interior of Lazzy's new room.

I explained to Lazzy that things would be like they used to be. At night time, there would be someone else in the lab to stay with them, and I would be going back home. He listened to me as I explained things, but in the end, I don't think he cared. He seemed mostly concerned with being near Della and Gloria, trading books and puzzles back and forth. I'm fairly certain it was harder for me to leave him than it was for him. During the entire drive home that night, I felt sad without him.

As I neared my driveway, the phone rang. Jack.

"Jack, hey. What's happening?"

"Hey, you have a minute?"

"I'm just pulling into my garage."

"Well, can you pull back out and meet me at my house? I have something I need to show you."

"Can it wait until tomorrow? It's been kind of a long day, and Sarah and I were going to get together for dinner."

"It's kind of important."

"Can you just tell me? Over the phone?" I asked. My body ached, and while I felt certain it was from the emotional strain of the past few days, the feeling of absolute tiredness pressed hard on me. Sitting there in my garage, the only thing I wanted to do was to go in and relax for the rest of the evening.

"I'd rather you see this in person," he said.

I took a deep breath, hoping for that second wind to hit me. "I'll be there in a few minutes," I said, throwing my car into gear.

"Great. Just come on in. I'll be in my computer room."

~

I opened the front door, and Bootles stood in the entryway, acting like he'd been waiting for me. He did a few figure-eights around my ankles. I followed him into the kitchen to get him a treat before making my way to Jack's computer room, knocking before I walked in.

Jack sat at the main console, one earbud in his right ear. His focus remained entirely on the computer screen in front of him, clearly working with a video. He waved me in and patted the chair next to him.

"I just have a few more clips to line up. I just got here a minute ago, so give me just a second."

"Why the urgency?" I asked.

"You'll see. I've been working on some different angles for about a week, and I happened to pull up a couple of more tapes today at work. And then it hit."

He went quiet, working away at his computer. As I watched him, I decided that he had become every bit as committed to solving this as anyone else involved. Even me.

All at once, the whole room was lit up by the monitors in front of us. Images of the CAR hallways popped onto the screens, one by one.

"Okay, watch this. This first one is of Martin Boyle, just walking down the hallway. Just on a normal day," he said. "And here's another. Watch it closely." Jack proceeded to pull up three or four more clips of Boyle, playing them side by side, simply walking around the halls.

"Okay. Boyle. Got it," I said.

"Hang on." Jack bumped my arm and then pulled up the next reel. It was the night of Lazzy's kidnapping, that old familiar tape where the person dressed in black pushed the large cart through the hallway. A brief segment showed them walking down the hall back to the lab area without the cart. "Now this," he said.

He pressed a button and played them side by side. It became immediately clear that Boyle and the person pushing the cart were one and the same. It was unmistakable. The way they walked, the manner in which they held themselves, and, of course, their physical proportions.

"Boyle," I said. "But we knew that, right? We've known he took Laz."

"Yes. Right. Boyle," Jack reiterated. "I have more."

I watched as he worked the keyboard and mouse. The screens went dark and then, one by one, began to fill up with more images. This time, they displayed Dr. Aubrey Keegan. As with Boyle, the various clips showed her walking through the hallways in an array of different outfits. They spanned several days or weeks.

Then Jack hit another sequence of keys. "And this."

The clip showed the day of the bombing, the empty hallway outside of the restroom. A moment later, the person, again, wearing head-to-toe black—their face covered with a mask, their head in a black hood, exactly like the kidnapper. But the walk was much different than Boyle's. As it played, next to the videos of Keegan, one could clearly see they were the same.

"You're kidding me. Keegan?" I said, nearly gasping.

A bag slung over her shoulder, carrying the bomb, no doubt. A gun in her opposite hand. She entered the bathroom door. We sat and watched the reel for the next 15 minutes, all the people passing the door, even entering the bathroom and coming back out. And then the explosion. I couldn't believe what I was watching.

"Jesus, Jack."

"Hang on. There's more."

The time stamp on the next clip he showed was the day of the shooting. Minutes before the assault, the assailant walked down the hall with two handguns, one in each hand. Once again, they were dressed in black, their face and head covered. There were no distinguishing characteristics except for the walk. Keegan. I sat in silence, watching the screens play the same clip on a loop. I had to let it all sink in.

"Have you shown this to anyone?"

"Not yet," Jack said, looking over at me, shaking his head slowly.

Chapter Thirty-Three

We sat in silence for quite a while. I don't know how long. I just remember leaning back in the chair and holding my head with both hands. It seemed incomprehensible to me that my boss, the renowned scientist Dr. Aubrey Keegan, could be responsible for these attacks. Granted, she was a mean and spiteful person to the core. And I couldn't stand the woman. Strike that. I could, in fact, stand her. I had learned to adapt to her during the short time we worked together. I suppose it would be more fitting to say that she could not stand me. Either way. The fact remained. Or at least, it seemed wholly apparent. Dr. Aubrey Keegan was responsible for both the bombing and the shooting at CAR.

"So you haven't given this to anyone?" I asked Jack, turning my chair toward him.

"Not yet. I've been lining up the clips and all. I wanted to make sure I had everything right. And once I got to a place where it was ready, I wanted to put it by you first."

"Why?"

"Well, for a couple of reasons. First, it was important to make sure that someone else confirmed what I was seeing before I pushed this forward. And I wanted to be sure it was someone I could trust. Fully. So here we are. And the other thing is this: I'm not sure who I should take this to first. Should I give it to my immediate boss, which would be Vargas? Or go over his head to Captain Huffman? Neither of whom ranks very high on my integrity meter. Or do I piss off everyone at Columbus PD and hand it over to the FBI?"

"I see why you were in a hurry to see me. I mean, this needs to go somewhere as soon as possible. But if you are asking me …" Just then, my phone rang. I looked down to check the caller. It was Sarah. "Do you mind if I just pick this up real quick?"

Jack nodded and motioned to my phone with his head.

"Hey, Sarah. Sorry, I'm late."

"Are you okay? Everything alright?"

"Yeah, I'm with Jack. He had to show me something."

There was a long pause on Sarah's end of the phone. I could tell she was disappointed. "Okay, well, I'm glad you're alright. I was worried. I'll let you go then," she quietly said.

"Hang on, this was really important, this thing Jack had to show me. But we're almost done. I'll be there in ten minutes or less, okay?"

"That's fine. Take your time." Sarah hung up the phone.

I glanced over at Jack, his full attention on his keyboard and monitor. "Well, Sarah doesn't get mad very often, but I think she's a little upset with me for not showing up on time. I should have called her on my way over here," I said.

"Well, you better get moving."

I gathered my jacket and headed to the door but stopped midway. "Jack. Thanks for doing all of this. I mean it." I started to leave once more but stopped again. "I never answered you. About who you should show this to."

"What do you think?"

"I'd say the FBI. All the way. I have never trusted Vargas. Maybe 'trust' is the wrong word. It's just that he never did anything to help with this case. And I'm not sure about Huffman either."

Jack and Bootles showed me to the door. As I headed for my

car, I tried to consume the enormity of what he had pieced together. I wanted the entire world to know immediately, yet I understood Jack's point of making sure that this evidence was handled correctly.

It only took me seven minutes to get home. I found Sarah seated at the table, reading a *People* magazine, of all things, and eating a strawberry Pop-Tart, the kind with the frosting.

"Did you make one of those for me?" I said, tapping her arm as I took my jacket off. I walked to the closet and hung it up and went back to the kitchen. Sarah remained in the same position as when I left her. I sat down across the table.

"Are you okay?" I asked.

She dropped the magazine, took another bite of Pop-Tart, and looked at me with a solemn face.

"I'm fine," she said as she lifted the magazine back up.

"Sarah, I'm sorry I was late. I'm even more sorry that I didn't call. But Jack called me right as I was pulling in and said he had something I had to see right away. He said it was urgent. So I went."

This time, she lowered the magazine all the way to the table, folded her hands in front of her, and leaned forward. She took a deep breath.

"It's okay. I'm sorry I got upset. It's just … Well … It's just a lot of things. I had a terrible day at work. And then, tonight, I expected you to be here. And when you didn't show up on time, I started getting worried. I don't know. There's been other things lately, and I was just hoping we could've talked some tonight."

"I'm sorry." I reached across the table and squeezed her forearm. She looked up at me and half smiled.

"I'm sorry. You've been going through so much lately too."

"It seems like things are clearing up a little, though. Don't you think?" I asked.

Sarah fiddled with the corner of the magazine and nodded.

"It's just that, well, today I found out at work that I might be getting relocated. Transferred. To Philadelphia. It's either move or find another job. Accura is moving its main office to Philly. So I might have to go."

"Oh no," I said. "That's terrible news."

"Technically, it isn't written in stone. But most of us here, at corporate here in Columbus, are getting moved over to Philadelphia."

I would miss everything about Sarah. Terribly. We did everything together. We relied on each other. A lump started to form in my throat. "I'm really sorry. I wish there were something I could do. But maybe you won't have to go. Or maybe you can get a city close to here."

She looked at me again, the corner of her mouth edged up slightly. She nodded. She continued to sit quietly, and I wasn't quite sure what to say next. It didn't seem like much was helping.

She got up and opened the refrigerator.

"Are you hungry? There's some leftover Pad Thai in here. I could warm it up."

"I'll fix something later," I said.

"How about a beer then? I'm having a beer." She came back to the table with two Heinekens, setting them down on the table and popping off the tops. She pushed one across to me.

Again, silence fell over us. Sarah stirred in her chair before getting up and walking to the chair against the wall where she'd hung her coat. She fished through one of the pockets, pulled out her phone, then put it back in her jacket before sitting back down at the table. Continued silence. I could tell from the look on her face that something much bigger was bothering her. Something deeper. I'd known her too long and too well not to notice.

"What's going on, Sarah? Something else is bothering you, and you're not saying it."

She looked over at me and smiled. Sarah had the most beautiful smile. She inhaled deeply.

"Look. There's something I've wanted to talk to you about for a long time. But the past few weeks have been crazy for you, so I didn't bring it up. Besides, It's just never felt like the right time. Anyway. Now this has happened with work. So I'm feeling like I need to tell you."

"You know you can tell me anything. God knows we have in the past."

She turned the magazine over on the table. And again.

"Rory, I care for you. I care deeply for you. For the past, what, five years now? We've been best friends. But more than that, we spend all our free time together. Just about. I mean, look at us. Hell, I babysit your bonobo at the drop of a hat." She looked down at the table and chuckled. "And everything else."

"I know," I said. "I love spending time with you. I've never had someone like you in my life. God, I love you for all those things."

She looked straight at me, nodding slowly.

"That's just it, Rory. I think I love you."

My face flushed. I could feel my neck getting warm. The thing was, as I sat there looking at beautiful Sarah, I'd had these same feelings before but pushed them aside. I knew her better than anyone else in the world, and she knew me. Neither one of us had had a serious boyfriend in all that time. Neither of us wanted one.

"Don't say anything, okay? Please. Just don't respond right now. I want you to take some time before you say anything. And I'm sorry this is coming out right now, but I needed to tell you. Now more than ever, with this work thing looming. My boss just sent me a text. We have a meeting in Columbus, Ohio. So I'll be gone for a couple of days." She looked down at her hands, turned one of the rings on her finger before looking up. "So maybe when I get back, we can sit down and talk. I'm asking you to take your time with this, please. And, besides, I might know more by then about whether I have to move away or not."

I reached over for her arm and squeezed it again.

"I'm glad you told me. We'll sit down when you get back."

Sarah went home to pack, as she had an early morning drive to the other Columbus. I sat at the table, feeling completely exhausted. I had this internal tsunami of emotions, an uproar of feelings, all crashing together in one giant mess. Everything in me felt like exploding. But where? To what end?

I got up, grabbed another beer from the refrigerator, and sat back down at the table, reaching over for Sarah's half-eaten Pop-Tart. I took a bite and washed it down with a gulp of Heineken. It wasn't the best combination, but I had a feeling that was going to be dinner for the night.

I felt completely numb, so I decided I wouldn't think about any of it. Instead, I grabbed another beer, headed to the living room, and flipped on the TV. I found old episodes of *Columbo* on Amazon and started binge-watching Peter Falk dropping his cigar ash wherever he went.

I woke to the sound of my alarm. Apparently, I had hit the snooze button the first time it sounded because now I was 15 minutes late in getting up. Not a great start for my first full day back on the job. I hustled through my shower and grabbed another one of those Pop-Tarts as I headed out the door, which immediately reminded me of Sarah and our conversation. My head was heavy from six too many beers the evening before, which upset me because I wanted to be sharp for work. I tried to clear my mind as I drove toward the lab. Then it hit me. The lab. I'd probably run into Keegan. How in the world could I face her knowing what I knew? Immediately, I felt my face get flushed with anger and anxiety, both at the same time.

I parked and jogged into the building. Morris was working the main metal detector.

"Good morning, Rory. Glad to see you back," he said.

"Morris! Good to see you. I'm running a little late, first day back on the job." I grabbed my things from the conveyor belt and gave him a little punch on the arm. "Talk with you later, okay?"

When I reached the lab, I headed to the cages first thing. I snuck up quietly so I could see what everyone was doing. All four of the bonobos were sitting on their respective floors, playing with various toys. Lazzy had constructed a little leaning tower with his favorite blocks. I walked front and center. "Good morning, ladies and gentlemen," I said.

They all seemed excited to see me, which elevated my mood immensely. I looked toward the main work counter and saw a new person sitting there.

"I'm Dr. Greene, the director of this lab. We haven't met," I said.

"I'm Terrance. Terrance Wilkie." The young man, probably early twenties, must have been six foot three, at least.

Terrance and I ushered the four bonobos over to the corner of the lab and sat with them while they interacted, sometimes with one another and sometimes with us. I kept my interaction time to a minimum and asked Terrance to do the same. Mostly, I wanted to spend this time observing their progressions, or regressions, since I'd been gone. And, of course, I needed to see how Della, Gloria, and Boris were handling their time with Lazzy. The 30 minute period went by quickly, and for the most part, everything seemed to be moving in a positive direction.

We were just about to finish up when Dr. Barber walked in with Dr. Keegan. They made their way directly to us, and I stood up. My stomach twisted into a knot as I tried not to show my inner turmoil. I attempted to keep my facial expressions neutral.

"Hello, Dr. Greene," Dr. Barber held out his hand, shaking mine. He was the kind of guy that shook with both hands. He would take you by the elbow with his left hand, squeezing it slightly, while he shook your hand with his right. His smile was always genuinely warm.

"It's good to see you," I said. "What brings you down to the fourth floor?"

"Well, I wish I could say that we just decided to come see you for fun. But the truth is, it is part of our new requirement by corporate. It's all in accordance with these Homeland Security guidelines we have to follow. One of us has to make the rounds to all the labs under our immediate supervision on a daily basis. Today is the first day, so both of us decided to come, just to get an idea about how much time it might take," he said. Keegan stood a few steps behind him, her arms crossed, scanning the perimeter of the lab like some bouncer at the door of a bar, checking the room for any potential trouble.

"Everything okay there, Dr. Keegan?" I asked, in my best attempt to act like everything was normal.

She gave me a look and a brief nod, furrowing her brows slightly.

"Well, we won't take up much of your time, Rory," Dr. Barber said.

"Have you met our new assistant?" I said. "This is Terrance. Terrance, I can't remember your last name. I'm sorry."

"I'm Terrance Wilkie."

Just then another assistant walked into our room from the testing area.

"And this young man over here is?" I held out my arm in his direction and nodded in anticipation.

"Oh, hello. I'm Julian. Julian Geer," he said, bowing slightly.

"Nice to meet you, fellows," Barber bowed slightly in return.

"Which brings up a hefty point right now. We're going to be replacing both of our former research technicians. Boyle. And, of course, Andy. Any news on the new researchers?"

I looked down at the floor.

"Nothing solid yet. But, Rory, I'm awfully sorry about the entire thing. I'm sure that must have been awful," Dr. Barber said.

"It's been pretty devastating. To all of us."

"Well, the good news is, I'm sure there are some interviews

lined up for this week. And a couple for next week too. Is that right, Aubrey?"

Dr. Keegan turned her head to us, looking like she had absolutely no idea what we were talking about. "I'm sorry. What were you saying?" she said.

"The interviews. For the lab technicians," Barber answered.

"Oh, yes. Sure." She started walking toward the door.

"Well, it looks like we're moving along now. I'm sure I'll see you around later, Rory. Nice to meet you, boys." And with that, Dr. Barber and Dr. Keegan left the lab.

I couldn't help but to think that the last time Dr. Keegan had been in my lab she'd probably been wearing a mask and holding a gun. Anger started to fill me, gripping my chest with tightness. I looked over, and Lazzy was standing right by my side. He grabbed my hand and led me to a chair in the play area. I sat down and looked at him. "What is it, Laz?"

He reached up and patted my cheek. And then he hugged me. I'm sure he knew.

Chapter Thirty-Four

By the time I pulled into my driveway, I felt almost too tired to move. There was something about standing on your feet all day that took some getting used to. My legs and back ached as I got out of my car. But more than anything, the emotional strain of the past few weeks had been weighing heavily on me, and I felt it. I stood and watched the garage door close slowly before walking into the house.

I couldn't have been in the kitchen for more than two minutes when the doorbell rang. I considered not answering it but let the thought slide away and headed for the door.

Jack stood on the front porch, six-pack of beer in hand. "Thirsty?" he asked.

"C'mon in, Jack." I turned and walked back to the kitchen. "I just walked in the door."

"I know. I saw you pull in. I've been waiting."

"Are you stalking me?" I laughed.

"Ever since we met." He laughed as he reached for a beer. "No, my date stood me up for dinner. And besides that, I wanted to drop by and tell you that the tapes got handed over right before I left work."

"Did you give them to Bishop?"

"Well, I was wrapping things up, you know, making sure all the files were saved in the right order and that I had everything on the disk. Anyway, I'm guessing Vargas must have been keeping an eye on me. He came in just as I was finishing things and asked to see what I had up on the screen. Of course, I couldn't hide anything from him at that point. Everything was disclosed. He was standing behind me at my console, patted me on the back, and then he asked for the drive, saying he'd give it to Huffman. I pointed out that it might be important to the FBI investigation, first and foremost, and he said he'd rather the arrest come from our department. Vargas was adament about it, saying that it would be better for Columbus PD that way."

"Well, shit. Now what?" I said.

"Now I don't know what. I can't really give this to Bishop now. They'd probably fire me for insubordination or something. I guess we just have to hope he'll move it along."

"But what do you think he'll do? Really?"

"I have no idea, but I'm hoping he plays it straight, takes it to Huffman, and then issues a warrant for Keegan's arrest."

I walked over to the table where he sat and reached for one of the beers.

"Mind if I have one?"

"I learned to share in kindergarten," he said.

"Not beers, I hope." I sat down and took a long drink from the bottle. It felt good. Tasted good. I needed a break, I thought.

"So let me ask you this. What happens if nothing happens?"

"What do you mean?" Jack turned his bottle in his hands while giving me a quizzical look.

"What happens if Vargas just sits on this information?"

Jack thought about it for a minute, continuing to twirl his bottle around. "I don't think he will. He can't, really. I mean, he knows I'll be expecting something to come of this. An arrest. Like he and I talked about. He can't just make this go away. And if nothing happens, well, I'll be asking questions. He knows how digital information works. He understands that I didn't hand over the only copy, like in some old black-and-white movie, when there was only one envelope with damning photos in it."

"So what will you do if nothing happens?"

"I'll either go to Captain Huffman or to Bishop and Neal. Probably to Bishop and Neal."

My phone started ringing, doing its buzzy dance on the tabletop. It was Maggie. I hadn't talked to her since she told me the truth about my dad, about Teddy Keegan, about all of it. She'd given me some time and space to absorb it all, but a lot had happened since we talked. I didn't have the energy to talk to her right then. "It's Maggie."

"Go ahead," Jack motioned toward the phone.

"No, really. Not tonight." I silenced the call and flipped my ringer off.

"What's going on there? Are you upset with her or something?"

"No, I just don't want to hear anything about anything tonight."

Jack raised his eyebrows at me. "Well, not hearing anything about anything sounds like a great idea. What do you think about hearing nothing while we pick up Sarah and go out for a pizza?"

"Sarah's out of town right now. Work stuff. But, you know, Jack? I'm feeling pretty beat. I think I just want to hang out around the house tonight."

"Would you rather be alone right now?" he asked.

I looked over at him and smiled sheepishly.

"I am a man of keen senses," he laughed. "Call me Sherlock. I can see the writing on the wall."

"Are you sure you don't mind?"

"Not at all. But I'd like to point out that I've been stood up twice tonight. I'm getting a complex," he laughed. "If you change your mind, give me a call." He grabbed his jacket and headed for the door, leaving the remaining four beers on the table.

"Good night, Jack."

"Good night, Rory."

Once the door closed, I sat in the kitchen chair, not moving, for a long time.

Work came early the next morning. By my choice. I felt compelled to go in first thing and spend some extra time with the bonobos. It seemed like I'd been away for so long, and so much needed to be brought up to date. For one, our research schedule had fallen way behind. But more than anything, I missed seeing those four faces, especially Lazzy.

The entire day moved along normally. Dr. Barber brought down the newly hired researcher, the one replacing Andy. The new guy, fresh out of college, seemed slightly overconfident upon our first meeting. Sherwood Bolling, a newly graduated product of Princeton. He probably would not have been my pick, but no one had asked me. I stepped back for a moment, realizing how quickly I had made assumptions about this guy without even giving him a chance. I would try to assess him purely on his work and behavior in the lab. Although, I have to admit, attitude can sometimes be more important.

At noon, I decided to go out for lunch rather than eat in the cafeteria. As I was leaving, the two new assistants, Terrance and Julian, were just a step in front of me as we went out the front door. I noticed them conferring as they walked. Suddenly, they stopped and turned around. "Hey, Dr. Greene. We're heading to Knott's Kitchen for lunch. Would you like to join us?" Terrance asked.

I was just about to say no when Maggie walked up. I introduced everyone, and we exchanged pleasantries. Then Julian invited us both. Maggie looked at me and shrugged her shoulders, so we accepted.

The atmosphere immediately felt welcoming and quaint, with bright yellow tablecloths throughout and the overwhelming aroma of baking bread.

"Had you two known each other prior to working at CAR?"

"No, we met on our first day," Terrance continued.

"Who hired you? I'm curious. Who's doing the interview these days?" Maggie continued her round of questions.

"Dr. Keegan pretty much handled the whole thing. I think for both of us. She did the initial interview. Then we both had one call back. And then just a brief orientation. Then she cut us loose. Just dropped us right in the center of the lab, into the throws of the day-to-day," Julian said. Terrance nodded.

"That's interesting. We have another new guy starting today. One of the replacements for our researchers. Sherwood is his first name. I couldn't tell you his last name right now. At any rate, Dr. Barber brought him into the lab today. I wonder why Keegan didn't do it?" I said.

"Dr. Keegan's not at work today. I sort of overheard Dr. Barber on his cell phone in the hallway. He told whoever he was talking to that Keegan didn't show up for work."

"What?" I asked. "Did she call in sick?"

"I'm not sure. It sounded like she just didn't come in. I heard Barber say it wasn't like her not to show," Terrance said.

I looked at Maggie.

"What's wrong, Rory?"

"I need to go make a phone call, guys. And Maggie needs to come with me."

We excused ourselves and went into the front receiving area of the restaurant. I filled her in, as best as I could quickly, about the evidence Jack found concerning Keegan, the bomber and shooter. Keegan, the murderer. I also told her that Jack turned it over the night before. To Detective Vargas.

"And now she's gone," I said, shaking my head, dialing Jack.

"Maybe they arrested her," Maggie offered.

"That's what I'm going to find out."

~

After a brief conversation with Jack, I learned they had gone to Keegan's home early that morning with her arrest warrant. The arresting team included Vargas, his partner Linda Patterson, and two uniformed officers. No one answered the door. They conducted a probable cause search and did not find any sign of her inside. Since that time, they issued an APB for Columbus and its vicinity. I asked Jack if there was anything I could do or should do. He told me to keep my eyes open and my phone handy.

Maggie and I discussed our options, which turned out to be none. We had to hope the police and the FBI would be able to track her down quickly. Feeling a bit helpless, we went back inside Knott's and continued our lunch with Terrance and Julian. Once we finished the meal, I made plans to meet Maggie later in the day. From there, I returned to the lab. Two Columbus officers were entering the building just as I headed in.

For the remainder of the day, I felt terribly nervous. I could barely work and kept an eye on the door for most of the afternoon. Finally, I couldn't bear the thought of another threatening incident, so I went directly to Dr. Barber's office. I asked if he would consider requesting a security guard to be placed at the lab door overnight. He granted that request without pressing me for details about my concerns. By the time I left, I felt somewhat relieved, knowing the bonobos would be safe. At least, I hoped.

Maggie had been in town for an afternoon meeting with her lawyer, who had moved here from Bloomington several years ago. I didn't ask any questions, but as such, we decided to meet at Mac McDonald's Pub, just down the street from the law office. She only had a small window of time. We sat as far away from any people as possible, which always seemed to be our choice in these places. Both of us ordered a beer and ate the breadsticks already waiting for us at the table.

"I mostly wanted to check in and see how you are doing after hearing about your dad. And about your … well … about Teddy Keegan," she said.

"God, Maggie, I wish that were just half of it. But to answer your question, I think I'm doing okay. Part of me feels completely upended by this new reality. But I'm not in some deep, dark place about the whole thing. I just feel … I feel … different. Deceived. Lied to."

"I'm sorry all of this happened to you." She reached over and grabbed my hand, giving it a reassuring squeeze.

"Maggie, there's something else, though. Maybe now isn't the time to bring it up. I know you have to leave soon."

"What is it? I've got the time," she said.

"Well … so I know you were with Eva for a lot of years."

She laughed and rolled her head back, looking up at the ceiling. "I always thought it was really something that you figured it all out when you were so young. And it never seemed to bother you one bit. It's just been one of those things that we never spoke about. But back then, I wanted to keep that part of my life separate from you. I didn't want your mom to say that I was a bad influence on you or anything. So Eva and I decided it would be best just to keep our relationship private and quiet. You understand."

"I do understand. I should've talked with you about it years ago. With both of you. And then look what happened. There we were at her funeral. I just didn't know what to say at the time. Instead, I just wanted you to know that I was there if you needed me."

"It felt better to have you sitting beside me. So, thanks," Maggie said, tearing up slightly. "So what is all this about? Why bring up Eva now?"

"How long were you two together?"

"Twenty-nine years."

"Were you friends first?"

"For about a year or so, I suppose. We met at school, at IU. We were in the same introductory English class during our freshman year. She sat right next to me that semester. At any rate, we started hanging out. We were in different dorms, but we all ate in the same cafeteria. At first, we just started eating together, then the library, then movies, and campus parties. Those sorts of things. And then, one night, we'd been to see the men's basketball team play. Isiah Thomas was the point guard that year. Man, he was awesome. Anyway, we were walking home, back to her dorm first, and she grabbed my hand as we walked. We were right behind Collins Hall, and I leaned over and kissed her. We were crazy in love. We just didn't know it until then. Not fully. But as soon as we kissed, it was game over from there." She rolled her napkin in her hands, looking down, smiling, a million miles away.

"That's so sweet."

"We were sweet. We were a great pair. Soulmates. Kindred spirits. Eva was the funniest, kindest, smartest person I'd ever met. I still miss her every day, even though she's been gone for almost 14 years."

"I wish I'd known her better," I said.

"Yeah, I regret how I handled that. I should have let you see our lives together, what we were like. There was no shame in it whatsoever. I just didn't want to upset your mom in any way."

"Mom. Dear sweet Mom. Let's not even go into that this evening."

"That's fine with me. But I'll ask again. Why the interest in Eva and me?"

I sat quietly for a long time, staring down at the table, trying to choose my words carefully. Finally, I decided that I didn't have to say any of this carefully.

"It's about Sarah."

Maggie raised her eyebrows.

"No. It's not like that. We're not together or anything. We've just been friends. Close friends. Complicated friends. But here's the thing. A couple of nights ago, she told me that she was having feelings for me. And the reason for telling me now was mostly because of her job at Accura. That's where she works, Accura World Bank. They are moving their corporate office to Philadelphia, and she thinks she'll probably have to move." I took a sip of my beer and looked around the room as if some sort of answer would appear. I continued with the story.

"I could tell she was nervous about the whole thing. But she didn't want to talk about it. She just wanted me to sit with this for a couple of days. She's in Columbus, Ohio, right now for work. At any rate, I'm sitting with it. It's been hard not to think about anything else."

"Well, if you ask me, you two sort of act like an old married couple. And, actually, I wondered if you two were a thing. Are a thing," Maggie said, rocking her head back and forth.

"Well, not admittedly. And, obviously, it has never come up before. She's my favorite person to be with. In the whole entire world. She's funny, and God, she's so smart. I love being with her. It always seems like the most comfortable place in the world for me. And now it looks like she's leaving." I looked off toward the door.

"So what are you asking me, Rory? Are you asking me anything? Or did you just need to talk, to let it all out? What?"

I thought about it for a minute before I answered.

"What would you do? I know it is kind of different, but were there times when you felt uncertain about things with Eva? Or did it all seem clear to you?"

"First of all, I can see how hard this is on you. You two are like peanut butter and jelly. You never argue. You're kind to one another, considerate, and caring. You two have been taking care of each other for years. And now that might be coming to an end. On top of all that, you've had a lot going on lately. Obviously. So now that Sarah has a problem, she might be feeling bad about bringing more bad news to the table. There's an awful lot going on here."

"Yeah, there is. I haven't talked to her since that night. She left for her trip and left me to think. I feel like the only way to answer all of this is with her," I said.

"You and I are in the profession of communication. Too bad we have all this experience with animals and not humans. But about how Eva and I handled things? Tender honesty. That was one of our biggest gifts to one another. Compassionate, tender honesty. So, yeah, you need to be honest with her. More importantly, you need to be honest with yourself. I think as soon as she gets back, you should sit down with her and talk."

We settled the check and gave each other a hug on the sidewalk. I watched her get in her car and waved as she drove off. I needed to call her tomorrow and thank her. Just for being her. For being my Maggie.

Chapter Thirty-Five

When I pulled up to Sarah's place, it immediately felt like a welcome sight. I looked forward to seeing her.

Normally, I'd just hit my garage door opener and pull into the garage. For a few years now, I had been using the extra spot in her garage, and she used the one at my house. But, for some reason, that night, I decided it would probably be better if I rang the front doorbell like any normal visitor would.

I stood on the doorstep, waiting for her to answer. As I peered through the side window, the only light I could see was coming from the kitchen. It took her a couple of minutes to come to the door.

"Hey, you. Why the front door?" she said, stepping onto the porch and giving me a hug. She was wearing a pair of dark blue PJ bottoms and a Pittsburgh University sweatshirt. They matched perfectly. Sarah always matched perfectly. "I had to check the camera to see who was out here."

"I don't know why I parked out front. Maybe I just needed a few minutes of the cold night air," I said.

"Come on in. Maybe I needed the cold air too. I've been standing at the freezer door for the last five minutes, staring down a pint of Ben & Jerry's Half-Baked for dinner."

"Ice cream for dinner? Must have been a bad meeting in Columbus."

She leaned back against the kitchen counter and crossed one leg over the other.

"Not really bad. It just turned out to be a big rehash, as far as I'm concerned. They gave us the reasons for the move, yadda. Gave us all a script, basically, that we are supposed to take back to our departments. Things to say when people question this big reorganization."

"Well, I'm glad you're back. I missed you."

Sarah smiled a bit sheepishly. "Thanks. I missed you too."

We ended up sitting at the kitchen table and talking. For hours. We talked about the past five years or so and fell into recalling fond memories of all the things we did. Things like picking up in the middle of one Saturday to drive up to the Indianapolis Zoo just to sit and look at the elephants. Or little things, like the time we burnt peanut butter cookies because we got too caught up in solving a crossword puzzle. We talked all around everything except for the big issue in front of us, which was "us."

Eventually, finally, I was the one to step into the light.

"Sarah. Listen. I've been giving things a lot of thought. In fact, for the past two days, it has never left my mind. In all my life, I've been more focused on science than my own personal life. Marriage has never been a priority. Kids, either. But as I look back on it, I never found the right person. In all the good, bad, and ugly dates I've had all my life, the guy that lasted the longest was Mark Burton, right after college. And that was for, like, five weeks or something." I paused briefly, trying to regroup. "I'm saying all this wrong." I took a deep breath and glanced out her kitchen window. It was dark out, and the only thing I could see was the kitchen reflecting back onto itself. I continued.

"What I'm trying to say is that I've never met the right person. Until you. You are my truest and dearest friend. But you are way more than my friend. You are right next to my heart all the time. We are inseparables, I think. I love it when we are together. When I'm with you, it feels like the safest place on Earth. I can tell you anything. And I look forward to telling you everything. And when something happens during my day, I'm like, 'I can't wait to tell Sarah this.' I like you. Everything about you. My life is comfortable with you and exciting with you at the same time. And … I think you and I make a pretty good pair," I said. "I guess when you said you might be leaving, it caught me off-guard. My mind had been through one thing after the other that day. I was up to my neck in nerves. But regardless of all of that, I've just never thought, not even once, about you or me moving away from here. I've come to rely on us always being here for each other. My life is better because of you. God, it is so much easier because of you too. And the fact of it is, I don't know what I'm going to do without you. I'm trying to say that I love you too. And even though this is all new to us, in a way, we'll figure it out. I think we're supposed to."

Sarah looked across the table and smiled. She looked so beautiful in that moment. No matter what she was doing or wearing or being, she always had this glow about her. She reached over and squeezed my hand.

"Thank you, Ror. I love you too."

"And if you have to move, we'll figure that out too. Maybe, somehow, you can stay in Columbus. Or, I can find a job in Philadelphia or wherever. Okay?"

She started crying.

"Or maybe you want to get out of town while the getting is good," I said, chuckling.

She laughed through her tears, nodding.

"I'm kind of nervous," she said.

We talked, laughed, and even cried for a long time as we continued to hold hands across the table. But by that point, it was getting terribly late.

I'd stayed at Sarah's many times before. This time, she offered again awkwardly. And I declined awkwardly. Our friendship had shifted, and we both knew we wanted to take things slow.

It was nearly three in the morning when I got up to leave, the night air even colder than when I'd got in. When I tried the ignition, my car would not start. It held all the signs of being a dead battery, with the "click, click" noise when I turned the key. Once again, Sarah's kindness came through, her unending, giving spirit. She told me to drive her car home, and she would get a neighbor to jump mine in the morning.

As I drove home, I felt a weird pit in my stomach. I hoped that dear Sarah really would be staying in Columbus. But it seemed to be something more. More like dread.

The next morning, I rolled into work early, once again, and spent time with the bonobos as soon as I arrived. I'd have to wait for Sherwood to start any kind of testing. I sat for a moment at the lab counter, staring at the cages. Della held a book in front of Gloria's face through their bars. She pointed at something on the page. Della. Showing something to Gloria.

Not only do bonobos communicate with bonobos, bears with bears, and bats with bats, but communication between species is happening all over the animal kingdom. Deer conversing with rabbits, or chipmunks handing out greetings to sparrows. I recently read a study about Madagascan spiny-tailed iguanas. They have these little well-developed ears, even though they don't communicate vocally. But their ears are there so they can hear the warning calls of the Madagascan paradise flycatcher. An iguana and a bird. These two classes of animals work together—these two species—even though they have nothing in common except the same general habitat. The other thing they have in common is the fact that raptors like to snack on them both. So the flycatcher will see these raptors and start screeching at the top of its lungs. "It's a raptor. It's a raptor." And the iguana, with its tiny ears, will hear the alarm sounding and take cover, on high alert for incoming predators.

All morning long, I'd felt like the iguana who had just heard the call of the flycatcher. Something in me felt on edge, and my intuition was right. It shouldn't have been any surprise to me when Jack called with the news. And, truthfully, I can't remember most of what he said during that conversation. Later, while at the hospital, the pieces of the story would come together, but it all felt like some nightmarish blur.

What Jack said was that Sarah had been taken to Columbus Regional Hospital. When I arrived, I learned she was in surgery and also in critical condition. She had been leaving for work in my car that morning, pulling out of the driveway, when someone, either walking or in a vehicle, shot her six times through the driver-side window. Sarah had been struck in the head, neck, and shoulder. A neighbor heard a crash and found my car, with Sarah in it, planted squarely into the trunk of a tree. Jack got wind of the story in the squad room and called me with the news.

As I walked into the waiting room, a couple of officers sat drinking coffee, talking, and waiting, with Vargas among them.

"Tell me everything you know," I said as I approached him.

Vargas looked up at me with a hardened stare. Finally, he spoke. "We don't know anything. A woman was shot, and she's critical. That's it."

"Do you have the shooter?"

"We don't have anything, Ms. Greene. Look, nobody saw anything. No one was out. Apparently, this woman's car wouldn't start. She asked the neighbor to give her a jump. He said that after it started, she pulled the car into the garage, door open, with the thing still running. She went back into the house. That was the last time anyone saw her before the shooting. We are checking to see if any doorbell cams caught anything. We've got people over there now. So right now, at this minute, we got nothing." He looked down at his watch.

I walked over to the nurses' station and inquired about Sarah's status. They had nothing for me either, except that she was in surgery. About 20 minutes later, Jack came in. He told me everything he had heard at the station, much of which I already knew. I wanted answers, and there weren't any to be found. My head felt surrounded by a thick fog. My vision and my hearing went blurry and dim. My stomach ached with emptiness. I didn't feel human.

The next few hours passed slowly. I waited. Jack waited with me. In circumstances such as this, time behaves oddly. Actually, through most of our lives, time does exactly what it pleases, depending on the situation. Like when you go on vacation to a beautiful place like Hawaii, soaking up the sun, enjoying the ocean, seeing the sites, and dining on the finest foods. Those seven days pass in an instant. Before you can blink, it is time to board the plane and head back home. And then there are times like in that waiting room at the hospital. Sitting, looking at my hands. Getting up. Staring out the window. Pacing the floor. Drinking a coffee. Surely, after all of that, a couple of hours have elapsed. And yet, when you look up at the clock, only nine minutes have gone by.

Time moved by painfully slowly that day, no matter what I did. Finally, after four hours and 52 minutes, a surgeon emerged through the double doors. I stood and walked directly toward him, with Jack just behind me.

The man looked down at the floor and drew in a deep breath. "Well, the good news is she pulled through the surgery. She's in recovery right now, but she's still in critical condition. I'm sure you are aware she was shot six times. Four of those bullets entered her head and neck area. The two in the shoulder were easy to remove. The other four, however, were in delicate areas. At this point, we have no idea how much damage has been done. Her brain has undergone massive swelling, and we are doing our best to control it. So, for now, we wait."

I wanted to know if she was going to live, and the surgeon answered honestly, saying he didn't know. I also asked to see her. They allowed me in for five minutes only.

The person lying there could have been anyone. Except, I knew her hands, her body, and every bit of her inner self. I knew Sarah still existed behind all those tubes and gauze and tape. I held her hand and whispered in her ear.

"I love you," I said. And then I left the room crying.

The next couple of days felt like some sort of vacuous, dark abyss. Sarah's parents had flown in from the East Coast the morning of the shooting. They were staying in town for now. But they announced that they might try to move Sarah, once she was stable enough, to a more comprehensive hospital, like Massachusetts General or Johns Hopkins.

I asked for a few personal days from work, which Dr. Barber granted without blinking an eye. During that time, I stayed mostly at the hospital, sitting by her bed, along with her parents. When they'd leave the room, I'd talk closely in her ear, telling her how much she meant to me. How much I loved her. Much to everyone's dismay, her condition remained unchanged. Sarah stayed unmoving, unresponsive, deep in a coma.

A couple of days after the shooting, while sitting at her bedside, I received a call from Dr. Barber, asking if I could stop by the lab and sign off on the month-end reports. As I left the building, a light snow started falling, and I remember thinking about Sarah. She loved the first snow of the season. She said there were angels in the sky, scattering their dusty magic down on the Earth, a way for the heavens to remind us they were there.

I walked across the parking lot, head tilted upward, feeling the flakes on my face. In an instant, a flash stung my eyes, a bombardment. My face skidded across the cold metal hood of a car, stopping at the windshield wiper before sliding back down again, across the hood, and dropping through the nothingness of air. My head hit the pavement. My body followed. Pain shot through every inch of me, from head to toe. All in an instant. And then everything went black.

~

When I woke, my back was resting against a large concrete column. My hands, tied at the wrists in my lap, looked slightly purple. I wiggled my fingers and felt a stinging, sharp pain run up my left arm into my shoulder. Both of my legs extended straight in front of me, and I could feel the cold of the concrete beneath my jeans. One of my shoes was missing. I tried both of my feet, moving them back and forth. I felt sore all over, but at least everything seemed to be working, except for my left arm.

I turned my head as far as I could, left to right, in an attempt to scan my surroundings—a large garage or warehouse, cold, dark, and empty. The windows in my range of sight along the one wall were soaped over. Some were broken. I tried to remember the sequence of events. I remember walking through the parking lot and noticing the snow. And then being upended by a car. At least, that is what I decided had happened. Everything swirled around me, and a wave of nausea hit me.

"It's about time, Greene," a voice said.

Keegan.

I reached up slowly, rubbing my eyes. They felt thick and bleary. I tried to focus on her, but my vision was slow to sharpen.

"Don't look so forlorn. You're fine. You've got a bump or two. That's all," she said, turning and walking somewhere behind me. She returned with a coffee cup from Starbucks. Standing over me, she took a long drink.

"God, how I love coffee, and this is still hot. I stepped out while you were napping."

"What do you want from me?" I asked.

Keegan leaned backward slightly, looking up at the ceiling as if she were trying to find the answer hanging somewhere in the rafters. She cocked her head to one side and gave me a long hard stare.

"What do I want? What could I possibly want? Since you're not too quick on the uptake, I'll tell you what I want. I'm sick and tired of you. For a long time now. So, what I want is to be rid of you. Entirely. And that whore you have for a mother. That's what I want."

My head pounded. Her words sounded garbled. Finally, I responded. "After all this time? You can't be serious."

She snapped her head, looking in my direction. "Oh, I'm dead serious."

She walked behind me again. I could hear a noise, but I couldn't make out what she was doing. I turned my head as far as I could, but she was out of my sight. Then she returned, this time with no coffee cup. A revolver dangled in her right hand.

"What are you doing? God, you can't be serious. You've done all of this, all of this killing and destruction, over what? Jealousy? Is that it, Keegan? It's been almost 40 years since your husband had that affair with my mom. Forty damn years, Keegan. Don't you think it's time to let go of that? There's no making this go away, no matter what you do."

She pointed the gun right at me. "I can make this go away. I should just shoot you right now and put an end to this blathering."

My words were failing me. "Listen, Keegan. It all happened so long ago. And this isn't going to change any of it. It's not going to bring your husband back or make that affair go away. I'm sorry it all happened. I really am. It must have been terrible for you. But we can't make the past go away. Besides, the police know you're behind all of this. The FBI."

"Shut up! God, you're just like your mother. You are as dumb as your mother."

I started to wiggle my hands despite the pain. I raised my knees up to my chest, hoping to mask the movement. "Well, to tell you the truth, I'm not real crazy about my mom right now either, so I guess we have that in common."

"I said shut up. I should have killed Mrs. Cory Greene the minute I found out about her and Teddy. The very minute. And, believe me, I had a plan back then. But the circumstances never worked out. It doesn't matter now, though. All this will be over soon enough."

"What do you mean?" I asked, all the while wriggling.

"Your dear mother is on her way here. I called her and told her I had you. That was over an hour ago. So, we still have a little while to wait."

"My mom is smarter than you think. I'm sure she's called the police by now," I said.

"Oh, don't bet on it. You see, I threatened to kill you. Besides, she doesn't know where I am. She's going to the dumpster behind McDonald's, where I left a cell phone. She's going to call me when she gets there."

Keegan walked behind me again. I wiggled, not getting much slack in my ropes.

"God, Keegan. Why did you have to hurt all those people? Why didn't you just take me from the start? Why kidnap Lazzy? Why the bombing? The shooting at the lab?"

Suddenly, her face popped around directly in front of me, smiling. I jumped.

"Because I wanted your death to seem like it was part of something bigger. Untraceable to me. I wanted you to look like a statistic. Part of a terrorist plot. Killing you outright might have come back to me. But if you blew up with some bomb? I'd be free and clear. And I still would be if you hadn't screwed things up. Twice. You were supposed to die in that explosion. When that missed, it was you I meant to shoot in the lab."

"You are out of your mind," I said quietly.

"My mind is perfectly intact. And the plan would have worked. But you had to start poking around into things. You and your friends. The police were supposed to handle this. And now look at the mess."

"Well, I would have let the police do their jobs if they had done them. But Detective Vargas wouldn't lift a finger. He just sat on his hands the whole time when Lazzy went missing. I had to get involved, all because of him."

"Vargas. The man's an idiot."

"You know him?"

"I know a lot about a lot of people. Not that it's any business of yours. But you couldn't possibly think I do this whole science thing for the sake of science."

"I don't understand what you mean."

"I work for a much bigger entity than CAR. Or any of these other horse and pony shows. You can't make any money playing with test tubes all day. You should know that. No, Rory. I've long been involved with a group you would not understand. We are the people who tell the government what to do."

She was right. I didn't understand. I dropped my head, trying to make sense of this moment. I heard her chuckle before she continued.

"Years ago, back in Indianapolis, Vargas was just some dumb beat cop. He wasn't making any money at that either. So he picked up this little habit of taking cash and drugs from people on the streets in exchange for him looking the other way. He got mixed up with the wrong people as a result. And, as with most of these cases, my organization had a handle on him from that point on. To this day. You see? Some things never change. He still takes money under the table. I threatened to expose him unless he agreed to stall this investigation. But he botched things up royally."

Keegan walked back and forth. She reached into her coat pocket, pulling out a pack of cigarettes. She lit one, drawing on it long and hard.

"Well, this day is just full of surprises," I said under my breath.

Keegan turned her head abruptly again, looking in my direction. She laughed.

"You really should get out more, Dr. Greene."

"So why did you take Lazzy? What could you have possibly gained by that?" I asked.

"Oh, mostly to see you suffer. Mostly. But also to make it look like someone from the outside was responsible for all of this. I enlisted Boyle to help me. I promised him a major promotion in the company and a transfer to anywhere in the organization he wanted. And, of course, I offered him money. But he proved to be careless. And a big loose end right from the start. So I had to shoot him."

I shook my head, shivering, wriggling my hands, looking for a way out. Then I thought about Sarah. I started crying.

Keegan walked up to me and bent over, smirking at me. I couldn't stand to look at her. I stared at her shoes as I spoke.

"Why shoot Sarah? What could you possibly have gained from that?"

"Your friend? I don't make them often, but she was a mistake. I thought it was you. Your car. I'd followed you over there the night before, and when it got late, I thought you were staying. So I went home and came back before dawn to wait until you left. You were supposed to be in that car."

I reacted with rage, pushing my back against the pillar with the force of my legs. I tried to get up, but Keegan walked over and hit me in the face with the revolver.

"Stay down where you are. I've had enough of this," she said.

Even though my head pounded, all the while numb and muddled, I could sense the anger rising in me. I felt a warm trickle of blood easing down my face. Moments ago, I hadn't understood how anyone could kill another person. But at that moment, I felt completely overwhelmed with rage, like I could actually kill Keegan. I also knew that I'd have to break free, somehow, or I'd wind up dead. I decided I'd keep trying, in small measures, to use my legs, pushing against the ground, forcing my back against the pillar so I could edge my way up. I repeated this, trying to give my legs strength, each time edging up a little further. But only when Keegan was looking away. I made up my mind to try to make a move. If she walked behind me once more, I would thrust myself upward and give her a fight, even though my hands were still bound.

She came back to my side, standing over me. "I learned a long time ago that people are expendable. There's only one person that matters in life. Number one. Everyone else is merely a stepping stone, at best. I didn't get to where I am by being the nice guy. That's exactly why you'll never get anywhere. You learned from your father. Not my Teddy, of course. But that stupid clod who raised you," she laughed. "Dear old Dad taught you well in that department. Well, here's news for you. You can't be nice and get ahead. But people like you are too dull to understand that fact about life." She looked down at her watch. "Your mother won't be here for a while, I don't imagine. Probably another hour."

"Look, you have every right to be angry about what happened. I mean, when you love someone and then find out they are with someone else? Of course, it is devastating."

She cut me off mid-sentence, forcing out a laugh. "Love someone? Are you kidding me? I never loved Teddy. He had connections when I met him. Connections I didn't have. That's the reason I married him. I spent as little time as possible with that dolt. But his affair with your mother? It was an embarrassment for me. Everyone in our circle knew about it and knew about you. I was mortified. So I got rid of him. Killing him turned out to be more than satisfying. It was exhilarating. All I had to do was cut the brake lines in his car before he left the house that morning. It all worked out so nicely. The State Patrol never investigated anything back then. Cause of death? Accidental car crash. And after he died, I received an outpouring of sympathy. Not to mention his life insurance policy. But planning your father's death was harder. In fact, I couldn't quite figure out a way to do it back then without raising some suspicion."

She reached for her pack of cigarettes and lit another, again blowing the smoke upward. Keegan looked as if her mind had gone someplace else.

"I never knew you smoked," I said reflexively.

"There's a lot you don't know about me."

“So why are you doing this now? After all this time?” I asked.

Most every time I asked a question, she’d snap her head in my direction, as if she had immediately become angered by the fact that I had spoken.

“Well, since we’re having a heart-to-heart here. I’ve had this plan for years, Rory. As fate would have it, I’d been assigned to work overseas, in Greece. My organization had me take a job as director of a research center there. Mostly pharmaceutical research. But then they decided they needed more operatives in the United States. Of course, I jumped at the chance when the position with CAR came up. They sent me right here. I knew you were on the staff at CAR, so it became my perfect opportunity. I found my anger about this whole situation hadn’t dulled one bit. And every time I saw you in the building, it got worse. It was like God was handing me this opportunity on a platter. So I began to put my plan into action. And that helped make everything better. In fact, it rejuvenated me. A brand-new purpose. The anticipation and the planning were every bit as fun as carrying out this whole big thing. But with all of that, I had to wait for the right set of circumstances. Then Boyle came along. And I could call in my marker with Vargas at any time. But you wouldn’t cooperate.”

“Me? What do you mean?”

“As long as we’re sitting here with nothing better to do, I suppose I can tell you. For the bombing, I had to study you and figure out your schedule. That part was easy. You are like clockwork. Every day, well, almost every day, you’d take your break at eleven. Without fail. You’d go to the vending area for a can of soda and a pack of cheese crackers. Then you’d sit on the bench in the hallway right across from that stairwell area. Every day. I had Boyle watch your movements in the lab. He took good notes. Anyway, off you’d go to the same place at the same time. But not that day. When I blew it up, you were supposed to be there. But you were nowhere near it. And then the damn shooting? It was risky. A bad idea, really. That was a lack of planning on my part. I hadn't accounted for all the variables, especially all the activity in the lab. When I started shooting, I didn't hit you on the first round. You disappeared out of sight, and everything was botched from that point. I had to get out of there quickly."

I didn't know what to say. I sat there, completely stunned by her cruelty and callousness. She walked around, recounting all these stories as if she'd been talking about fixing a pot of spaghetti. I couldn't believe her indifference to the lives of these people. And animals. I dropped my head down, shaking it in disbelief.

"You don't approve?" she laughed as she tossed her cigarette down to the floor, close to where I sat.

My chest hurt. Hearing all of this filled me with both anger and anxiety. And disbelief.

"No, Keegan. I don't approve. Do you even realize how many people you've killed? How many lives you've destroyed? By doing all of this? How these people's families must feel? Do you have any idea?"

"Oh, for God's sake. You're a bleeding heart, just like your father. Not Teddy. Charlie. Most people don't even like their families. And as for the people who died? Sooner or later, Rory, we all have to go. That's just how it works." She glanced at her watch again and walked over next to me. She pressed the muzzle of the gun against my cheek, grabbed me by the elbow, and squeezed hard.

"C'mon, get up. It's about time we go watch for your mother. It's back in the trunk for you, Dr. Greene."

It was harder to stand up than I had imagined. She pressed the gun into my lower back, shoving me forward. I walked a few yards and felt the blood returning fully to my legs. I decided this might be my only chance to make a move and quickly started planning my line of attack. Once we were outside, once she had her car keys in hand, I would body slam her with all my might. Head butt her. Whatever it would take.

It took only a matter of seconds until we were out the door. Even though the sky was heavy with clouds, the brightness of the day made it difficult to see. No matter. I spotted her car parked just a few yards away. It was now or never. Just as I moved to thrust my body into hers, an incredible noise rang out. A shot. And then a piercing pain in my shoulder. Another shot. I fell to the ground, hearing yet another shot.

I was moving toward the car, pulling myself along the ground, when I saw the pair of feet in front of me. I looked up, wincing. Jack.

Then I looked to my side. Keegan lay on the ground, her legs and arms splayed outward, her gun on the pavement.

"Jack!"

"Are you okay?"

"I'm shot. So, shit, no. I'm not okay," I said, rolling over and getting myself to a sitting position. "I think it's just my shoulder, but it hurts like a mother."

"I'm sorry," he said. "You moved."

"Jesus, you shot me?"

"I was aiming for Keegan, but you lunged toward her. Truthfully, I think you walked into it." He kicked Keegan's gun away from her.

"This isn't funny. You shot me, dammit."

"I think it skimmed you from the looks of it. I'm sorry."

The next moment, I heard sirens. Two cruisers came screeching in, slamming to a stop just yards from us.

"Hands where we can see them! Stay down on the ground and put your hands in the air."

Of course, we complied immediately. A few minutes later, things were sorted out. The ambulance arrived. As it turned out, Jack's bullet had, in fact, merely grazed my upper arm. I still had to make the obligatory trip to the hospital, where I was given four stitches, a bandage, and the comfort of Tylenol.

Dr. Aubrey Keegan was not so lucky. Jack had shot her squarely in the chest, the bullet lodging near her heart. I sat in the Emergency Room at the hospital answering the questions of two Columbus police officers. At the same time, Jack answered questions downtown, at his own place of work. For the first time, we had answers to give.

Chapter Thirty-Six

Several days later, Jack asked if he could take me out for dinner. We ended up at The Provolone Brothers, mostly because Jack was a huge fan of their pizza. In all fairness, I loved it too. We pulled into the parking lot just as late afternoon meets early evening. As such, we had our choice of tables and picked one by the fireplace. The smell of the burning wood drifted pleasantly through the room, occasionally bumping into the aromas of onion and garlic escaping from the kitchen. We ordered a large thin-crust cheese pizza, light on the sauce, and a couple of beers.

It was the first time we had a real chance to talk since I had been taken by Keegan. The police put me through a full interrogation to hear my side of the story. It all could be corroborated by evidence at the warehouse, the items in Keegan's car, and the testimony from my mother. She arrived at the McDonald's and called Keegan but did not get an answer. After 30 minutes of trying, she decided to go to the police. They brought her directly to me in the hospital emergency room.

Mom spent the night at my house. We hashed things out as best we could. She explained to me that she loved Dad dearly, but there had never been that burning spark. They were excellent companions, she said. They were better roommates than husband and wife. Mom also said that she never intended to be with anyone but Dad.

That was their pact, their agreement, their marriage. But then she met Teddy at one of their science group parties. From the moment she laid eyes on him, she knew he was the one. And he felt the same way about her. The two of them shared a soulmate connection. Her heart, his heart, became one.

She felt terrible about Dad. She realized that Charles "Charlie" Edward Greene cared much more for Corine "Cory" Anne Ladner than she did for him. She realized she had crushed his heart. But at the same time, she could not deny hers. And so it went.

As we sat there talking, drinking decaf coffee well into the night, I could feel my anger sliding away into nothingness. I saw on her face how much she loved Teddy Keegan. When she'd talk about him, her eyes would drift off somewhere into space, where she could see him again, somehow. Her love for him shone through, as genuine as it would ever come.

Mom recounted his death, his car accident, and said she had fallen into a deep depression after hearing the news. I didn't know whether I should tell her what I had learned, but decided it was better to be honest about all of it. And so I told her everything that Keegan had told me.

Mom started crying. She got up and went to the refrigerator, opening the door and leaning in. She stood there for a moment.

"You have anything stronger?"

"I think there might be some whisky in that cupboard right there. Jack brought some over one night. It should still be in there. Right up there," I pointed.

She found the bottle and poured a healthy tot into her coffee cup.

"You?" She held it up in my direction.

"No thanks. I'm still not feeling so great. Plus, I've had some pain pills. Did I mention I got shot?" I laughed.

We continued talking, sharing our stories, she about Teddy

Keegan, and me telling her the rest of what I knew about Aubrey Keegan and her horrible ways.

Jack and I finished our pizza. As always, he listened carefully and with concern, even offering insights here and there.

"Before we start on another thing," I said, "I've been meaning to ask. How in the world did you ever find me? In all the commotion, I never got the chance to ask."

Jack looked down at the table and shook his head briefly. He didn't answer.

"Well?" I looked at him raising my eyebrows.

"Well, I guess I have to tell you. I, uh, sort of put a tracking app on your phone. It's been on there a long time, actually." He shook his head again and held up his hand. "Now, don't think I was stalking you or anything like that. But when you first started getting those texts from the kidnapper when Lazzy went missing? Well. I decided to put it on your phone. I just thought it best because I was worried about your safety."

"You could have told me."

"I could have. You're right. But I didn't know how you'd react, and I worried you'd want me to remove it. And I didn't want to take any chances if someone was going to try to pull something. Well, something just like Keegan pulled." He stopped for a moment and glanced around the restaurant before starting again. "So, the day it happened I couldn't get a hold of you on your cell phone or at work, and I started to get nervous. So that's when I checked the location finder to see where you were. And it pinpointed you to an area in the old warehouse district when you should have been at the lab."

"How'd you know which building?"

"When I got down there, I tracked your phone coordinates to a trash can. Keegan made the mistake of not crushing the thing to pieces. She just tossed it. And, stupidly, it was just around the corner from where you were. It took me about five more minutes of driving around until I spotted the car. It was the only car down there, and that's when I decided to investigate."

"Good thing. But what took you so long?" I laughed.

"Yeah, I'm always slow on the uptake." He started playing with his napkin, rolling it on the table.

"Hey," I said. Jack looked up at me. "Thanks for saving my life."

Chapter Thirty-Seven

The trial for Dr. Aubrey Keegan did not happen until 14 months later. Immediately following her arrest, the story blew wide open in the media. For about a solid week, it was everywhere, from TV to newspapers to social media and back again. She had been arrested immediately but spent a couple of weeks in the hospital. From there, she was taken into the custody of the county jail. The authorities put Keegan on suicide watch and heightened security. I knew she would never kill herself. She liked herself too much. Besides, in her mind, she thought she was right. She believed she was innocent. Her fellow inmates would be much more likely to kill her with a shiv, given the scale of Keegan's likeability.

I returned to work after taking a week off, not only to heal physically but also to try to heal mentally, emotionally, and spiritually. Jack and Maggie were golden during those early weeks. I worried for Sarah more than I could say. I missed her. The chances of her survival remained fragile for a couple of weeks, but eventually she pulled out from her long coma.

For nearly six years, we had been constant companions. Her entire life had been overturned, as had mine. I didn't have words for how much I missed her. Her recognition of the world around her was not the same. Her memory was not the same. She said she knew me, but I wondered how much. Eventually, she was moved to a recovery center for a long road of work and treatment. I go there every day and work with her on her rehabilitation. We continue to hope that she will be well enough to come home. My home. Our home.

Once I returned to the lab from leave, I immersed myself in my work. Arriving early. Staying late. I grew closer to those little apes. Those bonobos. All four of them. Lazzy and I still had a special connection, but the other three became more a part of me than ever before. Of course, I knew I was breaking one of the commandments of research with animals. But I couldn't help myself. I needed them much more than they needed me.

One afternoon, after a question-and-answer session with shapes of objects, I let them play in the open area as I sat at the small table in the middle of the room, making notes. The four of them were energetic, and I knew they needed time to romp around. The note-taking consumed me, and I'd placed my entire focus on the work in front of me. So much so that I didn't notice Lazzy had pulled a chair up next to me. He patted my knee to get my attention. I began signing.

Me: Hello, Laz.

Laz: Hello, Rory.

Me: What's going on?

Laz: You.

Me: Me what?

He pointed at my mouth and then my eyes. Then he took his finger and traced his own face, a track from his eye down his cheek. Pointing back at me, he signed again.

Laz: Sad. Rory sad.

The following summer, I took a two-week vacation. I'd been seeing a therapist named Dr. Iverson ever since Aubrey Keegan went on her rampage. I'd been suffering from depression and anxiety as a result of all that had happened. After several months of therapy, Iverson suggested the trip. A pilgrimage of sorts. He said that I needed to find peace with each one of these people and that perhaps by visiting their resting places, I would be able to let go of the pain that I still held inside.

I started right in town, in Columbus, and visited the burial places of Hannah Shultz and Andy Turner, my two coworkers—and friends—who died at the hand of Keegan. From there, I drove to Siler, Indiana, to the St. Ignatius graveyard where my father, Charles Edward Greene, was buried. And finally, I drove to Bloomington, Indiana, where Teddy Keegan had been laid to rest.

I bought a bag of stones. Rose quartz, to be exact. It was the best thing I could think of, as Dr. Iverson suggested that I need a symbol of letting go. After much research, I decided on rose quartz, as it is known as the crystal of unconditional and universal love.

During my time with Sarah, the free spirit who was always admiring the secrets of the universe, I was exposed to a new way of thinking. In it, she always noted the expansiveness of the universe and the limited abilities of the human brain. She used to say—and often—"We don't know what we don't know." And she was right. All the scientific thinking in the world can't deny that fact. So, yes. I am a scientist. I work to discover facts. Yet, at the same time, the universe is a big place out there. Untouched and unknown. I am still learning. Hopefully, all of us are.

I went on my journey, with my little leather satchel filled with polished rose quartz stones on my passenger seat, and I drove to Columbus, to Siler, Indiana, and on to Bloomington. I laid a stone atop each one of their headstones and said my goodbyes. They weren't goodbyes, really. They were more like, "I'll see you the next time I see you."

And then, eventually, I went back to my life. Back to my work and all the people around me. To my friends. To Sarah. To the animals. To the world I was in. Through it all, I realized that everything is constantly changing and always moving. The entire planet and everything on it. We share all of this with everyone and everything. And all of it? All of it is in a constant state of motion and change. Every bit of it moving at its own pace. Just like my dad always said. The infinity about us is moving, one little molecule at a time. And we are moving with it.

- .... . / ..- -. -.. . .-. ... - .- -. -.. .. -. --.

www.ingramcontent.com/pod-product-compliance
Lightning Source LLC
Jackson TN
JSHW020255140825
89344JS00007B/218